ADVANCE PRAISE FOR *SUM*

A *Scary Mommy* Best New Book

A BookBub Best Romance

"Annabel Monaghan delivers yet another unputdownable love story about the messiness of life and lust. *Summer Romance* brims with heart, wit, and longing—the signature ingredients of my favorite beach reads. Anything Annabel writes, I'm reading it."

—Carley Fortune, author of *Every Summer After*

"A warm, funny, and bingeable five-star read."

—Abby Jimenez, author of *Yours Truly*

"Annabel Monaghan knows how to write romance, how to sweep you up and make you feel as though you, the reader, are falling in love. This is what romance books are all about. Ali is such a relatable protagonist and Ethan a perfect book boyfriend. I devoured it. Annabel has another hit on her hands."

—Sophie Cousens, author of *Just Haven't Met You Yet*

"How I loved this book! Annabel Monaghan has joined my shortlist of instant autobuy authors. Her writing is packed full of chemistry and warmth, and I could not put this book down. Ali is a heroine you will want to root for, and Ethan is completely swoon-worthy. I'll be recommending *Summer Romance* far and wide!"

—Paige Toon, author of *Only Love Can Hurt Like This*

"Summer Romance is a sweet, warm hug of a book. Annabel Monaghan's latest is like a chat with your best friend at the end of a long day—comfort personified. It's hopeful and fun, sprinkled with the kind of romance you wish for every summer."

—Elissa Sussman, author of *Funny You Should Ask*

SELECT PRAISE FOR *SAME TIME NEXT SUMMER*

A National Bestseller

A *Good Morning America* "Summer Breakout Pick"

Featured on *The View*

A *Real Simple* Must-Read Book of Summer

A *Glamour* BookTok Book
That Will Be Blowing Up Your FYP This Summer

A *Country Living* Best Romance Novel

A *Reader's Digest* Best Beach Read for the Perfect Escape

"This book has magic in it, encapsulating those big, heady first-love feelings, and it simply feels like summer."

—*USA Today*

"This may be the ultimate summer beach read."

—*Real Simple*

"Annabel Monaghan is topping the list as our new favorite romance author. . . . This just might be the ultimate beach read of 2023." —*Country Living*

"Bursting with the magic of first love, it's everything I want in a summer romance."
—Carley Fortune, #1 *New York Times* bestselling author of *Every Summer After*

SELECT PRAISE FOR *NORA GOES OFF SCRIPT*

A *Real Simple* Best Book of 2022

A *Cosmopolitan* 30 Best Romance Novels of 2022

A *Washington Post* 10 Noteworthy Books

A *USA Today* Top Rom-Coms

A *Southern Living* Beach Read

"A witty and poignant roller coaster that springs a delightful surprise." —*People*

"Monaghan's witty adult debut novel perfectly captures the apprehension and excitement of infatuation blended with life's complications." —*The Washington Post*

"The perfect escape from reality . . . In the best way."
—*USA Today*

SUMMER
Romance

ANNABEL MONAGHAN

G. P. PUTNAM'S SONS

New York

PUTNAM
— EST. 1838 —

G. P. PUTNAM'S SONS

Publishers Since 1838

An imprint of Penguin Random House LLC

penguinrandomhouse.com

Library of Congress has catalogued the G. P. Putnam's Sons
trade paperback edition as follows:
Names: Monaghan, Annabel, author.
Title: Summer romance / Annabel Monaghan.
Description: New York : G. P. Putnam's Sons, 2024.
Identifiers: LCCN 2024007476 | ISBN 9780593714089 (trade paperback) |
ISBN 9780593714096 (ebook)
Subjects: LCGFT: Romance fiction. | Novels.
Classification: LCC PS3613.O52268 S86 2024 |
DDC 813/.6—dc23/eng/20240223
LC record available at https://lccn.loc.gov/2024007476
p.   cm.

Hardcover edition ISBN: 9780593719855

Printed in the United States of America
1st Printing

Book design by Ashley Tucker

For my mom, Joany, who is still as close as my breath

SUMMER
Romance

1

SOMETIMES YOU JUST HAVE TO THROW SHIT IN THE pantry. Flour, garbanzo beans, Oreos. Just throw it in there and shut the door. Sometimes your kids are fighting or there's a capless Sharpie sitting right between the dog and your one good couch, so you don't have time to unpack your groceries according to a system. Sometimes you just need to wing it. These are words I never say to my clients. I truly do believe in the mindful storing of food, according to activity. Are you baking? Are you snacking? Are you breakfasting? But over the past few years, I find that I'm doing all of those things at once. In a dirty pair of sweatpants. I'm starting to think there aren't enough labeled glass jars to contain the mess that is my life.

It's no secret that I'm more than a little stuck. I'm in a holding pattern, like a plane trying to land in too much fog. I am here but also not here. Married, but also not. Instagram thinks I need to engage in some serious self-care to get me back to living my best life. They're obsessed with my cortisol levels and the depth of my meditation practice, but

I'm pretty sure this is a job for something bigger than the magnesium foot bath they've been putting in my feed all week. Today is the two-year anniversary of my mother's death, which makes it the one-year anniversary of the day Pete announced he didn't want to be married anymore. In fairness to Pete, he's never been one for remembering special dates.

I woke up that morning thick with grief. The calendar shouldn't have that kind of effect on us; there's no magic to the passing of three hundred and sixty-five days. It could have been a leap year and I would have had a whole extra day before I fell apart. I decided the night before that I'd make my mom's oatmeal chocolate chip cookies for breakfast. That's the sort of thing she'd do all the time: break up the monotony of life by doing something fun and unexpected. I was going to show my kids that fun doesn't die.

I left the butter on the counter to soften overnight, and I got up at six to start baking. It was late June, like it is now, and the sun was already up. I moved my teetering stack of unread mail into the sink to make room for my mother's mixer. I creamed the butter with the sugars and combined the flour, baking soda, and cinnamon in a separate bowl. I was crying by the time I added the three cups of oatmeal, wiping my tears with the sleeves of my pajamas. It's really unbelievable how much oatmeal is in this recipe, and for some reason that made me miss my mom even more.

This is how Pete found me. Crying into the Costco-sized box of oatmeal with my back to a sink full of unopened mail.

"Jesus, Ali," he said. Of course, he said this all the time.

But his tone wasn't angry like when he couldn't find a clean shirt or when one of his dress shoes had been filled with Cheez-Its and zoomed under the couch. And he wasn't sarcastic like when he waved his hand over the Leaning Tower of Paper and asked what I did all day. It was a soft, "Jesus, Ali," as if he'd run out of the energy to ever say it again.

I didn't usually react to Pete. His exasperation was sort of white noise in the background of my life. I sidestepped these comments and turned to the kids or the dog. Or my mother. But she'd been gone for a year, so I stood there crying. About the oatmeal, about the way Pete was looking at me and also not. And about the big chunk of my life I'd spent married to a man who would not cross the width of a kitchen to comfort me.

"I want a divorce," he said. When I didn't say anything, he said, "I don't want to be married anymore."

"That's what divorce usually means," I said. It was sarcastic and didn't even really sound like my voice. I felt pressure on my chest and a ringing in my head, like maybe I was going to leave my body. I have a memory of having had this feeling before, but it was when a doctor's voice put a time limit on my mother's days on this earth. Twelve to eighteen months. And I wanted to say, *Why not nineteen?* I was enraged by the arrogance of his specificity.

Pete left that night, and it's been fine. We act like we're on a reality show called *America's Best Separated Couple*. We are civil, almost warm, in front of the kids. He comes to get the girls for their Tuesday night soccer practices and Saturday games and takes them out for ice cream after, Cliffy in tow. Cliffy does not like team sports in any way, a fact that

Pete will not acknowledge, so he brings him to be his assistant coach. Cliffy packs crayons and a notebook. During the fall and spring seasons I go to the games, of course, and then we have an awkward goodbye in the parking lot during which I act like I'm in a hurry to meet a friend to do something outrageously fun.

I don't. Instead, I get in my car and talk to my dead mother. This is a new practice of mine, and I find it oddly therapeutic to lay it all out for her and just let my words echo off the dashboard. I wait for her to jump in with her red lips and wide smile to assure me that it will all be absolutely perfect in the end. But she doesn't, and I miss it the way you miss a lie. I miss the quick fix of her materializing at my door with a tray of chicken and the insistence that home life is easy and fun. It must be me, I would think, because I am finding this neither easy nor fun. The actual time with the kids, hunting stones in the creek out back or singing show tunes in the bathtub, was always easy and fun. But the rest of it—the house and the lawn and the appliances that take turns breaking and the plumber who says he'll come but doesn't come and charges my credit card anyway and the waiting on the phone and the explaining to the bank that yes, I had a broken toilet, and that yes, it is still unfixed, and then the explaining to Pete why he still has to use the kids' toilet in the middle of the night and his looking at me like, truly, I am capable of nothing. Neither easy nor fun.

But when she was around it was easier because I had a partner. She kept me company on Saturday afternoons, when Pete really should have been stepping up but needed to get in a thirty-mile bike ride. She was the one who helped me potty train and found the pediatric dentist that took our insurance. She was the one who caught my eye and smiled every time Cliffy said "angel muffins" instead of "English muffins." If I sounded stressed on the phone, she'd drop everything, pack a picnic, and take my kids to the beach so I could clean out a closet in peace. She was the only person alive who fully understood how restorative cleaning out a closet is for me.

My kids called her Fancy, because her name was Nancy, and it suited her. She was not a person whom I would describe as fancy; a lot of her clothes were hand sewn and she drove the same Volkswagen for twenty-five years. But she was prone to acting on a desire or a whim, anything easy and fun—a passing fancy. Sometimes her name plays tricks on me. A passing fancy. Fancy's passing. Cancer struck my Fancy. I am now Fancy-free. What I really need to do is Fancy myself.

Which is why this morning I tried the cookies-for-breakfast thing again. I did not cry as I added that extraordinary amount of oatmeal, and when my kids came downstairs to the smell of butter and sugar, they were tickled in a way I haven't seen them be in a long time. I felt like she was right there, with her long chestnut ponytail, dyed to match mine, and not a stitch of makeup besides her bright red lipstick, hatching an idea for an outing to the park or a science experiment called Baked Alaska. She'd clap her hands, bracelets jingling, and say, "You know what would be fun?" And this was rhetorical, because she was always the one who knew what would be fun. It's taken two years, but watching my kids eat those cookies this morning, I felt a bit of the heaviness lift. Just an easing in my chest that has given me the energy to hire my own services and tackle my pantry today.

I open Instagram on my laptop so I can see all of my posts at once—my clients' pantries look like they could belong to serial killers. Equidistant glass canisters labeled in my signature font. The images give me a quick dopamine rush. Bringing order to their homes satisfies a need in me that is so deep that I'm sure it's innate. As a child I wouldn't leave for school until my bed was made and my stuffed animals were arranged in order of size. My bedroom, my desk, my set of seven pencils. All of it washed me in stillness. The great thing about being an only child is that, at the end of the day, you find everything right where you left it.

I find it hard to believe that I was ever that person as I reach for the third nearly full box of cornstarch and place it at my feet next to a dozen open packages of crackers and stale tortilla chips. There is so much stuff on my floor that I fear it will rise up and engulf me. I will be swallowed whole by the Costco-sized box of granola bars that no one likes but I just can't throw out. Ferris rests his head on his paws, waiting for some of this bounty to come his way.

You have to make a mess to clean up. I'm always chipper when I tell my clients this. They're overwhelmed as I take every item out of their cupboards and spread them out on the floor. I am never overwhelmed in their houses. I talk as I go, and there's a forward-moving energy to my voice. "Now, we have everything out. Let's choose the items you use most often for breakfast!" In this way, I calmly guide them through the parts of their day, dividing their shelves into categories with pleasing storagescapes. Or I should say storagescapes™. It's a word I made up as an Instagram handle, and I'm trying to make it a thing. As I stand here in front of my pantry looking at all that cornstarch, I realize the calm I feel in those situations is because it's not my own mess. I don't resent the man who bought someone else's big jug of protein powder. I don't miss the mother who brought them that jar of Christmas chutney. My clients' messes are simple; my own mess is fraught.

I find a fourth box of cornstarch and it takes me down. I use one teaspoon of cornstarch once a year to make a pecan pie for Thanksgiving. How have I become a person who doesn't have the time or energy to check the pantry before she buys more cornstarch? How is it possible that I am a professional organizer who doesn't even make a grocery list? I ask myself this question and hear it in Pete's voice. He's asked me this before, and I can't remember how I explained it to him. You'd have to be here. You'd have to sit through a whole day of my life, right inside my head, to understand how that's possible. I'm not sure I understand it myself.

I give up and shove everything that's on the floor into a garbage bag. It's time to go get my kids anyway. It's the last week of school, and I just want summer to start already. Summer happens outside, and the mess of my garden is a much happier mess to be in. I find my keys under the camp T-shirt order form that was due last week. I find my phone under a buttered piece of toast. I've missed three calls from Frannie, so I call her on my way into the garage.

"You're going to flip," she says. I can hear the heartbeat of the diner in the background. Dishes hitting the counter and cutlery tossed into a plastic bin.

"Can't wait. What?"

"My parents are leaving the zip code."

I find this very hard to believe. Frannie's parents never leave Beechwood. "Like to go to the Home Depot or what?"

"They've won the Sunbelt National Sweepstakes. A two-week-long vacation in Key West."

"What? That's so fun! I can sort of picture them down there in shirts with flamingos on them." I'm smiling into my phone because I adore Frannie's parents. They have matching green pantsuits for St. Patrick's Day. They once showed up to an important city council meeting in powdered wigs and black robes. My mother referred to them as "that couple with the themes." They are the most enthusiastic people in the world.

Frannie and I weren't good friends growing up, but we were in the same grade, and everyone knows Mr. and Mrs. Hogan because they're a little eccentric and also because they own the two mainstays of our town—the Hogan Diner and the Beechwood Inn. Frannie and I reconnected after Pete and I left Manhattan and moved back to Beechwood, so I've been watching them to see how they'd age. I wondered if Mr. Hogan would tire of wearing his (now vintage) Beechwood High football jersey to every single home game. Or if they'd stop wearing their Yankees uniforms to the Little League Parade. There's been no sign of a slowdown yet.

"I know," she says. "They've gone completely nuts. My mom cut her hair into a bob an hour ago—she says it's more of a Florida look. They leave Saturday."

"There's going to be a lot of pink. And drinks with umbrellas, I think." I'm backing out of my garage and the sunlight surprises me. My geraniums are blooming nicely in the pots by my front door. I plant them on Mother's Day because they're the exact shade of my mother's lipstick, and they also have her stubborn resilience. Geraniums can handle a hot day much more gracefully than you'd expect. Don't overwater and don't be too fussy about them. Pick off the dead bits and new blooms will come. My eyes catch the coffee stain on my gray sweatpants, which used to be Pete's. I truly can't imagine how she would react to how poorly I've been coping without her.

"You okay?" Frannie asks when I've been quiet for too long.

"I'm fine."

"You let out a little sigh."

"I must be getting old."

"Stop with that, Ali. We're thirty-eight. We could be having babies, starting medical school."

"Why would you pick the two most exhausting things in the world as examples of things we still might get to do?" Frannie actually just had a baby last year, and it doesn't seem to be slowing her down all that much. She handles it all seamlessly while also running the diner. She's a different kind of person than I am, and certainly Marco is a different kind of husband.

"Spill it." I can picture Frannie cradling the phone in her neck and wiping down the diner counters after the lunchtime rush.

"Instagram wore me down, and I bought a bunch of floating aromatherapy candles last night. Do you think I'm a mess?"

"For sure. Tell me what pants you're wearing, and I'll tell you exactly how much of a mess you are."

I laugh. "No comment." Frannie's been trying to get me to start getting dressed since my mom died. I argue that, without my mom's help, I don't really have time for things as frivolous as an outfit. She argues that it takes just as long to put on a pair of jeans and a blouse as it does to pull on sweats and a T-shirt. I say, "For what?" She says, "For you." And we agree to disagree.

I pull into Beechwood Elementary's parking lot and get the last spot. "Okay, gotta go do hard time on the blacktop. Tell your parents congratulations and that I want photos."

As I'm pressing the red button to end the call, she shouts the two words that she truly believes will change my life: "Hard pants!"

Before I get out of the car, I say, "Mom." I rest my hands on the steering wheel, ten and two. "I'm so sick of being stuck. And I know I lean on you a lot, but can you work with me here? Like give me a sign?" She believed in signs more than I do, but I need help, so I ask. She doesn't reply, but I hear her laugh. It's her social laugh. The one that let people know she was amused. Not the body-racking, tear-inducing laugh she reserved for Will Ferrell movies and when Cliffy said "Massa-Cheez-Its" instead of "Massachusetts." Or "baby soup" instead of "bathing suit." She kept a tissue in the sleeve of her sweater in case something truly funny happened. You've got to love a person who leaves the house prepared to laugh.

Iris is on top of the jungle gym in conference with the A-one, top-dog alpha girls of the fifth grade. She's easy to spot in a purple tank top, orange shorts, and her soccer socks pulled up over her knees. Iris has a thousand looks that don't quite work, but she owns them completely. I pretend not to see Greer, who is sitting on a bench scrolling through her phone. She walks over from the middle school every day, to avoid the horror of being picked up by me. On the first day of sixth grade, I pulled up in front of the school, put down my window, and waved at her in front of her friends. So we don't do that anymore.

I stand in front of the kindergarten exit to wait for Cliffy. His teacher is outside already talking with the other parents, but I'm not concerned. He's always the last one out of the building. When he finally comes out, backpack secure over his SpongeBob T-shirt, he gives me the smile of a six-year-old boy who hasn't seen his mom in over six hours. This smile could power a small city, and every day I wonder when it will end. I wonder when he'll walk out of school, give me a nod, and then run off with his friends. I have never seen a forty-year-old man look at his mother this way.

Cliffy throws his arms around my waist and starts telling me about possums just as the clouds lower and the sky darkens. The girls spot us, and everyone runs for their cars. I grab Iris by the hand and laugh as the heavy drops of rain pelt my face. When we're in the car, I take a moment behind the steering wheel and smile at the rain pummeling my windshield. This is the sign I was asking for. A storm is a new beginning, and I want to stay in this moment. Greer, Iris, Cliffy, and me, cocooned in this car with the sound of rain filling our ears. We're all together, we're safe, and we're going to be fine. I really do feel ten percent better today. Maybe it was the cookies, maybe it was the forward motion of throwing out one garbage bag of old food. Maybe it's just time. Greer looks up from her phone and I can see a hint of the girl she was before things started to unravel.

My phone rings and Iris hands it to me with her I'm-still-eleven-and-don't-hate-you-yet goodness. "It's Dad," she says.

"Hi, Pete," I say with my phone to my ear. I never take Pete's calls on speaker in front of the kids because I don't want them to hear how casual he sounds when he cancels plans. "It's pouring."

"Yeah, I can see that. Listen, I didn't want to text you. I mean, it's been a year. I think we should go ahead and file for divorce."

I guess Pete does remember special dates.

I say, in my most chipper voice, "Great! Text me the details!" as if he's just invited me to a party.

When I hang up, Greer asks, "Why are you smiling?"

Because now I feel fifteen percent better. I'm going to make a real break from Pete. I'm going to figure out how to make my own money. I know exactly how many boxes of cornstarch I have now. "Fancy keeps sending me signs. We're going to have a champagne summer."

M Y MOM AND I USED TO CELEBRATE THE FIRST DAY
of summer by getting up before dawn to watch the
sunrise on the water at the Beechwood Inn. My first memory of this is from when I was four, the year my parents
divorced. We'd arrive in the dark, sneak around to the back
deck, and sit on the steps while the sun rose over Long Island in the distance. While we waited, she'd ask, "What do
you want this summer?" And I'd say into the dark: I want
to learn to ride a bike, or I want to beat you in chess. I want
to grow two inches. I want to be kissed. She'd keep saying,
"What else?" as I tossed my summer wishes into the dark.
There was no limit to the things I was allowed to want. After my last wish, she'd say, "You can have all of it," and I
believed her. And then, just as the sherbet sunrise was starting to erupt in the sky, she'd put her arm around me and
squeeze my shoulder. "Here's to a champagne summer,"
she'd say.

Beechwood, New York, is a small suburban town, just
north of Manhattan and just south of Connecticut, with

miles of coastline along the Long Island Sound. Our version of the beach is just the seashore where small waves
splash your ankles and deliver crabs. The water view ends at
Long Island in the distance, a finger of land that protects us
from the Atlantic. Because of our geography, our town feels
tucked away and drama-free. It's a town where you know
your mail carrier and your grocer by name, but if you want
something exciting to happen, you should probably go
someplace else.

We picked up my mom's first-day-of-summer tradition
again when I moved back to Beechwood, and, of course, we
brought the kids along. She'd smile at the water as my kids
shouted out their wishes. "What else?" we asked, over and
over. It was Iris's idea to start doing this on paddleboards
after my mom died. I resisted the change because a tradition is a tradition. But I could tell that the girls were feeling
more sad than nostalgic about it, and the change actually
felt good. Today's our second annual paddleboard sunrise,
and we park at the inn and walk the length of the dock to the
boathouse in the dark. My high school history teacher Mrs.
Bronstein, who now manages the boats there and insists I
call her Linda, gave me my own key years ago. We pull out
three paddleboards and launch ourselves into the water.
Greer is cautious, kneeling before she stands and staying
very still. Iris pops up and promptly cartwheels right into
the water. I straddle my board to keep it steady while Cliffy
lies on his back, head in my lap, waiting for the sun.

Summer is always marked by something. The summer
we moved to Beechwood. The summer Greer learned to
swim. These past two summers have been marked by death

and separation, and I'm wondering what our memory of this one will be. Cliffy tells the darkness that he wants to build a footbridge across the creek in our yard. Iris wants to score three goals in a game. Greer mutters her wishes to herself. "What else?" I say over and over. I want to make a wish too, but they're all jumbled in my head.

"Say something, Mom. Hurry up," Cliffy says. The sky is starting to brighten, but we can't see the sun yet. Iris is in a full handstand on her board. She is fearless and sure in a way that makes me wish she was a pill I could swallow. Greer paddles away, not too far, and then back again.

I haven't had fun since this boulder of grief landed on my chest. I want to laugh and be spontaneous about something as impossible as Baked Alaska. I want to clean out one single closet. "I want everything to feel lighter," I say as the sun appears and grants my wish.

"Here's to a champagne summer!" we all shout at the sun. Cliffy laughs, because it's funny to shout at the sun, but the girls and I are quiet, still a little unmoored out here.

E VERY MONDAY, I SPEND AN HOUR SITTING IN FRAN-
nie's little back office recording her deposits and organizing her bills while she tops up people's coffee at the bar.
It's been two weeks since I've been here because my kids
have been home, but today they started camp at the rec center, so I am back in my element. I can hear Marco at the
grill singing nonsense to Theo in his playpen. Theo always
smells like cheeseburgers, which I think is the only way to
improve the smell of a baby.

This is my favorite part of the week, sitting in this space
alone and making sense of this small business. Organizing
people's closets is a quick fix, but shoring up the chaos at the
diner is deeply gratifying. The fresh-bread delivery people
like to be paid in cash weekly, the dairy farm bills quarterly
or not at all, but the expense still needs to be recorded. The
utility bill is on autopay with Frannie's parents' personal
credit card. She leaves it all for me on tiny slips of paper,
faded invoices, and Post-it notes with question marks and

happy faces on them. Each week, when I leave, the problem
is solved and I am satisfied in the same way I used to be
when I was an accountant making the final closing adjustment on an audit.

Today I finish in forty-five minutes, so I order poached
eggs.

"What's happening with the divorce?" Frannie asks.
"Have you found a lawyer?"

"We're not doing lawyers."

"What does that mean?" Frannie tosses her rag into the
sink behind her.

"We've been living separately for a year, peacefully. We
still share a checking account and pay for everything out of
that. It's been pretty amicable, but with the new expense of
his apartment, we aren't putting anything into savings, so
we don't want to spend what savings we have on lawyers.
He's found a mediator."

"How absolutely new age hippie of you guys."

"It's nice for the kids to see things easy between us."

"Is he seeing someone?"

"I'd have no way of knowing. Is it time for that already?"

"It's not time for dating until you start wearing hard
pants."

I look down at my dirty gray sweatpants, which I think
are different from the dirty gray sweatpants I slept in. "I
know."

"And your overalls don't count." She's gesturing at me
with the decaf coffeepot in a way that I find mildly aggressive. "Don't try to hit me with the denim exemption; they're
soft and loose, and in their spirit they're sweatpants."

"They have hardware, like hooks and buckles. They're totally hard pants."

"Until you produce a pair of pants with a zipper, you will not be dating."

"It's the zipper that attracts a man. Noted."

"It might be just what you need," she says. "A date. Just to get you unstuck and past the firsts—first date, first kiss."

"Oh my God, stop." Just the thought of it makes me feel more stuck than ever.

"Can I go with you?"

"On a date?"

"No. To mediation."

I almost smile at the thought of Pete walking into a lawyer's office and finding Frannie by my side holding a big yellow legal pad. "No thank you."

"Well, you know my little brother's a lawyer, if you want to talk to someone."

This actually makes me smile. "Scooter's a lawyer? There's no way we're that old."

"He's thirty-six. He could be president."

"Scooter? Hilarious."

The bell over the door tinkles and Mr. and Mrs. Hogan appear in coordinating tracksuits and panama hats. "Oh, I forgot to mention, they're back," says Frannie.

"Girls!" says Mrs. Hogan. "So glad we caught you together." They sit down on either side of me and I notice they are wearing the same cologne. This is next-level.

"Welcome back! How was Florida?" I ask.

"Well, we just loved it," says Mrs. Hogan. "We were in a little bungalow on the water. It was like we could see all the way to Cuba. We made friends with the young people who bought the bar Hemingway used to go to."

"He didn't really go there," Mr. Hogan says.

"Well, true. But it's such fun to imagine that he did." She claps her hands together, and her smile is pure rapture. What I wouldn't give for one ounce of this woman's energy.

"The Fourth of July parade wasn't the same without you," I say. They always dress as Uncle Sam and a bedazzled Betsy Ross. The parade starts in town and ends at the inn, where the Hogans serve hot dogs and Cokes to anyone who makes it that far. This year Frannie had hotel staff in their regular uniforms serving everyone, and it sort of fell flat.

"I'm sure it was lovely," Mr. Hogan says. His eyes land on the translucent stain on the front of my sweatpants. The fact that it's maple syrup is known only to me, and I'd like to keep it that way. "Everything okay with you, Ali?" he asks.

"Yes, everything's fine. We're all doing great," I say, moving a paper napkin onto my lap and feeling it adhere to the syrup stain.

Mrs. Hogan gives Frannie a look. "Well, come for Funtastic Friday Night. We are celebrating our return. Bring the kids, of course. Scooter's even coming down."

"Sure, thank you," I say. I could use something Funtastic.

4

IT'S THE THIRD DAY OF CAMP AND I HAVE SIX THINGS on my to-do list today. I can currently remember two of them. One involves buying a less embarrassing pair of pajamas for Greer and another has to do with a lost retainer. As I listen to the glorious trickle of my coffee brewing, I take a moment to enjoy the certainty that managing Pete's dry cleaning isn't on that list.

Before I had kids, I was still on the list. I'd get up in the morning, make myself coffee, and go for a run or do yoga before work. If there was coffee left in the pot, then Pete could have some when he got up. If there wasn't, that wasn't my problem. We had the same job, the same paycheck—he still saw me as a grown-up back then.

When I stopped working, I started making the coffee to suit Pete. He liked me to add cinnamon to the grounds, which I think completely ruins the taste of the coffee, but I made it that way because he was the one going to work. It seemed like his coffee moment mattered more than mine.

Also, his evenings and weekends. It's hard to tell your partner you need a break when you don't have a job. Or if you
have a job that kind of looks like a hobby and doesn't bring
in a lot of money.

I almost added the cinnamon to the coffee on the first
morning that Pete was gone, but I poured it back into the
container and pressed the button with great ceremony to
brew my own, pure coffee. It was delicious in a way I can't
even describe.

I pour my own personal coffee now and twist my wedding ring around my finger a few times. I think of the cinnamon and how good it felt to stop that. I pull my ring off
and spin it on its side. When it lands, I open my spice cabinet and place it on top of the cinnamon. I take a deep breath
as the smell of coffee fills the quiet kitchen. I run my unjew-
eled, un-spoken-for fingers through my hair. Outside my
window, the geraniums are going strong. It's Wednesday
and I don't have to see Pete on Wednesdays. I have the
sense that I am a limb that went numb, and I am starting to
tingle again.

"You're looking at your mug like you're going to make
out with it," Greer says as she comes into the kitchen. This
comment is mildly mocking and sarcastic, but at least she's
talking to me. Greer has gone a little salty since Pete left.
She's twelve and unsure and probably angry at me for what's
happened to our family. I don't really know how to defend
myself. I've just completed a full year of being a single
mother, and she's just completed a full year of sixth grade.
Neither of us has had it so easy.

"I might," I say, and take another sip. Cliffy comes downstairs and gives me the smile of a six-year-old boy who hasn't seen his mom in ten hours.

"It's archery first thing at camp today, can we be a little late?" Greer asks. She is not enthusiastic about Beechwood Rec's summer camp. Next year she'll be old enough to be a junior counselor, so this year just feels embarrassing. I don't like being late, and I don't like my kids being late. But I just took my ring off and the chances are my kids aren't going to grow up and hunt for their own food.

I surprise us both by saying, "Sure. I'll go up and get dressed."

"Dressed?" Iris says, taking her seat in front of the third plate of eggs. I don't have to explain whose is whose: the manner of cooking—scrambled, sunny side up, and over easy—is like a place card.

"Yes, dressed," I laugh, and they are watching me. This isn't new. Since Pete left, they've been looking to me for clues about how I'm doing, how well I'm going to be able to steer this ship. Iris's big brown eyes peek out under the crooked bangs that she cut herself last week. She's wearing all green, including her socks, and it looks the perfect amount of crazy. And Greer, with my mother's wide smile and a face that is changing from girl to teen in a way that evokes both awe and panic. In September she'll be in seventh grade. This is the year she'll do a high-level overview of world history and sink into a Machiavellian hell. I can still feel the nightmare of seventh grade—the sudden and inexplicable abandonment by my friends. My mother putting me in the car and driving to Rockport to eat lobster rolls and walk around. We laughed at the corny sayings on needlepoint pillows and bought key chains with flip-flops on them. We had popcorn for dinner and stayed up late watching *Auntie Mame* under my grandmother's yellow crocheted blanket. I want to be that mother, both steering the ship to safety and being the safety itself. I'm going to need harder pants.

When I'm dressed in my overalls and my favorite blue and white striped T-shirt, I text Phyllis to see if she's awake. Phyllis is my ninety-four-year-old neighbor who lives in the too-close house next door. She has recently discovered the wide world of emojis on her phone. She replies with a coffee cup emoji, which tells me she won't want her eggs until later. I reply with the thumbs-up emoji, and she replies with the laugh-till-you-cry emoji, which almost never makes sense but seems to be her favorite way to end a conversation.

I drop everyone at the rec center for camp and take Ferris to the dog park. Beechwood's dog park is a giant lawn with hundred-year-old sycamore trees that ends dramatically at a seawall. Beyond that is the beach and then the sound. You can't see Manhattan from here, the view is just around the point, but I like knowing it's there. The park ends at the Beechwood Inn, bright white against the blue sky, with yellow umbrellas dotting the sand in front of it. A warm breeze comes off the water, blowing the lavender that's just starting to bloom. All of this feels like something I should enjoy, but, truly, the dog park is the worst. Ferris loves to run around and randomly sniff dogs' butts and force me into awkward conversations. It's like a cocktail party without the cocktails, and my desire to flee when everyone else seems happy to linger makes me feel like I'm the wrong kind of person.

Today, even though I am bolstered by my ringless finger and what some might call an outfit, I do not want to make conversation. When you live in the town where you grew up, every polite question is loaded with history. I do not want to look into the eyes of people who have known me my whole life and see their collective surprise that I am orphaned, separated, and not quite living up to my potential. I don't know how to respond to everyone's casual ten-thousand-pound question—*How are you doing?* Better than you'd think. I'm finally getting divorced, and look at my pants.

Ferris is being bullied by a pack of Chihuahuas and runs to me for comfort. I plop down on the wet grass and know that I'll be leaving the dog park with a dark wet spot on my rear end. Ferris is a fourteen-pound mutt with a long, wet nose and a mane of caramel-colored hair that he sheds like he's a flower girl sprinkling petals down the aisle. He places the weight of his little head on my thigh, and I rub that perfect spot on the back of his neck. He'll keep his head on my thigh for as long as I rub, and in this way we have a perfectly symbiotic relationship. His breathing steadies me, and I close my eyes to feel the light July breeze. *Mom*, I say in my head, *I got dressed.* I hear her voice: *Now, darling, wasn't that easy?* Well, it only took me two years.

Ferris snaps me back by jumping out of my lap and racing to the far end of the lawn by the entrance to the inn. I stand up to see what's caught his attention, hoping to God it's not a squirrel carcass he wants to roll around in. He stops by a guy with shaggy light brown hair, almost blond, who's holding a small black dog in his arms like a baby. A woman with a St. Bernard the size of Mike Tyson seems to be apologizing. As I approach, I mutter my mother's "Comparison is the thief of joy" under my breath. She's a little younger than I am, in jeans that fit and a pale pink blouse tucked in. As I get closer, I notice she's even wearing a belt. A belt! I can see now that this guy is handsome. He's wearing a faded green T-shirt and bright yellow swim trunks. He could be a teenager from a distance, but there's something about the way he carries himself that exudes a more grown-up kind of confidence. He's tending to his dog but is also being nice to the belted lady. It's almost like he knows by looking at her that whatever her dog did had to be an accident, because she's clearly got her act together.

Ferris is standing at his feet sniffing around, and just as I get within a few yards of them, it happens in slow motion: Ferris lifts his hind leg and pees all over the guy's left sneaker. "No!" I shout, when it's already too late. The realization spreads over his face, and he shakes his foot.

"Oh my God, I'm so sorry," I say as I reach them and kneel down to grab Ferris by the collar.

The woman looks down at me and then says to the guy, "Did that dog just pee on you?"

He shakes his foot again. "Feels like it. All the way down to my sock."

"I am so horrified," I say, because I'm so horrified. "I swear he doesn't do this. I mean he did it once when I brought my daughter home from the hospital. Because she was born, not sick. Anyway, she's his favorite."

"So maybe this is a compliment?" I look up and he's

smiling at me. It doesn't make any sense given the state of his shoe, but he almost looks glad to see me. He's probably about my age, though there's a lightness about him that makes him seem younger than I feel. His eyes are light brown, a shade darker than his hair, and there's not a hint of anger in them. It's possible that he's a guy who knows when a problem can be solved with a run through the washing machine. I'm taking in every detail of his eyes, mainly because I am trying not to look at his shoulders and the way his T-shirt stretches across his chest.

"Do you get peed on often?" the woman asks, and there's a weird flirtatiousness to it that annoys me. "Because I'd be freaking out." It strikes me as strange that she, with the great outfit, dry shoes, and potentially aggressive dog, doesn't have the grace to let me off the hook.

"I'm really sorry," I say again, and stand up.

"Honestly, it's nothing. It can all be washed," he says. There's almost something about him that I recognize. I don't recognize him, but the look. He's looking at me the way men used to look at me when I was younger. Like he sees me. I wonder if my wedding ring served as a cloak of invisibility or if maybe it's my nearly hard pants. I am at once terrified and delighted. These overalls don't even have a zipper.

The St. Bernard gallops off after another dog, and the woman reluctantly follows. I didn't check to see if she was wearing a wedding ring, but this guy is not. I don't think I've ever noticed a singles scene at the dog park, but maybe there is one. I run my thumb over my ringless ring finger and am struck by the fact that I am single, that I am a

person who would be part of a singles scene. It's as if that
fact has been buzzing around my head for a year, circling in
a way that I could faintly hear, and now it has landed. I am
single.

"So what's his name? The peeing bandit."

"Ferris," I say. "He's a rescue, he came with that name."
I look at the little dog in his arms, pressing his head against
his owner's chest. "What's his name?"

"Her name's Brenda."

"Brenda?"

"Yes, because she totally looks like a Brenda," he says
like he can't believe I didn't make that connection myself.
"She got walloped by that dog's giant paw, but I think she's
mostly just scared of other dogs. Maybe now that I've been
baptized by Ferris, he'll be familiar to her." His eyes rest on
me like there's no place else he'd rather look. He holds my
gaze until I have to look away.

"Really, I feel terrible."

"Stop. Maybe he likes me." Brenda is a dead weight in
his arms, and I envy her that kind of comfort. I like this
man with the big shoulders. I like his open expression, as if
there's a laugh waiting right behind his eyes. It's been a
really long time since I've noticed anything about any man,
and it's possible that I'm over-noticing this one.

"I haven't seen you here. Do you live in Beechwood?" I
might as well have said, "Come here often?" Why am I pro-
longing this conversation? We are not at a bar. I am not
good at being single.

"I'm just visiting my family."

I nod, and I can't think of anything to say. This is why

I can't stand the dog park. There's no context, no commonality except the indignities our dogs are inflicting on each other, or in this case, us. "Is she your first dog?" I ask. I immediately regret it. It's clear I'm trying to keep the conversation going, and the answer to this is either going to be "Yes" or a really sad story about a dog dying. That's the thing about dog stories, they only end one way.

"I've always had a dog, besides my freshman year in college," he says.

"That's a lot of responsibility. I mean for a college kid."

"I guess. It's sort of a habit. I don't think I'd know how to get up in the morning and do anything but take a dog out."

"Wait till you have kids," I say. That's a weird thing to say on a million levels. I don't know that he doesn't have kids. It also makes it obvious that I've surmised that he's single. That I thought about it. "I mean if you don't already."

"None of my own, no."

This got personal fast, and I want to know what that means. You either have kids or you don't. "I have three. Twelve, eleven, and six."

"Which one got peed on?" he asks.

"Eleven. Iris," I say. "She's adorable. I'm surprised all the dogs don't pee on her."

He smiles and it takes over his whole face. "I think you just called me adorable."

"I did not." My face goes hot, like prickly hot on my cheeks. I am totally out of control here. I meet one handsome guy in a decade and I completely lose it.

"You did—it's the transitive property of adorable. If you

play back everything you just said, it adds up to you thinking I'm adorable. I'm a little embarrassed for you."

I've been embarrassed for me since before this conversation began, but now that it's out in the open, it's sort of fun. I look around. "Where's the camera crew? You can't prove this."

"It's obvious to me, the dogs, I'm guessing everyone at the park. You're totally into me."

"I am not," I say, and fold my arms over my chest.

He laughs what I will admit is an adorable laugh. "I'm Ethan." He rebalances Brenda and frees a hand for me to shake.

"Ali."

He holds on to my hand for a beat too long. I have the strangest feeling that I want him to keep holding on to my hand. Also, that I want to spill my guts. I want to tell him that I took my ring off today. I want to tell him that I just realized I'm single and that I don't know how to be that thing. That I'm fascinated that he's borderline flirting with me and I'm wondering what comes next. How do people get past all those firsts? Do they meet for coffee? Or go straight to a meal? Is this what happens when you swipe right? There's something intoxicating about how he's looking at me like I'm someone I used to be.

To keep myself from saying any of this, I lean down and latch Ferris's leash to his collar. "Okay, well, nice to meet you. And sorry again about your shoe."

"It's fine. He's a cute dog."

"He is," I say. Brenda is sound asleep with her little black head in the crook of his elbow.

"She's going to be fine," he says, but I've been staring at his arms, not Brenda.

"Of course, okay. Bye. Sorry again. Nice to meet you." I turn to go and I can feel with each step that the back of my overalls is soaked from the grass. I'm definitely coming back to the dog park tomorrow.

5

AFTER THE DOG PARK, FERRIS AND I STOP BY PHYL-lis's house to make her eggs. Eggs, in a midlife plot twist, are my love language.

Phyllis feels like a not-quite grandmother and not-quite roommate. Our houses are called the Sisters because they were built for a pair of spinster sisters in 1919. Their parents lived in a giant stone house on the water where the summer people built, and when it became clear neither of their daughters was getting married, they ousted them into what is now a family neighborhood closer to town. Our houses were the first on the street—one sister wanted a brick Tudor (mine) and the other wanted one that looked like it was designed by Hans Christian Andersen (Phyllis's). Phyllis's house was actually my favorite house in Beechwood when I was a kid, because it looks like a fairy tale. My mom and I lived in an apartment above the dry cleaners in town, and, while we were happy there, it always smelled a tiny bit like kerosene. I always imagined Phyllis's house smelled like cookies. It's made of stucco with a tall pointy roof covered in hand-laid wood shingles. You can picture Hansel and Gretel wandering right through the rounded wood door. It's cozy and welcoming, with beamed ceilings and all of the original woodwork and hardware. Our houses were built uncomfortably close together so that the sisters could care for one another as they aged. I can see right into Phyllis's kitchen from mine, which is how I knew when she stopped cooking for herself.

Our houses would look like they were on the same lot except for the poorly maintained fence someone put up decades ago. It runs the length of our yards all the way down to the creek and is truly an eyesore. Six years ago, Phyllis had her handyman add a gate to the fence so that Greer and Iris could come over and enjoy her old swing set. Phyllis is old enough not to care about lawsuits and tetanus.

I've been checking in on Phyllis since we bought the house ten years ago, but I've started spending more time there since my mother died. It's not like she's a replacement mother, but I'll admit it's not super clear who's taking care of whom. The main difference between the two of them, besides the fact that Phyllis is not my mother, is that Phyllis hangs back and lets me come to her. When Pete left, she didn't panic or step in to fix it. She took my hands in hers, told me I was better off, and gave me her copy of *The Awakening*. She believes in the value of planting perennials rather than annuals, so that she'll have nurtured something that will outlast her. Her parenting and gardening mottos are the same: "Pull the weeds and let God do the rest." She has a confidence in the order of things and in the ability of all creatures to grow into their best selves that could feel naïve.

But if you talked with her for five minutes you would know that she is, like her garden, thriving beautifully.

When she's up to it, we spend afternoons wandering around her yard, and I've learned the basics of caring for perennial plants. I now have bushes of forsythia and hot-pink hydrangea that line the grassy path down to the creek, and also black-eyed Susans, gerbera daisies, and butterfly milkweed along the edge of my brick patio. Nothing needs to match in nature, and I find it totally counterintuitive the way my yard adjusts to death and welcomes whatever comes next. "Spring is always coming," Phyllis says. "It never doesn't come."

More often than not, when she's in the mood for fresh air, we sit out back and admire the giant weeping willow that sits at the edge of her part of the creek. She greets the tree with, "What are you crying about?" and then laughs at her own joke. Phyllis loves eggs, she loves my dog, and I think she loves me.

"Alice!" she shouts when I've let myself in. Like my mom, she insists that Ali is a narrow place behind a building that smells like garbage. "Where is *Wuthering Heights*?"

She is a reader, and her bookshelves overflow into piles that I worry may be a safety hazard. It would take me all day to find that single book, and I have a client in an hour. "I have a copy," I tell her. "Let me make your eggs, and I'll go get it."

She lowers her reading glasses when I've entered her sitting room. "Well," she says.

"Well, what?" Ferris takes his spot by her slippered feet.

"You look a bit like a farmer, and I still can't see a bit of your darling figure, but at least you're not in your pajamas. Much better." She's smiling at me, as if she's just paid me the highest compliment.

"Thank you," I say. "And I took my wedding ring off too." I hold up my hand to show her while grabbing last night's dinner plate and her water glass to take to the kitchen.

"Good!" she calls from her sitting room. "Good riddance!"

"Ferris seemed to notice," I call back. "He found the only single guy in the park and peed on him."

"You're surrounded by helpers," she says.

I scramble two eggs and season them with the smallest amount of salt I can get away with. I sit in the armchair across from hers while she eats.

"What is it?" she asks.

"What is what?"

"There's a buzziness about you. A shift."

"I told you Pete wants a divorce; I guess that was the first domino to fall. Then I took off my ring and sort of got dressed. And maybe that guy at the dog park was flirting with me? I don't know. It's got me feeling all teenage-y, like someone might ask me to the prom."

Phyllis nods at her eggs. "It's about time. You're young. You're a beautiful girl."

"Thank you," I say. "For humoring me."

When she's eaten and I've cleaned her kitchen while listening for the successful completion of her shower, I run home to find my copy of *Wuthering Heights* and leave it next to her TV remote. Phyllis will read all day until three o'clock, when she hate-watches Dr. Phil. She doesn't miss an episode or an opportunity to say, "He's not a very nice man."

From there I head to Jeannie Lang's. It only takes one intensely satisfying hour of work to revamp her front hall closet with uniform wood hangers and decorative hooks for baseball hats. I convince her to throw away a single black cashmere glove, as its match has been missing for over three years. I sometimes feel like a priest walking through people's homes. I come in and absolve them of guilt and restore their peace of mind. Yes, it's okay to let go of the hope that you'll ever learn to play that ukulele. Let's release it to its next owner. I post a photo with the caption *Coat rack goals*, and am the first to roll my eyes over it.

As I drive to the rec center to get my kids, the sky is a rich early-July blue and the leaves on the elm trees along Main Street flutter almost imperceptibly. My senses are on high alert, and I feel good. "Ethan," I say out loud. I like the way the word vibrates around the inside of my car. "Mom, I think he was flirting with me. Did you see it?" I wait for a response but just get a bubbly feeling in my chest. "Ethan," I say again.

6

O N THURSDAY MORNING, I DIG UP A PAIR OF JEANS that I haven't worn since before Cliffy was born and a white T-shirt that fits well but doesn't look like I'm trying too hard. I brush my hair, and at the last minute I put on lip gloss. I tell my reflection in the bathroom mirror, "You have completely lost your mind."

Ethan's not at the dog park. I know this because I have walked the perimeter and crisscrossed both ways diagonally. I have been approached by Greer's friend Caroline's mom, who is the worst kind of snob, and my mom's friend Mrs. Wagner. I have assured them both that I am absolutely fine, and I've exhausted all conversational avenues about the weather.

Ferris and I get back in the car. The sun has heated up my steering wheel and I rest my cheek on it. "Mom, seriously, what am I doing? I just spent an hour in lip gloss looking for a man who told me he doesn't even live here." *Why not*, she says. "There are a million reasons why not, Mom." And I sound just like Greer.

I drive to town to buy ground beef because I promised Cliffy hamburgers for dinner. I don't usually buy ground beef from the butcher because it costs a full three dollars per pound more than at the grocery store, but I do today. I tell myself it's a treat, but in truth I do it because a single man visiting his family is not going to be at the grocery store, but he might be walking through town.

Ethan is not in town.

I drive home with my overpriced beef, and my mom and I have a good laugh. *This feels a little like Where's Waldo*, she says. I am being absolutely ridiculous, but something about that quick dog park flirtation has me feeling unstuck.

When I get home, I see that Cliffy's forgotten his lunch, likely because it was blocked from view by the giant package of toilet paper I didn't put away last night. I get back in the car and find him at the far end of the rec center by the skate park and the tennis courts, where a group of kids have let loose a family of millipedes. Cliffy squeezes me with all of his strength, grabs his lunch, and disappears into the huddle.

I stand and watch because there's a breeze blowing through the old oak tree just behind them, and I like the way the sun feels on my face. It feels good here. I never intended to end up back in Beechwood. In high school, I imagined a more cosmopolitan life filled with taxis and bodegas. I'd say "handbag" instead of "purse" and learn to race down subway stairs in impossible shoes. I was going to make a lot of money and have a single spreadsheet that tracked the balances in all of my many accounts. A career in accounting would be a beautiful vehicle for bringing order to chaos, balance to unsteadiness. But I got pregnant with

Greer unexpectedly, and Pete and I got married. There were complications, and I left my job. Then we had Iris, and two kids and a dog started to feel like too much so far away from my mom. So we came back. Beechwood isn't what I pictured for myself, but it's a really nice place to live. The trees alone are worth it, and I'm rarely more than a mile from the water. An older couple is playing tennis on the courts to my right, in such an easy rhythm, back and forth. I like the rhythm of this life.

There are kids at the skate park, standing around the half-pipe. They're mostly teenagers, sort of watching and waiting their turn. I wonder if Cliffy's going to grow up and want to fly up a curved wall on a wheeled device with no seat belt. All eyes are on this one guy who skates up to the top of the half-pipe and flips up into the air and lands dead in the middle of his board. It's almost like a choreographed dance where the skateboard is his partner and he knows exactly where she'll land. I do not know why I just put that skateboard in the feminine. And I wonder if I've somehow just sexualized this skateboarder and the powerful way he controls his body, like he can fly. I walk closer, and by the time my hands are gripping the chain-link fence, I can see that the skateboarder is Ethan.

I feel the rush of excitement that comes from having found the thing you've been looking for. He hasn't left town, and it's a guilty pleasure to be able to stare at him from a distance. He is in complete control of his body as he moves up the half-pipe and into the air. There's an athleticism to this that I haven't associated with skateboarding before.

The strength and rhythm of his movement make me think, just for a second, that skateboarding is the sexiest thing in the world. The thought moves through my body as I grip the chain-link fence and watch.

There's a lightness to this man, and I have a feeling he knows how to have fun. I want to catalog every detail—the way his hair waves off of his face, how his navy blue shorts ride up the front of his legs and reveal the long muscles there. The way his white T-shirt grips the ridges of his back.

He finishes his turn, and I realize I need to go. This isn't me casually running into him at the dog park, where I have every right to be. This is me standing there ogling him while he's being oddly sexy wiping his brow in slow motion with the back of his arm. I have no way of explaining why I'm leaning against this chain-link fence watching skate-boarders. He's going to think I'm stalking him. Which, well.

I turn my back to the fence, and there's Cliffy's bug group in the distance screwing caps on jars. That's my out. I could totally just be an overprotective mother watching my kid enjoy camp.

"Ali?" He's right behind me, on the other side of the fence. He remembers my name.

I turn around and fail at trying to seem casual. "Oh, hey. Ethan, right? From the dog park?"

"Yeah, hi. What are you doing here?" He's out of breath and a little sweaty in the most appealing way possible. He's close enough that I can see gold flecks in his brown eyes. His hair is brushed back from his face, and the ends look like they've been dipped in blond, a leftover from last summer.

"Nothing really. Rec camp. My son's over there. I dropped off his lunch. Toilet paper." My voice trails off and I don't know where to look, because looking directly into his eyes is going to make me blush. I can feel the heat bubbling up right under my skin.

"Ah, rec camp. That sounds fun." His hands grip the chain-link fence and his fingers are right at my eye level. They're elegant, if that's possible. His hands are the hands of a man who works construction all day and then races home to perform a piano concerto. I may have had too much sun.

"I guess. They're releasing millipedes and I sort of wish I wasn't wearing flip-flops." Not an interesting thing to say, but it does give me an excuse to look down at my feet. "So what was all that? Are you a professional skateboarder or something?"

He laughs. "No, I'm just a lifelong skateboarder. For fun." He looks over his shoulder at the kids who are still skateboarding behind him and then back at me. I'm clutching the fence again, my fingers curled around the metal, and we're closer than we would be if there weren't a fence between us. He's looking directly at me, into my eyes and then at my hair. I am out of my body being looked at like that. I am out of time and in some other, lighter, freer body. I don't want to move.

"Why are you looking at me like that?" I hear myself ask.

He barely blinks. "I bet everyone looks at you like this."

"Just Cliffy." Weird, weird, weird. This man is flirting with me, I am positive of it. And I compare him to my son. I look away toward the campers.

"Who's Cliffy?"

"My son."

"Then that's definitely not how I'm looking at you." His eyes are smiling. I want this to be the part where he asks if I'm free for dinner. And then I say yes, my dinner plans were just canceled. And then I race home to call Frannie to babysit and help me find something to wear. I smile back at him, embarrassed for myself for a hundred reasons.

"Do you want to do something with me later?" he asks.

I am so surprised by these words coming out of his mouth that, for a second, I wonder if I said the thing about Frannie babysitting out loud. "Tonight?" I ask.

"Yes. Tonight." His eyes scan mine like he'll see my answer there.

He's asking me out. This attractive man who has beautiful hands and a brief history of flirting with me. This is a miracle, but it also feels like if someone told me I was going on safari in twenty minutes—I've always dreamed of going, but I'm not quite prepared.

"What would we do?" I ask.

"Something fun. Are you okay with surprises?"

I almost tell him that the last surprise I had was finding the carcass of a hermit crab in my bathtub. The surprise before that was Pete leaving. This feels different from those.

"Sure," I say.

"Sure? Sure's not yes."

"Yes," I say. And we're just looking at each other, like we both can't believe this just happened.

He smiles. "Great. I'll pick you up at seven?"

"No," I say, too quickly. "I mean yes to seven, but no to picking me up." He doesn't say anything. "It's just that I have kids. I mean I'm not married. I'm separated, but I haven't really been on a date, and I'm not sure my kids are ready for that. If this is a date. I mean, not to assume, it just sort of feels like one?" Where are all these words coming from? I can tell he thinks this is funny. "Say something."

He's smiling. "It's definitely a date."

"Okay."

"Meet me here at seven," he says. "Wear something casual. And you might want a hat."

7

FRANNIE'S NOT ANSWERING HER PHONE. MARCO AN-
swers the landline at the diner, and I tell him to tell her
to check her texts. Me: CODE RED. I met a man and I
have a date!! Can you guys please come hang out with my
kids tonight? I will pay you back in unlimited babysitting
hours for eternity. A DATE!

Frannie, finally: OMG, yes!

When I'm home and I'm outside grilling burgers for my
kids' dinner, I am completely overwhelmed by what's ahead
of me. On the one hand, this is a lucky break—me, taking
off my ring and getting to practice dating on a guy who's
only in town for a visit. By the end of the night, I'll be able
to check "first date after separation" off the list of things I
am dreading. Also, it could be fun. The last real conversation I had with a man was about shin guards.

I am sweaty and need to reshower by the time I figure
out what to wear. I would like to be in a dress for this date.
I'd like to be able to cross my legs without feeling the rub of

denim against itself. But a dress feels like too much, like I'm expecting a corsage or something. Plus, he said casual. As a compromise, I settle on a white sundress with a denim jacket over it, along with a pair of sandals that I have specifically chosen because they are not flip-flops. Sandals with a strap around the back will surely send the right signal about just how together of a person I am.

As I apply what I believe is the right amount of mascara, it hits me—I am infinitely more prepared for a safari than I am for this date. "So tell me a little about yourself," I say into the mirror, like I'm conducting a job interview.

I tell my kids I'm going to my book club and accept Frannie's enthusiastic squeeze of my hand as I head to my car. "I will be here, with all the time in the world to hear every single detail when you get back," she says.

"I don't want to act weird," I say. I grab Greer's red softball hat off the hook by my door and throw it in my bag. There's no way I'm going to really need a hat.

"Then don't," she says.

ETHAN'S WAITING BY a gray Audi station wagon in the empty rec parking lot. He's in pale blue shorts and a white button-down. He's casual but also dressed for a date. When he sees me pull in, he walks over to my car to open the door.

"I can drive," I say by way of greeting.

"I bet you're a great driver," he says. "But I'm driving."

"I didn't picture you as a station wagon guy," I say.

"You expected a minivan?" he asks. I start to say no, that I expected a Jeep or an SUV, but then I think maybe he's kidding. I want to be kidding too, but I have suddenly forgotten how to be kidding.

He opens the passenger door for me and I get in. His car is immaculate, and I'm immediately grateful that we aren't taking my car. I keep a lint roller in the glove compartment because of the dog hair.

He gets in the driver's seat and turns to me. "Ready?"

This feels like such a loaded question. Am I ready? I look at his hands on the steering wheel and his forearms where he's rolled up his sleeves. In the confines of this car, I can smell him—like pine and a candle burning in an old church.

"I am ready," I lie. He makes a left and heads down Magnolia Drive, out of Beechwood, toward Baxter. I smooth my dress over my knees and fold my hands. I am trying to think of something to say but my mind is blank. I can't even remember my job interview question.

We stop at a traffic light and he turns to me. "First date, huh?"

"Yes." I would give anything not to be this nervous. My heart is beating too fast and I have no way of controlling that without taking deep breaths, which, of course, would make me seem like I'm hyperventilating. Which I'm pretty sure is a dating no-no.

"I'm honored. When was your last first date?"

"I was twenty-four." I want him to keep asking me questions that I know the answers to.

"How'd that one go?" He looks over at me and his eyes catch mine in a way that's more than a glance. It's disarming, the way he looks right in my eyes.

"Fine," I say. But then I picture Pete in his biking shorts and make a face.

"What's that face for?" he laughs, and it relaxes me a little. It's the second time I've heard his laugh. It sounds like it comes from someplace deeper than his chest.

"We biked over the Brooklyn Bridge. That was the date. He was in these biking shorts and, I don't know, I don't really think they're a good look for everyone."

"They do make you think of an overstuffed sausage."

"Exactly," I say. And I turn to watch him watch the road. He has a slight bump on his nose that makes his whole face look strong.

He turns to me and the quick eye contact invites me in. "So then what? Besides the sausage pants, how was the date? I want to know what pitfalls to avoid."

"Well, so far you're batting a thousand with the appropriately loose clothing."

"Skateboarders don't wear a lot of Lycra," he says. "So then what? You rode across the bridge?"

"Yeah," I say. "It was exciting and exhausting. But also kind of weird. Like a first date where I'm following him around, sweating. No eye contact." This is actually a perfect metaphor for our marriage, I don't say.

"That is weird. Let's have so much eye contact tonight."

"So much," I say, and this makes me laugh.

WHEN WE GET to Baxter, he turns into the marina. "Did you bring a hat?" he asks.

"I did. Are we going on a boat?" I ask.

"We're going to a baseball game, by way of boat." He's smiling at me, waiting for a response, and all I can do is smile back. Part of me just wants to stay in this car with him where I can smell him and watch his hands grip the steering wheel, but the rest of me is excited to jump into the night. "We're nailing the whole eye contact thing," he says finally. I laugh again, and it wipes out the rest of my nerves.

We walk through the marina, and Ethan stops at a two-seater powerboat with a lounge seat at the back. "It's not mine," he says. "My friend loaned it to me because the traffic can be horrible getting to Connecticut." He says it like traveling by boat is the most normal possible way to combat traffic.

I take off my sandals and hop in just as he's extending a hand to help me. Full of regret over that missed opportunity to touch his hand, I settle into the passenger seat. He's all business starting the engine and untying the ropes from the dock. I'm a bit unsettled not knowing where I'm going, but also excited. I haven't been on an outing that I didn't plan since my mother got sick.

"Wait, what baseball is in Connecticut?"

He backs away from the dock. "Minor league. Rookie league really. The Southport Rockets. A guy I know is pitching." He puts the engine in neutral and turns to me. "Is this okay? I thought a surprise would be fun, but I probably should have asked you." There's a crease in his brow that I haven't seen before. It's the first time I've seen him unsure.

I'm crossing state lines with a total stranger because I'm hoping to remove a few firsts from my recovery checklist.

He makes a good point. But the air is summer warm, and the sun is as low as the stakes. Rookie-league baseball. A one-off date with a cute guy.

"No, this is great," I say and put on Greer's hat.

The ride up the coast to Southport is about thirty minutes. The engine is loud so we don't talk. I like the way the mist of sea spray is landing on my arms, how the wind in my face makes me feel free. I steal glances at him while he drives, and he catches me.

We dock and he cuts the engine. The new quiet is replaced by the sound of gulls and the crack of a bat hitting a line drive. He hops onto the dock and reaches to help me out of the boat. His hand feels strong and sure, and for a second, it seems like neither of us is going to let go. We make our way through the tiny marina, and the sound of cheering gets more distinct as we walk a block inland toward the stadium. We should be talking, I think.

"How do you know the pitcher?" I ask.

"He's from Devon. That's where I live."

"Massachusetts?" *Massa-Cheez-Its.* I hear my mom snort.

"Yes." He turns to me, and in this light, I can see he has a scar on his right eyebrow, but there's no crease next to it now. His face is completely open and relaxed.

The stadium announces itself with a forty-foot rocket out front. A wooden sign encourages us to **BLAST OFF INTO SUMMER.** An elderly man takes our tickets, and we find our seats in the front row, right by third base. I've never sat so close at a baseball game, but then again this isn't exactly

Yankee Stadium. Half the seats are empty, and there's a man a few rows back who is sound asleep. It's the third inning, and the Rockets are down one to five.

"How long have you lived in Devon?" I ask.

"Six years."

"And what do you do?"

"I'm a lawyer. You're good at dating—I can see you've mastered this part." He gives me a sideways smile and nudges me with his shoulder.

"Yeah, I'm a pro," I say. "Want me to guess your sign?"

He puts his feet up on the concrete wall in front of us and relaxes back into his seat. I put mine up next to his and lean back, happy with this view of his legs.

"Leo," he says.

"Knew it. Have you ever been married?"

"No."

"Why not?"

"I've never really dated anyone I wanted to marry, and also I'm told I'm unreliable." I turn to him and narrow my eyes. Unreliable. It's a good thing I'm not in the market for a husband, because this would be a deal-breaker. I wait for him to say more about this, but he doesn't.

A man comes by with a huge box strapped to his chest, and my unreliable date buys me an ice-cold beer and a hot dog.

"This may not have been the fine dining you were hoping for on your first date, but I promise the ice cream sandwiches are excellent."

We clink our plastic cups together and drink to that.

"There he is," Ethan says as a new pitcher takes the mound. We watch him warm up and then walk three players, followed by a grand slam.

"At least the beer's cold," I say. I take a sip and I can feel him smiling at me. I lean back in my seat and my arm brushes against his on the shared armrest. I am stunned by the feel of it, and I stay perfectly still to keep him there.

IT'S THE NINTH inning, the Rockets are down by twelve, and I've had two hot dogs and two beers. Ethan shells peanuts and hands them to me, while we watch the Southport Rockets let in run after run. We talk about nothing. It is a free-flowing, easy stream of conversation that feels like it's pulling me along, each topic leading to another. He tells me about the particular quirks of Massachusetts drivers. He likes San Diego but only to visit. It turns out we lived in the same neighborhood in Manhattan for a month more than a decade ago.

I tell him about my organizing business. "I'm running out of houses to organize in Beechwood, but I'm trying to make it a thing on Instagram."

"Because you're very organized?"

"Yes," I say. And immediately think of the full year of my kids' artwork currently on the floor by my front door. "Well, it's not so much that I'm currently organized, but I like to bring order to things. It helps me relax."

"Me too," he says, and it surprises me. "That's pretty much what my legal work is. I work mostly in housing and personal injury. Solving problems. Restoring balance. It feels good."

"Yes," I say. And before I've thought it through, I lean in toward him and say, "Yesterday, I took everything out of this woman's mudroom, wiped the shelves clean, and only put half of it back in so that there was space between every pair of shoes."

"That must have felt great. She must have been so happy." We're leaning on one another now, shoulder to shoulder, arms still sharing the armrest and heads nearly touching.

"Not as happy as I was."

He laughs, and I watch his mouth so close to mine. I don't know how much time you can spend looking at someone's mouth before it becomes awkward, but I'm probably pushing it.

"I'm glad you agreed to come with me. You're fun, and of course the alternatives were coming by myself or another night with my family."

"Is your family not fun?" I take a peanut from his hand.

"They're actually very fun. But you know how it can be."

I don't, actually. I don't really have a baseline for what most families are like. "I don't."

"They're great. They really are. But I'm the person in the family who doesn't quite fit in." He looks out at the field and then back at me. "The outlier, you know? I think maybe they always wanted me to be someone different."

"Different how?"

"Well, like a football player, for starters. My dad never got over the fact that I wasn't interested in football." He pops a peanut into his mouth. "It was like he hoped one day I'd come down for breakfast in pads and a helmet and make his dreams come true."

I think of Cliffy and feel a pit in my stomach. I know this is the vibe he's getting from Pete. "That stinks," I say, at a loss for better words. The best thing about my mom was that she saw me for exactly who I was.

"Yeah, and it's sort of still like that. They don't understand why I live up in Devon. I have a great life there, but it's like they're waiting for me to snap out of it, go back to working at a law firm in Manhattan, and bring my wife and two point five kids to Sunday dinner."

"No one ever tells you the point-five kid turns into a full kid, every time," I say.

He laughs. "Should we work on our eye contact some more?"

We lock eyes, and it's playful. He stepped into a vulnerable topic and stepped right out. I'd like to be able to do that.

WE GET ICE cream sandwiches on the way out and eat them as we walk back to the boat. They're the classic kind with thin chocolate wafers that stick to the roof of your mouth. They're delicious, and we lick our fingers and share napkins as the vanilla ice cream drips down our wrists.

As we approach the water, the moon casts a perfect stripe that ends at the dock. I stop to look, because it's magic the way it lines up so perfectly. A one-in-a-million chance, sort of like a handsome man passing through my town on the exact day I take off my ring. It's starting to feel like a champagne summer.

Ethan powers up the boat and we head out into the sound. He's driving slowly, and I'm glad because I'm not ready for this night to be over. After a few minutes, he cuts the engine.

"Are you in a hurry to get back?" he asks.

"Not even a little bit," I say, and smile, because it's true.

He smiles back. "Let's just float for a bit."

I follow him to the back of the boat, where he plops down on the lounge seat and puts his feet up on the center console. I do the same, and we are back to where we were in the stadium—reclined, shoulders touching, and leaning into one another.

"Comfortable?" he asks.

"Yes." It's odd how the space is so small again. The sky stretches above us and there's water as far as I can see, but I'm cozy here with Ethan.

"So what's your life like? Single with three kids?"

I turn my head toward him. He's looking at me with that open-faced expression, like he's ready to take on anything. "It's like you'd imagine it," I say.

"How do I imagine it?"

"Sort of hectic but beautiful. I have great kids. My husband. My ex-husband I guess. Pete, with the sausage pants. He doesn't really step in much." Okay, Rule Number One on a Date: don't say "husband."

"Does anyone help you out?"

Rule Number Two: don't say "dead mother." "My friend Frannie is great. She's with my kids tonight."

Something passes across his face. It's a slight expression

shift, almost a wince, that makes me think he's about to take this conversation in a different direction.

"What?"

"What, what?" he asks, and turns back to the moon.

"You looked like you were about to say something."

"No." He shakes his head a little. "It's nothing. I'm really glad we got to do this." And there's something he's not saying. It's almost like the words he wants to add are "just this one time." Which, of course.

We're quiet for a bit, and I concentrate on the feel of his arm next to mine and the slight rocking of the boat under me. "So where are you with your divorce?" he asks.

"It's imminent."

"Do you want to talk about it? I'm a pretty good lawyer."

"Yeah, but not in Manhattan, I hear." I turn to him to see if he knows I'm kidding.

He shakes his head and runs a hand through his hair. "Honestly, I think the whole reason I went to law school was to get my parents to take me seriously. But even back when I was a corporate lawyer, they still treated me like I was fourteen and maybe about to burn the house down."

I laugh. "Did you grow up around here?"

He looks away, back up at the moon.

"Did you grow up in New York?" I try again.

The crease is back in his brow. "Connecticut," he says.

"I'm a big fan of the Southport Rockets," I say. "So were you kind of a screwup in high school?"

"For sure." He meets my eyes and his face is open again. I feel that connection that's been building all night, like he's telling me something that matters.

"How so?" I ask.

"In a quiet way. I didn't make a big splash about it. My acts of terror were mostly against myself." He looks back to the sky, and I know this is something he doesn't want to talk about. I want to know more, and I want to keep hearing the sound of his voice.

Instead, we're quiet for a while. I listen to the sound of the water lapping up against the boat. I watch our bare feet next to each other on the console. I watch a cloud pass over the moon above us. I try to memorize this fun night with this fun man. A night like this could easily never happen again, and I want to be able to look back and remember it—the sound of the water hitting the boat, the stripe of moonlight, the press of his shoulder against mine.

I turn to him just as he turns to me.

"So how'd your first date go?" he asks.

"So much eye contact," I say.

He smiles, just a little. There's a sadness to it that's totally out of place. "I'm glad I got to be the guy."

The water keeps lapping up against the boat in a slow rhythm. The moon keeps laying its rippled stripe down the middle of things. And Ethan keeps looking at me like he's going to kiss me any second. But he doesn't.

He takes my hand, and it startles me. Both the strong feel of it and the way he's entwined our fingers like this is something we do all the time. He feels soft and strong at the same time, and I think the whole construction-worker-turned-concert-pianist thing may have been spot-on.

"I'm going to get you home," he says, and sits up, releasing my hand.

We're back in Baxter more quickly than I'd like. He cuts the engine and ties up the boat. And as we walk back down the dock to the car, my mind reeling, he takes my hand again.

We're quiet on the drive back to the rec. He parks next to my car and gets out. He's definitely going to kiss me now. I am loopy with anticipation. He comes around to my side of the car and reaches out his hand to help me out. I get out, and he doesn't let go. We're facing each other, and I take a small step forward, just to make my consent crystal clear.

"Thanks for tonight," he says. "It was perfect." And he does not kiss me.

8

WHO'S FEELING FUN-TASTIC?" MRS. HOGAN GREETS us at the door the next night in a pineapple-print sundress and, more notably, Carmen Miranda's fruit head-dress. Cliffy lets out a little squeal of delight. I think he would love to live in a world where everyone was as playful as the Hogans. Iris beams. Greer averts her eyes, embar-rassed for herself, Mrs. Hogan, and everyone on earth who has ever considered eating fruit.

"Well, I am now," I say, giving her a hug and pressing my face into the side of a plastic banana. This banana is reality. I am not in a life with soft, entwined hands and too-close lips. I am in a life with plastic fruit. I need to embrace my reality and recalibrate after that date. In addition to not kissing me, Ethan did not ask for my phone number. I am officially bad at dating, like I need a seminar, and that's that. "You look fabulous."

"Just a little something I threw together. Florida's made Charlie and me eternally tropical."

We walk into the foyer and take off our shoes. I always

think of this house in the feminine; she is one of the oldest houses in Beechwood and she is a grande dame. She is the only residential home right in the center of town, and her neighbors are city hall to the right and the library to the left. She is made of whitewashed brick, and her oversized leaded windows keep everything light. Her floors are a dark mahogany, and the oak staircase was carved by the same artisans who were building the local Episcopal church that same year. She has small rooms off of other rooms for purposes we'll never know. There's even a four-foot-tall closet under the front stairs, exclusively for children's coats. I grew up admiring this house, and I always feel like she demands and deserves my respect. So we take off our shoes.

Mr. Hogan calls from the kitchen, "Where's my head thing?"

"Right on the table," Mrs. Hogan calls back. "Come on in. Frannie's got drinks on the patio. I hope you brought your bathing suits."

Greer holds up a tote bag in response, and we make our way through the kitchen out to the backyard. There's an outdoor seating area against an ivy-covered brick wall, and a small outdoor kitchen. Frannie's standing by the sink transferring a pitcher of piña coladas into a carved-out pineapple with a spout on one side. She looks up and shrugs. "My dad's invention." And to my kids, "Hi, guys, you want to swim before dinner? Something tells me it'll be funtastic." She rolls her eyes and gives me a hug.

My kids run inside to change and I take a sip of my drink. It's strong, and I make a mental note not to finish it.

"So spill it. The date. Where'd you go? All of it," Frannie says. She, Marco, and Theo were sound asleep when I got back, so I sent them home without the download.

"It was good. Or maybe great. I don't know. He's just this perfect guy, like from a movie. The kind who tunes in and isn't all about himself. He asks follow-up questions."

"Okay, so he's a unicorn. Or he's hideous. Attractive men don't ask follow-up questions."

"He's so attractive. Like with this hair and these eyes." I really don't know how to describe him.

"Everyone has hair and eyes, at least at some point, Ali."

I ignore her. "He's sexy. He has these beautiful hands, like a construction worker who is also a concert pianist. But something's off. He didn't kiss me and I feel like there's something he wasn't telling me."

"Like he's married?"

"I would be shocked." And as I say it, I am actually shocked because Ethan walks onto the patio.

I have to be imagining this. I look back at my drink, which is, in fact, strong, but I've only had one sip. It's definitely him and he's standing at the French doors. He's in a navy blue T-shirt and white shorts and is holding a bag of ice in one hand and has Brenda cradled in the other arm. He seems relaxed, not at all like he's just stormed into the Hogans' house uninvited. My heart is racing, and I try for a deep breath but can't quite catch it. Now he's giving Mrs. Hogan a kiss on her cheek.

"What?" Frannie is saying. I don't take my eyes off of him. "Ali, what? It's just Scooter."

"Scooter," I say. No, no, no, no, no, no. There is no way Scooter is the guy whose gold-flecked eyes I stared into last night. There is no way Scooter owns the beautiful fingers that wrapped around mine in a way that made heat pool low in my belly. Scooter has a mullet and a skateboard. Scooter was suspended his freshman year for stealing a freezer full of ice cream sandwiches from the cafeteria. Omigod. Of course the first guy I go on a date with in fourteen years turns out to be Frannie's weird little brother. I thought I was getting my life together—checking items off my recovery list—and here I am, a fresh hot mess.

"Yeah, it only took him forty-five minutes to get a bag of ice. Classic," Frannie says.

Ethan looks up and sees me. It is not an *Oh yay, there's the woman I held hands with last night* look. It's more like the look you'd have on your face if bats started flying out of your toilet.

I don't know how to organize my face or where to look as he walks toward us.

"Ali," he says.

"Scooter," I say. It sort of sounds like an accusation. I'm holding his gaze because I'm a little angry, and I don't want to let him off the hook. There is no way on earth he didn't know who I was last night. I mentioned Frannie, and he winced.

"Hi," he says. There's a slight cringe to the way he's looking at me, as if he's embarrassed to have been caught impersonating a guy who is not Frannie's brother.

I can see Frannie watching us in my peripheral vision, back and forth, like she's waiting for the ball to land. Mrs.

Hogan calls her over to the grill, and she hesitates before walking away.

"You said Connecticut," I say.

"I can explain," he says just as my kids run over, soaking wet. Cliffy throws his wet arms around me with the unnecessary exuberance of a six-year-old boy.

"Cliffy," Ethan says.

"Hi," Cliffy says.

Frannie comes back with a *What did I miss* vibe.

"And these are my daughters, Greer and Iris," I say, trying to recover. "This is Scooter, Frannie's little brother. And his dog, Brenda."

"You know Brenda?" Frannie asks.

I sure do. He must have known who I was all along. I thought he was going to kiss me and he was—what? Tricking me? I need to change the tone of this conversation so that I don't burst into tears or break something.

"We met at the dog park. Ferris kind of picked Scooter, if you know what I mean." I give Iris a look.

"Oh my God, Mom. Tell me Ferris didn't pee on him," says Greer.

"Yep, picked him out of the crowd. Soaked him down to his socks." Maybe he deserved it.

Ethan is visibly uncomfortable. His brow is creased, his face is closed, and he looks like he wants to bolt. He turns to the lawn, where there's a kids' play tunnel and a bunch of dog toys. "So I'm trying to train Brenda to run through that tunnel," he says to my kids. "Supposed to be good for her brain. Want to help me?"

"Yes!" says Cliffy, and runs toward the toys.

Ethan follows him. *Coward,* I think. Greer and Iris look at each other and then at me. "Go ahead," I say. I really need to not be with my kids right now.

When they've run across the lawn, I say to Frannie, "Okay, so, weird about Scooter."

"You mean about Scooter being weird?"

"No, about him growing up to be a full-sized man."

"Happens to most boys, I think. But deep down, he's still the same Scooter who got high and set fire to the basement rug."

"Huh. I would never have recognized him. I thought—" I don't know what it is that I want to say here. I thought I was going to run into him again this morning, which is why I hunted around the floor of my closet to find a pair of white jeans and a yellow linen top. As if wearing white jeans to the dog park is a totally rational thing to do. I thought maybe all that effort was going to lead to another date and an actual kiss. I am clearly delusional. "He doesn't match my vague memory of an undersized kid on a skateboard."

"We left for college when he was, what? Sixteen?"

"I guess. Wasn't he kind of a weirdo? Like a skate rat?"

"He's totally still a weirdo, and he still skateboards," she says. "But then again, he probably remembers you in hard pants."

"I was wearing hard pants when I met him, and you didn't say anything about this." I gesture to the tank top and skirt that I'm wearing. I wait for her to mention that the skirt has an elastic waist so it basically behaves like sweatpants.

"Progress," she says.

We're quiet for a bit, watching Iris crawl halfway into the tunnel to coax Brenda through while Ethan ceremoniously places a bucket hat on Cliffy's head. Iris and Cliffy crawl through the tunnel, and Greer waves a stuffed bunny. Brenda doesn't budge.

"It's nice to see them having fun," I say to change the subject.

"I was going to say that about Scooter."

"He seems like the kind of guy who's always having fun. Looking like that and skateboarding around." Tricking single mothers into thinking he's someone else. That's next-level unreliable.

Frannie gives me a sideways glance. "He's thirty-six years old and a lawyer, Ali. People even call him Ethan, if you can believe that."

"Crazy," I say. I'm watching him squat down and give Brenda a treat for doing absolutely nothing.

"He came because my parents summoned him, but I think mostly he had to get away for a bit."

"Why?"

"Bad breakup."

In addition to the tornado of emotions I'm trying to tamp down—anger, sadness, embarrassment—I hate this girlfriend who got to hold his hand whenever she wanted to. And I also feel sorry for her. Down by the pool, Cliffy and Iris chase poor Brenda through the garden. Greer and Ethan are watching and talking, and I would give anything to know what they're talking about.

"Poor woman." I can't imagine having those eyes on you all the time and then not having them there at all. Well, actually, I can.

"I think she broke up with him." I didn't see this coming. What more could that woman possibly have been looking for? "She realized he's not ready to be a grown-up." Ah.

MY KIDS GIVE up on Brenda and jump back into the pool, and Ethan joins us on the patio. "So," he says, and grabs a beer from the cooler between us. I search his face for the remnants of the easygoing guy from last night, but he's tense. As he should be.

"Scooter," I say, with emphasis.

"How weird is he with that dog," Frannie says. "I mean, who adopts a dog with mental health issues and tries to fix her with circus tricks?"

"Me, I guess," he says. His free hand is in his pocket and his shoulders are pitched forward. He is not even a little bit comfortable in his skin.

Mrs. Hogan calls to Frannie from the kitchen, and she leaves us there looking at each other.

"I'm sorry," he says. In the daylight there are still little flecks of gold in his eyes.

"So what was last night? A joke?" I'm loud-whispering, but I sort of wish I were shouting. "Were you messing with me?" This thought tightens my chest.

"I'm really sorry. It was so perfect last night, and I knew it would be ruined if you knew who I was. I was about to tell you a bunch of times, but I didn't want to give up how you were looking at me. I don't think you ever looked me in the eye in high school. And I wanted you to." He takes a step toward me, as if he's going to take my hand. He's Ethan again, confident and in command, and I am struck by the fact that time is a powerful thing. It's made him so strong and sure, and it's made me unsteady. This must be what they mean by the law of conservation of matter: maybe he found everything I lost.

"Well, now I know," I say, and sip my too-strong drink. "Scooter."

"I should have said something after the game, and I was going to when we were on the boat."

"Boat?" Frannie is back. "When were you on a boat?" She's looking at Ethan, and then at me. And I see the realization roll across her face. "You said 'sexy,'" she says to me.

"She did?" Ethan asks, eyebrows raised.

"Oh my God," says Frannie.

Before I can defend myself, Marco joins us on the patio with Theo in a sling. "Is it me, or is this family getting weirder all the time?" He gives me a hug and I bury my nose in the top of Theo's warm baby head. He smells like cheeseburgers.

Mr. and Mrs. Hogan are assembling plates in the outdoor kitchen and call for us to sit down. I find my palm tree place card and sit to the right of Mr. Hogan, who has now found and donned his fruit hat. Ethan is across from me and I try not to look at him.

Mr. Hogan raises his cocktail. "To Florida!" We all clink glasses.

"And to having Scooter here," says Mrs. Hogan. "It's so wonderful to have you back, sweetheart."

"Thank you, Mom. It's always good to be home."

"Which is why you're never here?" asks Frannie. It's interesting to see this dynamic. I know Frannie as an adult and a mom and a restaurant manager. I don't know her as an older sister, who's potentially a little prickly.

Ethan rolls his eyes and takes a sip of his beer.

"His work is in Massachusetts," Marco says. "It's not like he can be popping in for Sunday dinner every week."

Mr. Hogan cuts his steak and admires the piece on his fork. "Well, it was nice when he was a real lawyer and lived in Manhattan. We saw more of him then."

"I am a real lawyer, Dad," Ethan says in one breath, like he's said this a million times already today.

"Of course, I know. I mean like with a firm. Like before." Mr. Hogan reaches over and pats Ethan's hand.

"It's wonderful that you've found something to keep you busy, sweetheart," says Mrs. Hogan. "Just wonderful. And I wish it was closer to home, but no one knows how great it is to start fresh more than we do. Right, Charlie?"

Mr. Hogan agrees. "We sure had fun in Florida."

I look across at Ethan and see the tension in his face. It's exactly as he described it, just without the two point five kids. I suspect this is a decade-old conversation in the Hogan family—Scooter, the problem child who didn't move back home. He leans back and runs a hand through his hair. He catches me watching him and rolls his eyes the smallest bit. It feels oddly intimate, like he and I are the only two people at the table who know how he feels. But I look away because I don't need to be sharing intimacies with a guy who held my hand under false pretenses.

Cliffy climbs onto my lap and takes off my charm bracelet. He lays it flat, like he always does, and runs his fingers over the events of my life, the tiny charms that my mom designed to document it: fairy, ship, soccer ball, graduation hat, University of Michigan, graduation hat, business suit, wedding dress, baby girl, dog, baby girl, little brick house, baby boy.

Frannie says, "Well, we're glad you're back. It wasn't exactly convenient that you guys went away for the first time ever at the beginning of the inn's busy season."

Mrs. Hogan smiles and nods her fruit to her husband. He puts down his glass and says, "Well, that's something we want to talk about, and partially why we wanted Scooter here." He looks across at Mrs. Hogan for encouragement and she smiles. I feel pressure on my chest watching this silent communication. Pete and I were never like this. Not even at the beginning. For the most part, our communication bumped off our kids or was rerouted and diffused by my mother. I don't think we ever talked with our eyes. This is something I should have known enough to want. *Comparison is the thief of joy, honey.*

Mrs. Hogan takes over. "We're going back Monday." And she smiles with the brightness of the tropical sun, clasping her hands together as if she's waiting for us to cheer.

"I don't understand," says Frannie.

"She said they're going to Florida on Monday," explains Iris.

"Yes, but why?"

"We've talked about this," says Mr. Hogan. "We think we may have been in a rut. And that trip to the Keys made us feel young again. We found a little house right on the water. So we're moving to Florida. You all are welcome to visit whenever you like, you included," he says, with a wink to my kids.

"No one moves to Florida in the summer," says Ethan.

"We love it there," says Mrs. Hogan.

"And we're going to get a boat and learn to fish," says Mr. Hogan. "So we're not going to run out of things to do."

Frannie places her napkin on the table. "Just wait a second. I don't understand. Are you selling the house? Are you never coming back here? What about the inn? You need to be here for the summer rush at the inn. And what about Theo?"

Mr. Hogan looks to his wife for permission to go on. "Well, that's the other thing. We're retiring. Harold Webster is stepping into the role of general manager at the inn."

"And of course we'll be up to see Theo," Mrs. Hogan adds.

"Harold Webster is a beach attendant. He stacks chairs," says Frannie. Her voice is measured, like she's using all of her energy to restrain herself.

"Yes," Mr. Hogan agrees. "He was a very competent beach attendant. And now he's general manager. And you and Marco are around—you can help fight fires."

"Marco and I are running the diner. Seven days a week. And we have a baby, if you haven't noticed." Her voice breaks, and I think she's going to cry.

"Honey, this is doable. The inn practically runs itself," says Mrs. Hogan.

Greer's looking at me like she wants to run. This is a tense family moment and the chance of tears seems pretty high. We shouldn't be here for this.

Ethan refills Frannie's wineglass. "This is a lot," he says. "I'll keep doing the legal stuff, but to be clear, I'm not going to be able to be physically here to help."

"We know, Scooter. You've told us a thousand times. You're not going to help," Frannie says, and takes a too-big sip of wine and wipes her mouth with the back of her hand. "What about the house? Are you selling the house?"

Mr. Hogan says, "We're giving Scooter the house."

"What?" Ethan pushes himself back from the table.

"And we're giving Frannie the diner," Mr. Hogan says. "We've had them appraised, and they're roughly the same value. Your mother and I are keeping the inn, of course, and we'll keep an eye on Harold from Florida."

"Wait. What am I going to do with this house?" Ethan asks. "I'm not moving back here." It comes out as more of a plea than a statement, as if the next thing out of his mouth will be, *You can't make me.*

"Sell it. Get married and fill it with kids. Do whatever you want. It's yours," says Mr. Hogan.

"I don't think Scooter's in any hurry to get married, dear," Mrs. Hogan says.

Frannie is staring at her plate. Marco puts his arm around her. When she looks up, there are tears in her eyes. "It's very generous, thank you. I'm just not ready to lose you." It was the last thing I said to my mom, selfishly. As if her suffering and imminent dying were somehow about me and how unready I was. But it was true: I have never been less ready for anything in my life. I wrap my arms around Cliffy.

"Jesus, Frannie, they're not dying," Ethan says. "They're retiring and moving to Florida. It's kind of what people do."

"Then you should sell the inn," Frannie says. "Take the Beekman offer. It's just too much to manage without you."

"Why aren't you getting married?" Cliffy asks.

"Cliffy." Greer heaves a sigh. "Personal boundaries?"

Ethan looks around the table and gives Cliffy a sideways smile that doesn't reach his eyes. "Apparently, I'm unreliable. Just ask anyone in Beechwood."

9

IT'S SATURDAY AND PETE'S TAKEN THE KIDS TO SOCCER. Frannie texts me: Sexy? Scooter???

Me: He said Ethan. How was I supposed to know? Won't happen again

Frannie: Ok, good, because weird. But I'm glad you went out at all. We'll find you someone normal

I look at my phone for a few seconds, at the word "normal." It morphs in front of my eyes into something negative. Normal is a man walking into my kitchen and making me feel absolutely nothing. Normal is just getting through a conversation so it can be over. Normal is someone like Pete.

I get back from Phyllis's and decide not to go to the dog park. I do not need to be hunting down a man who so quickly inspired black-hole-sized fantasies in my mind while also completely lying about who he was. I am finishing my second cup of coffee and deadheading the geraniums by my front door when his station wagon pulls into my driveway.

Ethan gets out and leaves the windows down for Brenda in the backseat. "Hey," he says from the end of my walkway.

His hands are in his pockets, and I'm a little relieved that he seems nervous. I don't know if he's nervous because now I know he's Scooter, or because now he's the one doing the stalking.

"Hi," I say.

"I hope this is okay. My mom told me where you lived. I was going to take Brenda to Beechwood Point and wondered if you guys wanted to come."

"My kids just left with their dad," I say.

"Oh, okay." But he doesn't turn to go. "Are you and Ferris free?"

There is no reason in the world for me to go on a second excursion with this man. I am humiliated thinking about it. But he takes a hand out of his pocket and runs it through his hair in a way that makes me think, *Yes.* Yes to the way his hand runs through his hair. Yes to making him explain himself. Yes to getting another taste of that lighter way I feel when I'm with him. I'm in the house grabbing Ferris and a leash before I've had a chance to think it through any further. It's been a week of tiny steps forward, though I now wish one of those steps would have been washing my hair this morning. I stop at the mirror by the front door and put my hair into a braid.

I get into the car and say, "So where are we going exactly?"

"The very tip of Beechwood Point."

"Of course, you're a local. The Fairlawns' house?"

"To the right."

"The Schwartzes' house?"

"To the left."

"There's nothing between those houses."

He's smiling. "You'll see. I owe you a really big apology, and I think I need a better setting than the front seat of my car."

"Agreed," I say, and look out the window.

We drive down by the water and pass the dog park and the inn. Beyond the inn is more public shoreline and then about twenty waterfront homes that end at Beechwood Point. It's all private property. "Okay, so now that you've met my children, you also know I can't get arrested, right?"

"We won't get arrested."

"Because we're not breaking the law?"

"No, we're totally breaking the law. But I've done this a million times. You never get arrested for break-in a million and *one*."

I turn to the window and grip Ferris tighter. I have been out of my comfort zone since the day I met Ethan, and there's a bit of excitement mixed in with my nerves.

"Not much of a rule breaker?" he asks.

"Exactly never."

"Today's your day." He pulls up in front of the Schwartzes' gray stone mansion. "We're here." When I don't move, he says. "If we get caught, I'll take the fall. I'll say I kidnapped you."

I roll my eyes and get out of the car. We walk our dogs past the Schwartzes' tall hedge and black iron fence. The air is damp and thick here closer to the water, and there are no cars on the road. This part of town feels like a gothic novel, with giant old homes and a murder of crows keeping watch. I don't know where we're going, but I can feel the excitement that comes with taking a risk creep right up my spine. Ethan stops at the end of the Schwartzes' fence. To the right is the Fairlawns' house. He moves toward a wall of ivy between the two houses and turns back to me. "Through here."

As he cuts a few of the vines with a pocketknife, I realize that we are at the Ghost Gate. Or at least that's what we used to call it when we were kids. It's a rusted-out gate between those two houses that leads to a sandy path. Before these vines grew in, you could see the first few yards of the path where it turns into a grove of trees. In high school, kids used to talk about what was back there, but the one kid who actually tried to find out got caught on the security cameras and was arrested. Sort of the way we're going to be arrested today. I should turn back immediately, but I don't.

Ethan pushes the gate open just wide enough for us to get through, and I grab his arm. "Again, single mom. Not really up for prison time."

"We'll be fine." He's looking down at me and it feels like he's daring me to follow him. Daring me to do something incredibly reckless that might end up wonderful. I notice I'm still holding on to his arm and quickly let go.

"Seriously. Look. There are two security cameras, one on each side." I wave at them for good measure. "Let's just get out of here."

"I really want you to come with me. My big apology isn't going to land right if you're not there." His tone is light, but his eyes are pleading with me. "Would it make you feel better to know that when I was sixteen, I reoriented those security cameras so that they miss the exact spot where we're standing?"

"You did not."

"Look at them." And I do. They're trained on the edges of the gate.

"No one's ever noticed?"

"Well, no one's ever moved them back. See? I'm a problem solver. Come on."

We push through the gate and close it behind us and let the dogs run ahead down the path. We turn into a row of maple trees that touch branches overhead so that the path is darker but speckled in sunlight. I stop and look up at the canopy. I want to spin around in that space. I want to lie down in the path and be speckled myself. I turn and he is watching me, a smile on his face.

"It's amazing," I say.

As we walk through the leafy tunnel of green, the water appears in the distance. Our dogs race ahead and then back. I thought I'd seen every corner of Beechwood, like I'd worn this place out until it was threadbare. I know every street, and I know most of the people. I have never seen this patch of heaven before.

When we emerge from the trees, we are at the water. There's a small crescent of beach maybe twenty feet wide, covered in white sand and shells. We are enclosed on both sides by tall beach grasses. The sky is a dark July blue, and ahead of us is a perfect view of the Manhattan skyline.

"Wow," I say. Because, *wow*. "This is beautiful. I've never seen it from here. I knew the city was right there, but I've never . . . wow."

I turn to him and he's watching me take this in. "Yes, beautiful," he says.

We sit down at the center of the crescent of beach, and I feel like we are two pearls in the center of an oyster. We are close enough to the lapping waves that I can feel the cool air off the water on my legs, but we're not close enough to get wet. The sun is warm on my face, and the only sounds I hear are gulls, the waves, and the splashing of dog feet.

"Did you and your friends hang out here in high school?" I ask.

"I usually came by myself."

I still can't picture this man being an awkward teenager. "And what did you do?"

He nods at the skyline in the distance. "I daydreamed about getting out of here. So escape fantasies mostly."

"I had those too." He turns to me as if he wants to hear my escape fantasies. "I just wanted to go and become my own person." I needed to go out and see who I was separate from my mom. I wanted to know I could take care of myself.

"You were always your own person, Ali." He's looking out at the water and then turns back to me. "I remember one Halloween you and your friends came into the diner for late-night pancakes. Your friends were a sexy nurse, a sexy vampire, a sexy cat, and you were a pumpkin. Do you re-member that?"

"I do."

"Not a sexy pumpkin either. Like a big orange one with

a black toothy grin. I just remember thinking you were the coolest girl ever."

I love hearing this. I love that I was once that person and that someone remembers. I want to tell him about how my mom convinced the tailor at the dry cleaner's downstairs to let her use his sewing machine for that pumpkin, but I don't. I'm not good at mentioning my mom casually—my voice always breaks.

"So was the city what you hoped?" he asks.

"Yep. I went and got a grown-up job and everything. Accounting. It was like organizing someone's mudroom times a thousand. I loved it."

"Why'd you come back?"

"It's kind of a long story. I was dating Pete for about a year and got pregnant, so we got married. I kind of panicked because Greer was born prematurely, and I quit my job. And then I had Iris a year later. I thought coming back here might make my life easier, with my mom here to help."

"That wasn't that long of a story," he says.

I smile at the water. "I guess not."

He rests his forearms on his knees and watches the water. My forearms are on my knees in the same way, and if I leaned a bit to the left our shoulders would be touching. There's heat coming off him now and I imagine I can feel the blond hair on his arms brushing up against my skin. The distance between us feels like nothing, a whisper.

He's quiet for a second as a gull swoops down and plucks something off the beach and flies away. A large sailboat passes in the distance and momentarily breaks the skyline.

"I wanted to kiss you," he says. "Thursday night, and at

the skate park, and at the dog park. And a million times before that, actually."

"Oh?" It comes out high-pitched. I am taken aback by what he's said and how easily he's said it.

He laughs. "Don't be weird about it, I'm trying to apologize. I was a little bit obsessed with you when I was a teenager. And when I ran into you and you looked at me like I wasn't Scooter, it felt really good. I should have told you before we went out, but it just kept getting better and better. It felt so easy."

"It was very easy," I say to the water.

"It was maybe the first time I've ever really felt like myself here. Which is something, because I lived in Beechwood for eighteen years. Every time I come home I have this sort of uneasy feeling that there's something I need to apologize for, but I forget what it is. But with you, I felt good. I didn't want to break the spell. But I couldn't kiss you while I was lying." He turns back to the water. "I planned to get your number from Frannie on Friday morning and come clean, but I chickened out. And then there you were at dinner."

I replay that night in my head, but with him telling me he was Scooter as we sat on the boat. I probably would have kissed him anyway.

"Okay, Scooter," I say. "I forgive you."

"Thank you," he says. We look back out at the city and we're quiet for a while.

"So what were you hoping to escape from?" I ask.

"People calling me Scooter, I guess." He turns to me and his eyes search my face. "And yet here we are."

"I've seen you skateboard—the name suits you."

"That's not why they call me that." He looks back at the water and waits a bit before he spills it. "They call me Scooter because I never learned to crawl."

I laugh. "Cliffy did that for a while. He'd sit and kind of scoot on his butt toward what he wanted. Eventually he figured it out."

"Well I didn't, apparently. I just scooted until I walked. And my grandparents thought it was hilarious, so the nickname stuck. A person's got to get out of a town where he's named for his first missed milestone. Kind of gives the place a weird vibe." He stretches his legs out in front of him and leans back on his elbows. "But mostly the same reasons. I wanted to find out who I was, get a real job. Find a woman."

"And did you do it?"

"Eventually. All but the woman. It's easy to find a woman, nearly impossible to find *the* woman."

"I always wanted someone to think of me that way, that I was the one," I say.

"Come on, Ali. I'm pretty sure every guy at Beechwood High thought you were the one."

"Not even close."

"Maybe it was just me," he says, and looks back at the water.

My face goes hot and I pull my knees closer to my chest. I'm sure I've misheard him, and now I don't know what to say.

He goes on like he's said nothing. "You got married, you must have felt like you were the one then."

"Not really. I think Pete liked the idea of me. He liked me at work. He liked me in a suit being good at things and then on the weekend doing power-couple activities. But life's not a day job and planned activities. It gets messy."

"So messy," he says, and the warmth and fun leave his face. I want it back. "Is that why you're divorcing him?"

I don't answer. I don't want to tell him that in all those miserable years, it never occurred to me to divorce him. I just kept regrouping and shifting gears every time things got worse. I sort of thought we'd just muddle through like that forever.

"I'm divorcing him because he's divorcing me," I say, finally. "It's the first decision he's made in a long time that I've really respected."

"I say you let Ferris pick the next guy." It's an adorable thing to say, and he's said it lightly, like it's a joke. But all I can think is: *Okay.* He smiles and I want to reach up and run my fingers over the creases of his eyes. I want to touch the sharp corner of his jaw.

"How long are you staying?" I ask.

"I was going to leave tomorrow, but now with the whole Florida thing I don't know. I need to clean out that house in order to sell it, and that could take all summer."

He's going to be here all summer, my mother says. Not that I needed that clarification. I heard him say it in my stomach before it actually hit my ears. This man with the shoulders and the hands and the steady gaze is going to be here all summer.

"And I don't know what your schedule is like, but I'd like to see you. Maybe try for a second date?"

"I'm not sure," I say.

"About what? It's a second date, you don't need to be sure about me yet."

I smile at him and look back at the water. "You're not a person for me to date. You live in another state, you've already told me you're unreliable. Also, you're Scooter."

"Remember when I said I'd meet you at seven and then I showed up at seven? Maybe I'm totally reliable when it comes to you."

We're looking at each other, and I feel like I could watch him watching me all day. Maybe I could go on another date. "I'll think about it," I say.

"Fair enough. And, in the meantime, if you have time, I really do need help with the house. I could use an organizing expert."

"Sure, I can help you."

"Okay, name your price, because I'm sort of desperate."

"I can't charge you," I say as a text comes in on my phone. It's Pete: Back in 10. Lost the scrimmage, had pizza.

And maybe it's the sight of Pete's name on my phone, maybe it's the word "pizza," but the spell is broken. I am cast from this secret paradise Ethan's created for me. "I'm sorry, can you get me home?"

PETE'S CAR IS in the driveway when we get back to the house. He still has a key so I didn't really need to race home. I'm a little disoriented. I feel like I walked through a wormhole and then back again. I grab Ferris from the backseat and hop out of the car.

"Thanks for the field trip," I say.

"It was fun."

I don't want to close the door.

"Let's start over," he says. "Can I call you tomorrow?"

I look over my shoulder at my house. "I have my kids."

"Of course," he says. "Then you can call me." He pulls out his phone and waits for me to give him my number. I do and he texts me, while I'm still standing right there: Call me.

"WHERE WERE YOU?" Pete asks as if it's any of his business.

"Walking the dog," I say, hanging up the leash. "How was it?"

"We lost," Iris says. "The refs were totally blind."

"Also, we were awful," says Greer.

"Both things are true," says Pete. He picks Cliffy up to give him a hug and kisses Greer and Iris on the tops of their heads. It's poignant every time, this act of saying goodbye to people you used to live with. There was always a heaviness after I'd spent a day with my dad, like we were family but not as much as we used to be.

"Thanks for lunch," Iris says.

"Yeah, thanks, Dad," says Greer.

I see this register on his face. He is not a person they used to thank. Food and essentials just happened, like they were their birthright. "Of course," he says. "See you guys Tuesday night. We've got to work on our offense."

The air is strange when he's left. Everyone's quiet and we could really use a dose of Fancy. I try to imagine just what she'd do to change the energy. "Well," she'd say, and clap her hands together. "I know just what we should do." And we'd all lean in, waiting to hear what kind of fun she was about to hatch.

I work with what I have. "I was going to grill chicken tonight, but what if we turn it into a picnic and eat at the beach?"

"Let's ride our bikes," says Cliffy.

"We should make cookies," says Iris.

Greer's looking at her phone. "What?" she asks when we're all looking at her.

"A picnic tonight, at the beach," says Cliffy.

"Fine," she says.

Cliffy's in the hall closet pulling out an already-sandy bucket and shovel. This is the same closet where we hang our good coats. "I'm going to find a horseshoe crab," he says.

"You're not bringing it home," says Iris. "They stink."

I take the butter out for the cookies and turn on the oven. I know they're going to argue about this for a while, but at least no one's thinking about Pete anymore.

10

O N MONDAY, AFTER I'VE ORGANIZED FRANNIE'S BOOKS, I head straight to the Beechwood Inn to get the single kayak from the boathouse. It was Linda's idea that I start kayaking regularly after Pete left. When I came back from my first ride alone in a canoe with my kids, she told me it was time to build myself back up.

The five of us used to take a canoe out on Sundays, and Pete and I would paddle us around the tip of Beechwood Point. Greer would yell, "Faster!" and we would get going pretty fast. The first time we did this after Pete moved out, I could feel their collective disappointment that it was just me paddling. They yelled, "Faster!" until my muscles ached and I had to admit that that was the best I could do. Since then, I've been taking out a single kayak whenever I have the chance, and I haven't been this strong since high school. It's funny, what you'll do for your kids but not for yourself.

Linda taught me the basics of technique—the difference between working to the point of exhaustion and doing it right so that it's effortless. I used to wonder if that was the

difference between my difficult marriage and Frannie's easier one—maybe I was doing it wrong. Like maybe I could
have altered my technique and things would have felt right.
I certainly should have known how to paddle a canoe because I've been out on the water my whole life. My mother
used to take me out on Sunday afternoons, and I'd sit in the
front and enjoy the view while she paddled behind me. It
was fun and it was easy, being carried along by my mother.
But she did all the work, and I feel oddly unprepared for
being thirty-eight.

This past year I've been on the water regularly unless
it's been dangerously windy or cold. In January, the cold air
felt like shards of glass, and I liked moving through it and
imagining that it made tiny cuts in my skin that pierced
through the numbness.

Of course, July is more comfortable and easier to dress
for. I launch the kayak into the sound and hop in wearing
shorts and a tank top. There's no breeze today, but I create
one as I paddle faster and faster along the shore. I love the
burn I feel in my abdomen and my back and the sound of
the wake I'm leaving behind. My to-do list evaporates on
the water and is replaced by a feeling—strong, forward
moving, in full command. It's a feeling that I remember
from being younger and boundless, and it comes to me as I
paddle, only to disappear when I'm back on dry land. I try
to hold on to it the way you try to grab a dream at first light,
but it's gone the second I get into my dirty car.

Today, as I cut through the water, I am replaying Ethan's
and my urine-soaked meet cute at the dog park, the way he
looked at me in the ballpark. I'm trying to hear him say

something about my being the one, but I can't remember the exact words. I've been falling asleep imagining myself leaning in to kiss him. And the kiss I imagine is one I've never had before, but it's like him—easy and warm. The palms of my hands seem to know what his hair would feel like to touch.

I find it hard to believe that that guy is Scooter, famous for setting his basement on fire and self-diagnosed as unreliable. For a single mother of three, an unreliable man is as welcome as a lice infestation. But there was a time when it didn't matter that a guy wasn't your forever guy. There was a time when I could just dabble and try someone on for a while. What if I was the sort of person who could just go out with someone a few times and maybe run my fingers through his hair, just to know what it felt like, without worrying about how it would end? What if I was a person who could be easy about things for a bit? *Such fun,* my mother whispers over the waves. *A summer romance.*

I remember a summer romance that I had with Jimmy Craddock the summer after my sophomore year of college. I was home, working at the rec center camp, and I had two months before I'd be going back to Michigan. Jimmy was tan and a good kisser. For two months, that was plenty. There was no planning for the future, there was no trying to fix him. We could just enjoy it, because it was just for the summer.

I am so lost in this memory that I paddle a lot farther than I intended. I turn around and head back toward the inn, focusing on the widow's walk, which is the only part that is visible above the tree line. The Hogans never let anyone on the widow's walk, because when we were in high school, they caught wind of Frannie's plans for an off-season kegger. They bolted the door to the old stairway permanently. I've always wanted to see what life would look like from up there. I imagine it has its own weather pattern, because the inn's flag flaps in a breeze that I don't feel down here. I try to conjure a widow as I pass, her hair wild in the wind, looking longingly out at the water.

I myself am a ball of unfocused longing. When I'm quiet I can hear my heart yearning for impossible things. I want a perfectly pared-down home, and I want to hang on to every scrap of the past. I want a break from my kids without missing a single minute of their lives. I long for a partnership, and I long for freedom. I long to be enmeshed with someone without losing myself. I want all of it. Maybe that's the essence of a summer romance: it's the impossible thing—a love affair with no reality check. I let this lighter, easy feeling roll over me as I paddle. Jimmy Craddock has been in and out of the penal system for years, but he really was very cute.

When I pull up to the dock at the inn, my body is spent in the best possible way.

"How was it?" Linda asks. She's standing outside the locker with a clipboard and a zinc-oxide-covered nose.

"Great, but I may have gone too far."

"You deserve it," she says. My mother would have said the same thing.

11

"THERE ARE NO LIMES AT THE INN," FRANNIE SAYS when I've picked up her call.

"This sounds a little too New Testament for eleven a.m. on a Tuesday." I'm at the dog park with Ferris, watching him socialize. Ethan isn't here, and I know this because I wandered around this place for thirty minutes looking for him. I know I could call him, but it seems so forward, like I'm calling to ask for a second date that leads to a kiss. I think if I wanted it less, I would have called by now.

"Harold doesn't understand how to do the ordering. It's a system, one my parents came up with. And honestly, Ali, it's not that hard. He just doesn't know how to use it because he's not a general manager. He's a beach attendant." Frannie sounds a little unhinged.

"Do you want me to go to Costco or something?"

"I need to get over there and show him how it works, but I have Theo here and Marco can't run the diner alone with a baby on his hip."

"Got it. I'm free. Want me to come get Theo? Or actually, I'm right next to the inn. Come now, and I'll meet you."

"I'M REALLY NOT stupid," Harold says while we're waiting on the front steps. He's fidgeting with the stiff collar of his shirt, and I can only imagine how he longs to be back on the beach, where the work is straightforward and the uniform is unstarched.

"She doesn't think you're stupid. I don't speak French. Not because I'm stupid but because I never learned how. You'll get the hang of it."

Ferris lifts his head off my lap and alerts me that something exciting is happening just before Ethan comes into sight. He's walking from the parking lot in a white T-shirt and red swim trunks with a giant bag of limes in each hand. He smiles when he sees me, like I'm the thing he's been looking everywhere for.

"Pretty," he says, and then turns to Harold. I scan myself for what he could be referring to. "So I got some frantic and mildly aggressive texts about limes? I went to Costco. Has Frannie gone insane?"

Harold takes the limes. "I don't know, man. It's about a lot more than limes."

"Harold hasn't had a chance to learn the ordering system, so Frannie's on her way here. I'm going to watch Theo."

Ethan squats down to pet Ferris. He hasn't shaved, and he has the tiniest bit of stubble on his jaw. He looks up at me and says, "A baby, a dog, and Ali Morris. I'm staying for this."

I'm standing here in front of the man who I held hands with and with whom I want to have a summer romance, and I am tongue-tied. I'm trying to get the word "okay" out when Frannie pulls up. She leaves her car right at the entrance, like she's in a fire truck and time is of the essence. "I'm sorry I yelled," she says to all of us, pulling Theo out of his car seat. "It's just too much. I don't think Mom and Dad know what they're asking of us."

"Yeah, wait till you see how much stuff is in that house," Ethan says. "I went through a single cupboard yesterday and almost ran away to Florida myself."

"It can't be that bad," Frannie says. "Here, take Theo. I'll text you when we're done." She thrusts the baby into my arms, but he reaches for Ethan instead.

I know just how Theo feels, so I hand him over. Frannie and Harold disappear to the offices around back, leaving Ethan and me standing there on the steps with our charges.

"They carry him too much," he says.

"Right?" I agree.

"I try not to give parenting advice, because what do I know."

"Well it's true—he's like a marsupial," I say.

"Let's go onto the beach and let him crawl around."

"I have the dog," I say.

"I know the owners."

We walk into the inn and I have the same sense of awe that I've had every single time I've been here. It's as if by walking through the double oak doors, I am retrieving a piece of my heart. My mother is by my side, and we're celebrating something—a birthday, a big soccer season, a good

grade. Table for two on the patio, please. My mother gets
the crab cakes, and I order a steak. It's where she surprised
me with my charm bracelet and my very first charm, which
she designed after my third-grade play. After dinner, we
stashed our shoes under the deck and walked down the
beach while the sun set. I ran my arm through the water
and watched the tiny fairy charm shimmer wet in the light.
She held my hand and reviewed every performance in the
play. She sparkled with the thrill of it, as if she'd waited her
whole life to have a child in a school play. Which, after seven
miscarriages in twelve years, she probably felt like she had.

The Hogans had just completed the big renovation before my mom's last birthday, so she got to see it as it is today.
I remember our collective relief that the renovation was
mainly just tweaking and updating. The spirit of the place
is the same as it's always been, and I am oddly possessive of
it. Reception is a long white desk that must be a hundred
years old. Beyond it, floor-to-ceiling plantation shutters are
open so that we can see straight out to the sound. The floors
are original but have been restained a dark cherry, making
the bright white walls and shutters feel like an explosion of
light. The chandelier at the entrance is made of seashells,
and they sway a bit with the motion of the ceiling fans.

Ethan carries Theo through a sitting area toward the
back deck. I carry Ferris out of respect for the new sisal rugs.

He leads me down the steps where my mom and I used
to welcome the summer. We walk down the beach toward
the water. Ethan puts Theo down and we each take one of
his hands and let him kick at the hot sand.

"This is pretty good, right?" he asks.

"It's pretty good," I say.

Theo lets go of our hands and plops down onto the sand. We sit cross-legged on either side of him, forming two half circles that should attach at our knees. Ferris crawls into my lap. Ethan's squinting against the sun and showing Theo how to shovel sand into a heap with his hand. I run my eyes across his brow and along the angles of his cheekbones. It is an inarguably beautiful face, but when Theo makes him smile it is something else, something clear and warm. I'm trying to connect this to anything I remember about him from high school, but I can't.

"How's the house coming along?" I ask.

"It's a nightmare."

"I love that house."

"It's a good house. Crazy location though, right in the middle of everything."

"Super convenient to the library," I say.

"Yeah, that was huge for me growing up." He's kidding. Theo puts a handful of sand into his mouth.

"What do we do?" Ethan asks.

"Let him," I say. Theo wipes the sand from his tongue with a sandy hand and laughs.

The wind blows my hair into my eyes. I pull a hair tie off of my wrist and put it into a ponytail. I can feel Ethan watching me, and when I look at him he looks away like he's been caught. I have a feeling that starts mostly in my chest, then moves throughout my body. It's unfamiliar, and I almost want to call it pleasure. I like being with this man. There's nothing complicated or messy about that. It feels good. I am emboldened by this feeling.

"I'd like to see you too," I say. It doesn't come out quite as bold as I'd hoped. "Like you said the other day, while you're here."

He doesn't blink. He just holds my gaze like he could keep me here with the sheer power of his eyes. "Good," he says. We're smiling at each other and I'm feeling goofier than I'm comfortable feeling, so I look out and smile at the water.

"What are you guys doing?" Frannie has appeared out of nowhere. And we're busted. I feel like a teenager who's been caught making out in a car. She has her hands on her hips like Wonder Woman and seems imposing against the backdrop of the clear sky and water.

"Babysitting," Ethan says.

"Okay?" she says.

We are sitting way too close to one another. I lean back and turn my body toward Frannie, but I can still feel his eyes on me. "Did you get it all straightened out with Harold?" I ask.

"Mostly," she says. "I think he gets it, but I don't think he wants to get it. I don't think he wants this job." She reaches for Theo. "Thank you for watching him." Neither Ethan nor I make any move to go. It's a few seconds before we both realize we don't have any reason to stay on the beach.

12

FIVE HOURS LATER I HAVE BEEN SWEPT BACK INTO MY slightly complicated reality. It's soccer Tuesday, and I'm barbecuing hamburgers so I can feed the kids before Pete picks them up. I shake off a daydream that Pete will show up early and take them to dinner, or even just arrive with a pizza.

Besides being out on the water, I think this Tuesday-night break is the thing that keeps me sane. Pete coaches the girls' soccer team (Iris is quite good and plays up a year), so he can't really back out. There are a million things I could do with this time, but I usually collapse on the couch with a bowl of popcorn and watch Netflix.

I have to see Pete one extra time this week because we are meeting with the mediator on Friday. We are supposed to bring our financial records and tax returns. Pete has made a complete list of our assets. There's a savings account and a brokerage account with a few stocks and both of our 401(k)s. Two cars and we have some equity in the house. It's an upside-down state of affairs. We are dividing the things that don't matter. It's the things that aren't on the list that tell the story of our marriage. The travel books we bought and never used, the collection of tiny cleats that were too cute to give away. The Etsy quilt I had made out of the girls' soccer jerseys. He was excited because he thought I made it, and I laughed, explaining how much work it was just to collect the jerseys and mail them to the Etsy woman in Oregon. He seemed disappointed that I hadn't gone to more trouble.

We're eating at the kitchen counter when Pete shows up. He's in his biking shorts and matching top that smooshes his body in that way I find vaguely repulsive. He kisses the girls on their foreheads and gives Cliffy a squeeze. "I need to get changed before soccer," he explains to them, not me. "I'll be right back."

And with that, he bounds up the stairs into my bedroom, presumably to undress while silently judging my unmade bed and yesterday's unfinished crossword on the table next to it. He'll use my toilet and come downstairs with a remark about the aromatherapy candles I've lined up at the foot of the bathtub.

I am defensive, and I feel my chest tightening and heat racing from my gut to my face. *Take a deep breath*, my mother says in my head, and I do. I place my hand on my pounding heart and am shocked by the fact that the pilot light of my anger is flickering more fiercely with him in my bedroom than it did when he left a year ago. I've adjusted, and I'm doing just fine on my own. He doesn't get to know what that looks like.

He's back downstairs in his gym shorts and Beechwood

Soccer T-shirt, and he looks annoyingly less gross. "'Arugula,'" he tells me. "Six across: it's 'arugula.' Saw you got stuck." He places his hands on the girls' heads and says, "Ready to go?"

They're still eating, so no. I'm annoyed that he's rushing them, and, more acutely, that he's invaded my crossword puzzle. "Yesterday sort of got away from me," I say. "How'd you have time for a bike ride after work?"

"I took the day off. I met with a Realtor. I've rented a bigger place."

I haven't been through the numbers, but I'm pretty sure there's no extra money. There's no way I can stay here and he can afford a bigger place. "How's that going to work?" I ask. I'm using my nonchalant voice so as not to alert my children to the fact that I am feeling hyper-chalant.

"We'll rejigger some expenses," he says without looking at me. "Come on, girls, cleats on." And he looks over his shoulder at me with the closed-mouthed smile that I've seen him use with car dealers and his dad. He's lying, and I know I need a lawyer.

13

A S SOON AS THEY'VE LEFT, I RUN UPSTAIRS AND change into a T-shirt that doesn't have ketchup smeared down the front. I put on lip gloss and roll my eyes at myself in the mirror. I drive the half mile to the Hogans' house and park on the street. His station wagon is in the driveway, and I realize that I haven't thought this through. I'm not sure that Ethan and I have a dropping-by kind of relationship. He could be in the shower, he could be hosting a barbecue.

I text him: Hey it's Ali. I had a quick question and I was wondering if I could stop by for a sec

Ethan: Since you're parked right in front of my house it's sort of hard to say no

I could not be less cool. I text back: Haha coming in

He's opened the front door before I've made it all the way down the walk, and he's smiling in that self-satisfied way you smile when you've caught someone doing something dumb. Also in that smile: pure delight.

He's in the same red swim trunks and white T-shirt as

earlier, and it's unfair how good he looks. He steps aside, and I walk into the foyer, taking off my shoes.

"So what's this? Spontaneous second date?" he says with a half smile.

"No," I say.

"No?"

"Well yes. But not today."

He crosses his arms over his chest. His forearms are tan and muscled, with that gold dusting of blond hair. So much about Ethan is gold. "If you came over here to break up with me, this is going to be the worst almost-relationship of my life."

"No," I say. "I mean I know you're joking. Yes to a date another time, no to breaking up with you. Not that we're dating." I wish someone would shove a sandwich in my mouth to shut me up. I walked in flustered because of Pete, and now I'm standing in the awkwardness of how much I'd like to reach out and touch him. He doesn't seem to feel awkward at all. He seems kind of amused, like he knows he has the upper hand.

"Come in," he says. "You look like you're about to flee, and that's the last thing I want." He leads me into the grand living room with its caramel-colored velvet sofas. The curtains are ivory silk with thin gold stripes to match the oriental rug.

"The place looks great," I say. "Looks like you're ready to sell."

He crosses the room and starts opening cupboards in the oak-paneled walls. There are boxes and crates and baskets full of dried flowers. One of the cupboards contains nothing but Mr. Hogan's high school football memorabilia. When he's opened six cupboards, he says, "So this is what I'm dealing with. And when I say it's the tip of the iceberg, you should believe me."

"It's doable. Is there a lot they want to keep?"

"They don't want anything—they're all about this clean-slate, Swedish-death-cleaning thing."

"It's a very nice thing," I say. I think about the excruciating process of cleaning out my mother's apartment. I dread cleaning out my dad and Libby's house and sort of hope that's going to be Libby's kids' problem one day. I think of Phyllis's daughters sorting through all those books. I think about my own kids trying to wade through the too-small-cleat museum I've been curating.

"Yeah, I thought I could toss it all, but I've been through a few boxes and in every one of them there's something important. Like a thousand magician's scarves and the original deed to the house. Or a box of *People* magazines with my grandparents' baby photos at the bottom. So I need to go through it all. I just got totally overwhelmed." He looks at the open cupboards and I recognize the panic on his face. "Can we go outside?" We walk through the kitchen and he grabs two beers from the fridge. "Nuts?"

"A little," I say.

He smiles and pours almonds from a jar into a bowl. It's nice, this small gesture.

We walk out onto the covered area of the patio and sit in two armchairs that are facing one another. There's a matching couch against the wall of ivy, and part of me wants to lie down there and have this whole conversation like I'm at a therapist's office. "It's so weird that you own this house now. Scooter Hogan, lord of the manor."

He winces. "People, for almost two decades, have called me Ethan. I beg you."

I spot Brenda lying on the grass taking in the last of the evening light. "How's she doing?" I ask.

"She's good. Now come on. Why are you here? You seem a little rattled." He's leaning forward with those golden forearms on his muscled thighs, holding his beer with both hands, his long fingers toying with the label.

I try to pull myself back on course. "It's about my divorce." Just saying the word out loud feels like I've thrown cold water over myself.

"Okay. And I'm sorry. I don't think I said that before." He looks up from his beer. "Well, I don't even know him. Are you sorry?"

It's a bigger question than I thought he was going to ask me. I absolutely could not stand Pete tonight. But I loved our family unit and the comfort of another adult walking into the house at the end of the day, even if for a long time that adult was my mom. I liked waking up in the morning to the sound of another person breathing. But in the past year, there hasn't been anything about Pete in particular that I've missed. I've just missed him as a placeholder. So, "No."

"Okay, then I'm not sorry either."

"We're going to mediation on Friday. It's all been pretty easy. We've been separated for a year, just living apart and paying bills out of the same accounts we always used. We used to put some money into savings each year, but now with Pete's apartment we're just getting by."

"Makes sense."

"Yeah." I fold my legs under me like I'm at a slumber party and I just got to the spooky part of the story. "But tonight he came by and told me he's just rented a bigger place. And he wasn't really making eye contact. We never talked about it, and I'm sure it costs a lot more, and he said we could 'rejigger some expenses,' which I assume are the kids' and mine." I put my beer down on the table next to me. "Scooter, I'm an accountant. Or I was. I wore a suit and had an assistant. I was good at it. And I've completely handed the reins over to him. I don't even know the name of the mediator. He was going to pick me up and drive me." And with that, there's a hitch in my voice and it's very likely that I am going to cry. I sit back in my chair and watch Brenda breathe.

"You need a lawyer."

"The problem is we go Friday. I don't really have time to hire a lawyer." It's a statement that's also a question and a cry for help.

He doesn't say anything. He just nods and goes into the house. He returns with tissues and a yellow legal pad. This has the effect of a doctor walking into the examination room in a white coat; suddenly he's legit.

He takes a sip of his beer. "This isn't that complicated, and I can google what I need to know between now and then. I can tell you right now that Pete's trying to get his personal expenses up so that when it comes to alimony he gets a bigger piece of the pie. I know that from watching TV, not from law school."

Of course that's what he's doing. "Tonight I felt like I

was seeing it all for the first time. Like I just walked into the room and was like, wait, is this my life? How—and when—did I give up control of every single thing to this man?"

"You trusted him, you were a family. Listen, I'll go with you on Friday. I'll bring all my TV knowledge and back you up. He'll need to sign something saying it's okay for you to bring a lawyer."

"And what's he going to say about your fee? He's not going to okay that. The first thing we agreed to was that we can't afford to pay lawyers."

"We're going to barter services."

And suddenly I'm in a porno. My face goes hot, and I am sure that Ethan with his gorgeous legs and shouldery shoulders is suggesting we swap sex for legal services. I'm twenty percent flattered, twenty percent intrigued, and sixty percent horrified that my life has come to this.

"You've got to help me clear out this house." Oh. "I can't sell it with all this stuff in it, and I can't go through it all alone. It paralyzes me. And it could be fun. Extra time I can see you between all of those dates we're going to go on." This catches me off guard, and I smile.

"It does not paralyze me," I say. "I can totally help you." The thought of cleaning out this house makes me feel newly confident, because this is something I know how to do. Which is not something I can confidently say about sex.

"Okay, deal," he says, and reaches out to shake my hand, his eyes smiling in a way that makes me think he saw me blush. His hand is cool from the beer bottle and he holds on for a second too long. "I'm going to start googling New York state divorce law, and you tell Pete you're bringing an ambulance chaser for moral support. You have my permission to tell him my name's Scooter. In this one instance, I think my alter ego's going to help."

I don't know why he seems excited about this, though showing up with a skateboarder to mediation might be fun. I look at my hands and feel overwhelmed by how much there is to do.

"I think I know what you need."

And just like that, I'm back in the porno. "What?"

"Skateboarding." Wrong again. "When I'm wound up or anxious, I head to the skate park. I'll show you."

14

H E GRABS TWO SKATEBOARDS FROM THE BACK OF his car, and we start walking the two blocks from his house to the rec center. The sun is low, almost gone. It's soupy humid and the crickets are cricketing in a way that reminds me of a hundred summers past, riding my bike around town until the streetlights came on. It was my favorite part of the day, the thing you could always count on.

A couple about my dad's age is walking toward us. "Well, if it isn't Scooter Hogan. Staying out of trouble?" the man asks with a laugh.

I feel Ethan stiffen next to me, like a full-body wince. "Hi, Mr. McDermott," he says. "Mrs. McDermott. Do you know Ali Morris?" They don't and we say hello.

"I hear you're still up in Massachusetts figuring out what you want to do."

Ethan lets out a hard laugh, the kind with pain wrapped inside. "Good news. I figured it out," he says. "Have a good night."

We continue on to the skate park. "I'm starting to see what you mean," I say.

He shakes his head and runs a hand through his hair. We walk a half block before he starts talking again. "So the thing I want you to know about skateboarding is that it's more than a sport."

"Is it really a sport though?" I give him a sideways glance.

He stops, and I'm happy to see the lightness return to his face. "Of course it's a sport. But it's also a way to move through life. A way to approach things."

"Wait, are you going to Mr. Miyagi me and make me wax your car?"

"Probably," he says, and smiles. He looks at me for a second, and I swear I can see impure thoughts race through his mind. We start walking again. "It's about finding balance and then mastering a trick that you're sure is impossible. It's about looking at something that can't be done and being willing to go after it anyway. It's about speed and perseverance but also grace and control." He stops because the streetlights pop on. He looks up at the light and the particles of summer that it illuminates above us. "I love that so much." Then back to me, "Ali, no joke. You're made for skateboarding."

"You've known me for one week, Scooter. You don't know what I'm made for."

"I've known you a long time," he says. His gaze is heavy on me, full of a million things unsaid. It's like he knows a thing that I don't know. Like he sees something I don't. He takes my hand and entwines our fingers. I feel it all over my body and briefly forget where we're going. He gives my hand a squeeze and then lets go. "Come on," he says.

We keep walking until we get to the gate of the skate park, which is, of course, locked. Ethan picks the lock with his pocketknife like it's something he's been professionally trained to do and walks in and switches on the lights.

"Just to be clear, we've broken in and now we're turning on the lights?" I'm going to need a map and a compass to find my way back to my comfort zone. Skateboarding, breaking and entering. The thrill of it bubbles in my chest.

"Yes. This is important." The half-pipe is in the center of the concrete park, illuminated by tall halogen lights. Around us is complete darkness, as if we are in the center of a spotlight on an empty stage. The crickets chirp from just beyond the chain-link fence on every side, and fireflies flash in the corners of my eyes. The sweet honey smell of tuberose and lilies hangs in the air.

He catches me taking this all in. "Admit it. It's pretty cool."

"It is," I say.

We walk to the half-pipe, and he sets our boards down. He gets onto his. "It's unsteady to stand on wheels. It makes no sense, right?"

I nod.

"Do it anyway," he says.

I step onto my board and it feels like a banana peel. It's going to slip out from under me and I'm going to be flat on my ass. He reaches for my hand and I lose focus as I close my fingers around his again. I squeeze it involuntarily, maybe to intensify the feeling. Maybe to keep it there.

"I'll steady you, bend your knees," he says. His body is close enough to mine that I can smell the faint mix of pine and sunscreen on his skin. He rolls me back and forth a few times. "See? You're doing great. Now hop off and back on; try to keep your feet by the bolts."

Hopping off is easy, hopping on is terrifying, and I grab his other hand.

"Not bad," he says. "Now let me roll you around a little." With both of my hands in his, he walks sideways, cruising my board along. "Feel okay?" he asks.

I squeeze his hands in response. I don't want to talk. I like the sound of the wheels on the concrete and the feel of Ethan so close, holding my hands. I am immersed in my senses—the thickness of the night air, the electricity coming off of Ethan's hands. The smell of the grass and the blacktop in the stale air. He stops me and we are face-to-face. With the few inches the board gives me, we are eye-to-eye. And I know that I will kiss this man. As many times as he'll let me.

"I want to turn you around," he says.

"What?" I don't know why everything sounds dirty.

"Get off the board and face the other way." Right.

I hop off and turn around and get back on the board facing the half-pipe. Ethan is right behind me and takes both of my hands in his again. I can feel his chest against my back, and I want him to wrap our hands around my waist and stay there. He talks directly into my ear. "So the point of skateboarding is to master the impossible trick. You can get hurt in a ton of different ways. You've got to control the fear. At some point, I'm going to send you to the top of that ramp and you're going to skate down, and you're going to trust that it's going to work out just fine." I can feel his breath on my cheek as the sound of his voice moves through my body. "Because if it doesn't work out it's going to be all concrete and broken bones. Which is why you need to practice like crazy and then be graceful and present."

I let out a breath. I don't want him to move.

"Tell me, Ali. Are you thinking about Pete and his apartment right now?"

"Not at all."

"That's the thing about skateboarding. It's the ultimate terror ride, so all the other stuff just floats away."

I turn around in one step and don't topple the skateboard. This is mostly because Ethan catches me around the back as I turn. He says, "So, in that way, it's about mindfulness and progression. Just tiny steps forward." We are eye-to-eye, nose-to-nose, and finally his chest is pressed against mine. I have stepped into something completely unfamiliar and unexpected. And I want to take another step forward.

15

WHEN I GET HOME, PETE'S CAR IS ALREADY IN THE driveway. It's blocking the garage, and it occurs to me that he's not being thoughtless: it would just never dawn on him that I wouldn't be home, right where he left me.

Greer and Iris are peeling off muddy socks and cleats in the kitchen. Cliffy's in my arms. Pete has helped himself to a Gatorade from the fridge. "How was it?" I ask.

"It was good," says Iris. "We're going to kill at the scrimmage Saturday."

"Kill? Really?" says Greer with an eye roll.

"Why don't you two go get showered?" I say.

When they've gone upstairs, and Cliffy has turned on SpongeBob, I busy myself fake cleaning up the kitchen. It's basically the act of moving things from one spot to another, like a Coney Island shell game, to feign busyness. "So," I start. "I wanted to ask you. I'm feeling a little overwhelmed with everything and all the details, do you mind if I bring someone with me on Friday?" I take the dishes out of the sink and stack them on the counter. I move the pot I used for the broccoli into the sink.

"Like a buddy?" he asks. It's really unbelievable what a child he thinks I am.

"Like a lawyer," I say, and turn around.

"Ali, we've been through this. We can't afford lawyers and there's nothing to even argue about."

"No, of course not. But I just sort of feel like my mom did when she had to go to the doctor all the time, that it was good for her to have a second set of ears. I'm going to be managing this house all by myself and I really want to do it right. Like make sure I understand the details." I hate myself for sounding so incompetent, while I also like feeling a bit subversive. Like I've snuck Old Ali in her navy suit into a Trojan horse.

"How are you paying a lawyer? I didn't approve that."

Um, how are you renting a more expensive apartment? I didn't approve that. A decade of rage simmers just under my chest. It's a familiar feeling, like it wants to get out but doesn't know how. I place my hands on the kitchen island between us and take a deep breath. When I look up, my face is as soft as I can manage. "No, it's not like that. It's not even a real lawyer. Frannie's kid brother, Scooter, is a PI attorney and he said he'd come with me and take notes if I helped him organize his parents' house."

Pete laughs and downs the rest of his Gatorade. "Scooter?"

"Yes, that's his name. Can you imagine?"

16

I TELL ETHAN I'LL PICK HIM UP ON FRIDAY BECAUSE I have the urge to drive. I feel like I am sick of being in the passenger seat.

I pull into his driveway just as he walks out wearing a powder-blue tuxedo and ruffled white shirt, straight out of a 1970s prom photo. His pants are an inch too short, and his expression is serious. He opens the car door, takes a deep breath, and says, "What do you think?"

I am stunned. I try to imagine Pete's face when I show up with him as my lawyer. "Scooter. What the hell?" I burst out laughing. It's the last thing in the world I thought I'd do today, and the laughter wipes out the morning's nerves.

A smile creeps up the corners of his mouth. "Okay, this was worth it already. And, God, the look on your face is priceless. I have no clothes down here, and all of my dad's suits are too small. I found this in his closet, and it called out to me." His smile is huge now, like he's successfully executed a practical joke. "You hired Scooter, might as well go all in."

"Pete's not going to know what to think," I say.

"That's the plan," he says.

WE DRIVE THROUGH town and I can't help but feel self-conscious about how I'm dressed. If Ethan's playing the part of Burt Bacharach in Vegas, I'm playing the part of downtrodden housewife. I'm in a denim skirt (that's a hard skirt) and a T-shirt with a cardigan in my bag in case of air-conditioning. I want to be in my navy suit or even in Mrs. Hogan's Carmen Miranda costume. I just don't want to look like a doormat.

The mediator's name is Lacey. She's younger than I am, which is fine except for the fact that she's blond and charming. She greets Ethan with a smile that tells us she's in on the joke about his outfit, and I have the weirdest urge to tell her that, no, it's just our joke. We introduce ourselves, and she shows us into an office that feels more like it's for therapy than for divorce. She has several paintings of covered bridges on the walls, which I'm sure are subtle metaphors for our journey into this next stage. We join Pete at a round table, which makes me feel, wrongly, that there are no sides.

"Pete, this is Scooter," I say.

"I didn't know Frannie had a kid brother," Pete says. He's in khaki pants and a white polo shirt and is eyeing Ethan suspiciously.

"I live in Massachusetts," Ethan says. "Haven't been around much. Thanks for letting me sit in on your meeting." He takes his legal pad out of his briefcase and carefully places a pen on top. He smooths the ruffles on his shirt and gives me a serious look, and I bite the inside of my mouth to keep from laughing again.

Lacey starts by explaining how this is all going to go. Today is the first of three meetings. She asks us both for verbal confirmation that we are going to split all existing assets in half and gives us each a copy of the asset list that Pete put together for our review. The house, the checking account, the savings account, a brokerage account with barely anything in it, the 401(k)s, two cars, a jar full of gold coins.

"Looks right," says Pete.

"When did you two buy these gold coins?" Ethan asks.

Pete looks up from the paper and narrows his eyes at him. "Why?" he asks.

Ethan turns to me for an answer. It's a funny moment, because it's been a long time since anyone has asked me to chime in. I hear my mom answering for me, and I feel it like an ache in the back of my heart. When it comes to anything with Pete, I've gone silent.

I say, "We didn't, my mom left them to me." I remember taking the ceramic cookie jar full of gold Krugerrands from the apartment and placing it on my kitchen counter next to the coffeemaker. It's a treasure in plain sight, just like she liked it. They're worth about sixty thousand dollars, an inheritance from her mother that she never touched.

Ethan is looking at me. "I'm sorry," he says. "I didn't know that about your mom."

"It was two years ago," Pete says, like two years is

forever. Like he can't believe my mom being dead is still a thing.

"Well, I'm sorry," Ethan says, and turns back to his list. "Then that's separate property." He crosses the coins off the asset list. "What's next?"

Lacey nods and crosses it off her copy too. Pete lets out a breath, and we move on.

Lacey says, "You've agreed to split the house. What's the timing on that?"

Pete says, "I've agreed to let Ali and the kids stay there until Cliffy is eighteen, then we sell and split the proceeds."

"Twenty-two," says Ethan.

Pete drops his pen on the table and leans back in his chair. "Twenty-two what?"

"I think you two should consider keeping the family home until Cliffy is twenty-two. It's disturbing to come home from your freshman year in college to a new place. From what I can tell an eighteen-year-old is still a kid."

I have removed and replaced the cap on my pen about a thousand times. I am watching Pete watch Ethan. I am also reading his mind. Pete does not like being made to look like a jerk. I sometimes think the only reason he coaches the girls' soccer team is so that he gets credit for participating and to distract onlookers from the fact that those are literally the only hours he spends with them now. I also know that Pete's parents divorced and sold their house as soon as he left for college and that he was totally traumatized by it. He knows that I know this.

"Twenty," he says. And we agree.

AFTER AN HOUR of reviewing bank statements and filling out forms, Ethan and I shake hands with Lacey, nod to Pete, and make our way downstairs and onto Delaney Street. It's July–in–New York hot and humid, and I stand for a second and let the sun warm the air-conditioning off my skin.

"Feel good?" he asks. He takes my hand, gives it a too-quick squeeze, and lets go.

"Yes."

"That was oddly satisfying." He smiles at me. "I don't know why, but it's super important to me that Pete thinks I'm completely insane."

"Well, you're off to a good start, and thank you for saving me half the gold coins. I think I knew they were mine, but I'm not sure I would have said anything."

"Why not?"

It's a bigger question than I feel like exploring at noon in the middle of town. "I don't know. Maybe I've gone quiet."

"I'm really sorry about your mom. I remember her. And how you guys were together."

"You do?" I look up at him and have the feeling she's here with us, like he's summoned her. I wait for her to say something in my head, but she doesn't. What I really want, I realize, is to hear someone say her name.

"I remember you guys at the diner, and seeing you around town. Always talking about something, and I'd think, wow, who talks to their parents that much?"

I smile. Me, that's who. We were so close. "It's been really hard." People are walking past us on the sidewalk and

I've backed up to the hardware store to get out of the way. Ethan leans against the wall next to me. "We lived right there," I say.

"Right where?"

I motion to the small yellow door across the street, next to the dry cleaner's.

"I didn't know that," he says.

"Yeah, my parents moved into that apartment intending to buy a house and fill it with a million kids. It ended up just being me, and they divorced when I was little, so my mom and I stayed there." I don't say "seven miscarriages" because that always makes people uncomfortable.

"Then we were practically neighbors, both living in town."

I give him a look that says *not exactly.* "Yeah, we liked it. That's why we were always at the diner. I worked at the dry cleaners sometimes. I helped the tailor." I don't say how much I love ironing, because that always makes people think I'm crazy.

"And then you moved back and bought a house and filled it with a million kids."

"Yes," I say. "I did." I look up to the picture window above the yellow door. Beyond it was our little black kitchen table with two chairs. She worked at that table, sketching her designs on four-by-four pieces of card stock. At the end of the day she'd secure her stack with a binder clip, and I'd either never see the designs again or one of them would be the featured jewelry item at Macy's that season. She never seemed to care much about which designs sold, she just loved the process and formed her own opinion about what was good. "Alice!" she'd call from that little table. "I made a frog! Doesn't he just sparkle?" My mother believed that when something came together in exactly the right way, it sparkled. She thought this of some of her designs, most of her big ideas, and all of my kids.

When I don't say more, he lets it go. "What do you want to do now, besides clean out my entire house? I own you now." He takes my hand, just barely, and runs his fingertips over mine.

This makes me smile because I'm actually dying to go through that house and make her open-house ready. It's my favorite kind of quiet, satisfying work where you see your progress as you go and you know when you're done. My boss used to tell me that I was the only person he ever knew who saw beauty in accounting, but I loved it for both the process and the moment that everything balanced. The thing about motherhood is that day to day there's no measurable outcome. The mark of a successful day is just getting everyone back in bed.

Before I can stop myself, I reach out and brush my fingertips over his again. I love the way that whisper of a touch moves up my arm.

"Let's start with lunch," he says.

WE SIT AT the bar at the diner and wait with serious faces for Frannie to come out and see us. "Oh hey, sis," Ethan says when she comes out of the kitchen.

"Good God, Scooter," she says, placing a stack of pancakes in front of the man at the other end of the bar and walking toward us. "Tell me you didn't wear that getup to the meeting. Please."

"He did," I say. "And he's a damn good lawyer too. Saved me thirty thousand dollars' worth of gold coins. And got me two more years in my house."

Ethan seems very pleased with himself. "Who knows, maybe I'll wear the whole Carmen Miranda costume to our next meeting."

Frannie laughs. "What did Pete think of you?"

"I'm not sure I'm his favorite," he says.

"Oh, I like this very much," says Frannie.

"WANT TO COME in for a beer and a swim?" Ethan asks as I pull into his driveway. "As fun as it was messing with Pete today, I think I'm ready to get out of this tux."

That sounds so lovely and gluttonous. How I would love to spend the rest of this summer day floating in a pool with this handsome man. I want to get Pete out of my head and just lean into this, the easy conversation and the way he makes me feel like I'm lit from the inside. *This is what easy and fun looks like.* "Thank you, but I need to get my kids from camp."

"Okay. What's tomorrow?"

"Saturday."

"I know. I mean, what happens? Does Pete take the kids? Can you come by?"

"I'm not sure, I'll ask him." I don't know if he means can I come by to help with the house or come by to just hang out. Those words, "just hang out," make me feel like a teenager.

Ethan turns to me in the still-running car and his expression is serious. "Ali. At some point you've got to hold him to a schedule. If you're going to share custody, you're going to need him to be accountable for certain days so that you can make your own plans."

I let out a laugh. "I don't really have a lot of plans." I make eggs, I kayak. I replace people's wire hangers with wooden ones.

He leans toward me, just an inch, but I can feel the space between us crackle. There's energy to it. The hum of my car idling surrounds us, and I'm having a hard time knowing what's vibrating. He is so ridiculous in that tux, but I want to know what it would feel like to brush my cheek against his. I'd just like to know what it would feel like to have my face close enough to his so that I could feel his skin against mine. I want to feel his hands in mine again; I want to feel them tug on my waist. He's looking right in my eyes like he can hear my thoughts, and I have to break eye contact. I turn to my steering wheel and say, "What?"

Ethan keeps looking at me. "I know you're in there, Ali Morris. You are the most confident girl in the room."

"Are you getting affirmations off of Instagram too?" I'm still looking at my steering wheel.

"That's how I remember you. In total control because you were completely yourself."

I smile at the gearshift. "Well, that was a long time ago."

He raises his hand like he's going to touch me, but he

doesn't. "That's how I remember it. You were the girl who said what you wanted, wore what you wanted. I see you in the cafeteria grabbing a snack before soccer, walking by Jen Brizbane and her awful friends and not even noticing them. And my lame friends would say, 'Show me more, Ali Morris.'"

I laugh.

"And you're still that. I saw it the other night when you were with your kids, and even when you were trying to hop on that skateboard. Just so natural and sure of who you are."

"Thank you," I say.

"When I was a kid and had no idea who I was or who I could be in the world, I liked seeing how confident you were."

I meet his eyes, and for a second I feel like I'm the girl he remembers.

"Cliffy definitely thinks you're the coolest girl in the room," he says.

This makes me smile. "Ferris does too," I say.

"Ferris has great taste." He opens the car door and the spell is broken. He leans back into the open window. "Okay, enough with the pep talk. You owe me thirty thousand dollars' worth of organizing and a second date. Text me your schedule later." And he straightens the collar of his ridiculous suit and walks into the house.

17

THE KIDS AND I ARE SITTING OUT BACK AFTER DINNER, listening to the slow trickle of water in the creek. We have a wrought iron sofa with green cushions that's tucked against the house, and it's exactly the right size for the four of us. Phyllis just texted me a moon emoji, followed by a laugh-till-you-cry emoji, so I know she's gone to bed. I text Pete: The scrimmage is at two in Greenville. What's the plan?

Pete: Your lawyer's a piece of work

Me: Yes. So what time are you getting them and how long are you keeping them? I need to work tomorrow, so it would be good to know.

Pete: Can I just let you know in the morning? I might do a long ride in the afternoon but I'm not sure.

This is how it is, how it's always been. The fact that I'm going to have to repeat this conversation to Ethan makes me cringe. My schedule/plans/wants are entirely dependent on Pete's being satisfied first. My ability to repay my debt to Ethan and, more important, get my second date depends on whether Pete decides he wants to go cycling. The worst part is that I'm uncomfortable asking him for this small courtesy.

Me: Let me know as soon as you decide

Not for the first time today, I try to retrace my steps to figure out how I got from being the girl Ethan remembers to being the woman sitting in this place right here. The most disturbing part of the balance of power in my relationship with Pete is that I was complicit, chipping off pieces of myself and offering them to him until all that was left is who I am now. Because when things first started feeling not-quite-right between us, I panicked. That wedding dress charm was firmly affixed to my bracelet, and we'd promised all those wedding guests that we'd stay married forever. I was determined to make it work.

I probably wouldn't have married Pete if I hadn't gotten pregnant with Greer. We'd only been together a year and we were both working so much that it still felt like date night whenever we were together. I had my own place in the West Village and my own money. I had work friends and a handbag that I bought at a sample sale downtown. I loved how Pete was all in on everything—his job, his bicycling, his weekend soccer league. I loved how he was sort of single-minded about where he wanted to go and how he wanted things to be. I loved the deliberate way he hung up his suit at the end of the day, first the pants folded along the crease, then the jacket fitted perfectly to the specially designed wooden hangar. Always hung up, always facing left. Pete was a person next to whom things made sense.

But then I was pregnant. I was terrified, and my mother was elated. She couldn't get over my good luck, "getting" pregnant like it was something that happened to you rather than something you pursued with all of your life force. Once I got used to the idea, I was excited too. I hatched a new plan where I'd be married with a baby and still be great at my job. At home, Pete and I would wade through all that happy chaos you see on sitcoms, but with the ease and order of the couples in *Real Simple* magazine. We got married, and it wasn't until I was on bed rest and had to ask Pete for help that I realized he was all in on everything but me. It was as if he saw my needing him as a weakness or a breach of contract, and he was annoyed. When my maternity leave was over, Greer had only been out of the NICU one week, and I had a minor panic attack at my desk on my first day back at work. I knew that Pete was never going to step up when we needed him. I told myself I was lucky we could afford for me to quit my job, and I did. Pete took another step away.

My new plan was to be a great stay-at-home mom and wife. There is no shortage of chaos to be smoothed out in a household with a baby. I ironed onesies and stacked them in piles according to the rainbow. I strained vegetables and jarred them for the week. I consolidated our household finances into a spreadsheet that fed into tax software. I adopted Ferris for reasons I'll never understand. It had something to do with Greer's first word being "dog" and me feeling guilty for getting pregnant again so quickly. Things still weren't right. Then Iris was born just sixteen months after Greer, and she came into the world in an easier way. I waited for him to notice how beautiful our family was. I waited for him to look at our daughters the way he looked at his new road bike.

My mother said come to Beechwood. She always said come to Beechwood. It was her dream to have me back home with my family. I resisted because moving home felt like giving up, and I knew it would be harder to go back to work once I'd left the city. But she was lonely, and eventually I warmed to the idea of the girls out here collecting crab shells in the Long Island Sound and drinking milkshakes at the counter at the Hogan Diner. I loved the idea that they'd know her in the intimate way you know a grandparent that you see every day. Maybe they'd even get to know my dad. I thought maybe I could find part-time work as a book-keeper, just to make some money and feel like I was making sense of something. So we moved, and my mom brought me the little brick house charm as a housewarming gift.

Things still weren't right.

The first time I saw my mom notice how bad things were in my marriage, there was actual fear on her face. My life with this man and these children was her dream come true. The opposite of this dream was her worst fear—me being alone. She was always hung up on my being an only child, but it never bothered me.

She helped with Greer and Iris, and I tried to set up our home. After living in the city, I couldn't get over the size of my pantry—three feet wide with five shelves. My mom, the girls, and I went to the Container Store for the first time all together and ran our hands over the glass containers and beige shelf liners. I spent a hundred and fifty dollars on organizing gear for that pantry, all of which sat in two identical bags in my garage for years. Pete came home tired from the train, baffled by the noise and the mess and the fact that he had to get back on that train again in the morning. What baffled him more was that I didn't. I saw my work as keeping people alive. He saw my work as going to the playground and lounging through naptime, the work of a child. At some point Pete and I stopped talking other than in a transactional way. There was so much silence in all that noise.

Cliffy was our last shot at making it work. Maybe if we were outnumbered, we'd see this family as something bigger than ourselves. Something big enough to hold on to. But a third child pushed me more deeply into overwhelm, and Pete offered to take over the family finances. I was stunned by this offer of help, the first in years from what I remembered. I would have preferred that he take over the grocery shopping, but that wasn't on offer. So he did, and I kept on with the kids and the house and the river of laundry that flows aggressively into my basement. And when my mom died, I went completely numb. It's been an unexpectedly painful consequence of her death to realize that, in my home, my mother was the freshly painted shutters that kept anyone from noticing the foundation was rotten.

Greer laughs at something on her phone. Iris has gotten up and is dribbling the soccer ball down by the creek. Cliffy's head is heavy on my shoulder. It's so peaceful here without Pete. I wonder how my mom would react to knowing her worst fears have been realized, and that it's absolutely fine.

PETE SHOWS UP to get the kids at one on Saturday without texting beforehand. It's an act of aggression, and I know this because I've known Pete for fifteen years. Pete's selfish, but he likes to announce himself. *I'm on the 5:26 train. Leaving the gym now. Home in 20.* This always felt like an act of self-importance, like he wanted to be preceded by some guy with a horn to herald his arrival. Greer and Iris scramble to get ready, and Cliffy tosses some markers and a watercolor set in his backpack. I ask Pete when they'll be back.

"Not sure, I'll text you." He nods to the kitchen island, where my broken laundry basket rests on the mountain of unopened mail. "Love what you've done with the place."

I hold his gaze for a second. There's a whole marriage's worth of things to say, but I say, "Come on, guys, let's go."

When the kids are in the car, I stand between Pete and the driver's door. It's like my body knows I have something to say, and it wants to force the issue.

"I need to know when they'll be back, because I have things to do today."

He responds as if I'm hard of hearing. "Got it. I'll text you when we're on our way."

"What if I'm not home?"

"Where would you be?" he asks. Fresh rage simmers. It doesn't boil, but it's a strong simmer. I sort of like the way it courses through my veins and turns my chest into a hot, beating molten burst of fire.

"I'd be working." Or with a friend. I'd be swimming or drunk at a bar or lying on a massage table or serving soup to the homeless. Maybe I'd be riding my goddamn bike all over kingdom come. "I'd be out, as in not here." My voice is shaky and betrays just how seldom I've spoken up for myself in the past few years.

"Jeez, Ali. Relax. I'll text you."

18

WITH SHAKY FINGERS, I TEXT ETHAN THAT I HAVE A few hours. He tells me to come over. I don't want him to see me like this. I want him to flirt with me through a fence and say something about my being the one. I want him to give me a look that tells me we're in on the same joke. But maybe now that he's seen me around Pete, that's too much to ask. I'm not the Ali Morris he remembers.

I find him seated on a box in the middle of the living room surrounded by other boxes. "I literally can't start," he says.

"It's a lot," I say, as I do to every client when they shut down. I acknowledge their feelings and then inspire them to move forward. I saw this in a YouTube video on personal coaching.

"Are you okay?" he asks, getting up and walking toward me. I have the sense that he's going to reach out for me and then doesn't.

"I'm fine. Pete's an ass."

"Didn't he take the kids?"

"He did, but he also did this thing. It's this dismissive thing. It's hard to explain." He narrows his eyes at me, like he's concerned. His face is so open, like he's ready to take in whatever I have to tell him. It's almost hypnotic, the way that draws me in. But I don't want to be this Ali right now, the one who was just told to relax in front of her children. I straighten my shoulders. "We're going to make four piles— one to keep, one to throw out, one to donate, and one to sell." I still feel the adrenal rush of wanting to murder Pete with my bare hands, and saying these words that I've said a million times in my calming voice is settling me.

"Okay," he says. "Where do we start?"

"How about with the box you were sitting on?"

He stretches his arms over his head. His T-shirt rides up and reveals a bit of his sculpted stomach. I take in a little breath at the sight of it and shift my attention to the box.

"How long can you stay?" he asks.

"I don't know. A couple of hours, maybe more."

"He didn't tell you when he's bringing them back?"

"No." I rip the tape off and pull out a bubble-wrapped ceramic turtle. "And I'm super pissed off. At him, at myself."

He turns to me, and I really don't want to hear what he has to say.

"I know, Scooter. I used to be in control. I get it. Now, keep, toss, donate, or sell?"

WE WORK IN relative silence. (He keeps the ceramic turtle, which is adorable). At first I empty boxes and ask which pile he wants things in. Then he starts opening his own boxes and making decisions without me. He gets three phone calls, which he takes in the kitchen. I can't hear what he's saying but I can tell by the tone of his voice that it's personal, that he's placating someone. I wonder if it's the old girlfriend and think he must have been exceptionally unreliable to keep her from wanting to run her hands across his stomach all day. I'm sure she's blond. She's completely put together in outfits entirely made of silk because, of course, she doesn't sweat. She buys designer toilet paper just two rolls at a time and has never set foot in a Costco. Just the thought of her and her fancy toilet paper makes me want to wring that ceramic turtle's neck.

His phone rings again, and he takes it in front of me. "Hey," he says. "Yeah, that's fine. I'll see if Vince can come fix it in the morning. Okay. Thanks." And he hangs up.

"Everything okay?" I ask, because I'm nosy and also delighted that that didn't sound romantic.

"Yeah, fine. It's just some kids I know from skateboarding. The lock on the skate park fence is broken."

"Ah, and I know how strongly you object to breaking and entering."

"It's the amateurs that break the locks," he says. "I'm a pro."

He opens a box that holds an old adding machine, a cowboy hat, and a set of porcelain chopsticks. He shakes his head and puts the whole box in the donation pile.

"But why are they calling you about the lock?" There was something so casual about the way he spoke to whoever was calling.

"They call me for everything. I told you, I'm a problem solver. I'm like their uncle who knows how to get things done."

"And you know them from skateboarding?"

"Everything I know, I know from skateboarding."

BY FIVE, I still haven't heard from Pete, and we've emptied two of the oak cabinets in the living room. We've only found a handful of things he wants to keep. It's a critical rule of cleaning things out that you stop every few hours for a major break. If you go too long, you stop looking at what you're sorting through and just start throwing everything away. I call it StuffFatigue™, and it's a real problem.

Ethan seems like he's in the zone, but I get two beers from the kitchen and tell him it's quitting time. "Thank God," he says, and follows me out to the patio. It's a cloudless day and the early evening sun is making the pool sparkle. No one should be inside going through boxes.

We plop down in our two facing armchairs. "A happy life accumulates a lot of stuff," he says.

"Any kind of life does," I say, and we drink to that.

"I bet your house is organized like a military locker."

I choke back a little beer. "No."

"Seriously?"

"The cobbler's children have no shoes," I say.

"Fascinating."

"It's a lot easier to work through other people's problems. I think I must be very attached to my own."

Ethan's looking at me like he's waiting for me to say

more. He has a nice way of knowing when to dig and when
to give a little space. I wonder again what's so wrong with
him that his girlfriend broke up with him. Now that I've
seen two square inches of his stomach, it makes less sense
than ever. "So why'd your girlfriend break up with you?"
I ask.

He shrugs. "The usual reason."

"Your fashion sense?"

He smiles, and I love that we have a joke. "I need to
grow up."

"Because of the skateboarding?" I ask. This blonde
doesn't know anything about what's sexy. "There must be
more."

"I didn't prioritize the relationship."

I look at him for a minute, registering his steady gaze
and the gift of his undivided attention. He seems like a person who takes care of things that matter to him: his dog, his
car, his parents' belongings. I wonder what mattered to him
more than his relationship with this annoying woman.

My phone beeps, and it's Pete: Great game, Iris scored
two. I'm going to take them for dinner and then to sleep at
my place. Text you in the morning.

I'm delighted that they had a great game and that I don't
have to make dinner. "Pete's keeping them overnight," I
say. I lift my eyes to his and see all the possibilities associated with what I've just said dance across his face.

"Oh," he says, finally, and then goes inside.

I am free for the entire night. I am a single woman, free
for the night. I'm glad he's left me alone because my breathing has gone uneven, and I need to get up and pace a little.

I circle the pool once while Iris texts a full play-by-play of the game.

Ethan comes back out with a plate of sliced tomatoes, fresh mozzarella, and sliced salami. Under his arm is a baguette. "Look, a picnic," he says. He walks over to the outdoor kitchen and pulls two wineglasses from the cupboard. He opens the wine refrigerator, chooses a white, and carefully opens the bottle.

He sits down and pours us each a glass. My senses are on high alert. I can actually feel my heart beating in my chest. My mind is scanning the situation for clues as to what's coming next. Beer, my mind tells me, is for friends hanging out. Wine is a date.

I need to get a grip. There is no reason for me to feel afraid of the way I want to run the tips of my fingers along the inside of his forearm. I have not been attracted to a man in so long that I am becoming obsessed with this guy's forearms. I laugh a little at that. I must be losing my mind.

"What?" He sits down and pours us each a glass of wine and I rip off a piece of the baguette.

"This is just so lovely."

"Thank you," he says. "Why would that be funny?"

I rip off another piece of the baguette and make a little sandwich out of the mozzarella and salami. He's watching me. He's assumed what I now know is his you-have-my-full-attention pose. Leaning forward, golden forearms resting on thighs. It feels like an invitation to spill my guts.

"It's just that you're this man with wine and the lovely food, and then you're also Scooter who stole the ice cream sandwiches."

"It was a dare. People really need to let that go. I was fourteen, and I did my time."

I smile and look down at my wine. "You really helped me yesterday," I say. "And it's been a long time since I've felt supported like that, like someone was in my corner."

"I'm glad I got to be there, but you could have totally handled that on your own."

There's no way. "I'm not so sure," I say, and now wish that I hadn't steered the conversation back in this direction. I want him to lean forward again so that I can study his eyelashes, darker than his hair.

"Of course you could," he says. "You're the architect of your own experience."

I narrow my eyes at him. "That was in my high school graduation speech. 'I am the architect of my own experience.'" Of course he would have been at Frannie's and my graduation. "I can't believe you remember that." I can feel all of those nerves again and the way my mom fixed my cap and hugged me before I lined up with my classmates. I was so nervous, and she told me I was going to knock 'em dead.

"It really resonated with me. I was a sophomore and was hanging out with total screwups because I didn't know what else to do. And my parents had pretty low expectations of me after the basement fire and, of course, my failure as a football star. Those words sort of made me realize I didn't have to keep being who everyone thought I was forever."

"Wow," I say. I try to remember what sort of experience I was hoping to create when I wrote that speech.

"It's funny how you're meeting me for the first time, and I've known you forever," he says. He leans forward again, so I do too. He's very close, and I can feel that crackle between us, like the air is suddenly thick. One thing I know for sure—I am no longer numb. I can feel his eyes on mine. I can feel the space between our mouths. The longer we linger here, the more intense it gets, and I find myself moving by half millimeters toward him and then back again, just to feel the crackle against my lips.

"You know," he says, and I can almost feel his mouth as it moves. "I have a thing where I won't kiss a woman who refuses to call me by my real name."

He's looking me right in the eye, waiting. His eyes are searching mine for an answer, and I'm sure he sees it there. I have wanted to kiss him since the moment my dog peed on him. He smiles at me the tiniest bit, and I smile back. "Ethan," I say.

I've barely gotten the word out before his mouth is on mine and my lips part and I am lost. His hands wind through the back of my hair and pull at my neck to bring me closer. I underestimated the thrill of kissing someone for the first time. I didn't account for the taste of him and the brush of his slight stubble against my face. I did not consider what it would feel like to breathe in his scent up close, my fingertips tightening on his shouldery shoulders. I have the sense that I could eat this man. Everything around us has gone quiet, the kind of quiet when the pin's been pulled from the grenade. Just before the explosion.

He deepens the kiss and I hear myself groan. He pulls away, my face in his hands, and looks me in the eye. His breaths are shallow. "Wow," he says. He brushes his thumb over my swollen lips and I feel it throughout my body. After a few beats he says, "I'm going swimming." It's a dare, and I wonder if he knows that right now I would follow him anywhere.

He gets up, takes off his shirt, and walks to the pool steps. I run my eyes across his shoulders and his chest, and I know that he knows I'm watching him. His eyes catch mine and we both know I'll never call him Scooter again. I finish my wine, and without thinking about it, I take off my shorts and T-shirt and dive into the pool in my bra and underwear. The water shocks my already heightened senses, and I love the delicious way it moves across my skin. When I'm close to the bottom of the pool and the cool water has touched every part of me, I realize that I forgot to be self-conscious about my perfectly fine body. I forgot to notice what underwear I was wearing. Most of it comes from a package of six that I get at Costco, cotton in shades of beige with one blue pair that's particularly dowdy. In February and September it's on sale, so I stock up. At this moment I don't feel like a woman who buys her lingerie at the same place she buys laundry detergent and peanut butter pretzel bites.

I come up for air, and he's getting into the pool. I swim from the deep end, underwater, to where he's standing submerged to his shoulders. It's too deep for me to stand so I place my hands on his shoulders to stay afloat. There's some reality where my holding on to him is just playful. Or me trying not to drown. He looks at me like he thinks this is neither of those things and puts his arms around my back.

"So," I say, and wrap my arms around his neck.

"Yes?" He pulls me close so that our stomachs are touching. I can feel this going from zero to sixty very quickly. My body is screaming at me to jump in, but I need to contain it.

"This," I say, and gesture between us, "this is a summer romance." My voice catches as he moves his mouth down my wet neck.

"It's whatever you want," he says, right before he presses his lips to mine, first featherlight and then with intent.

"Can this just be kissing?" I ask against his mouth.

"Yes. Whatever you want, Ali Morris. I mean it." He kisses me again.

"It will get so complicated otherwise." I'm saying this thing, which is intended to slow us down, while exploring his bottom lip with my mouth.

He nods.

"And no touching in public. My kids."

"Okay, I'll just keep you here," he says against my skin, and I shiver. I move my hands down his back, exploring the muscles there and feeling his breathing speed up as I do.

There's a beeping, and it reminds me of the sound of my alarm during a really good dream. He keeps kissing me and I keep pressing myself against him. Then I hear the beeping again. It's my phone.

I kiss him quickly and move toward the steps. He grabs my hand and pulls me back toward him. "You don't need to get it."

"I have kids. I always need to get it." I squeeze his hand and get out of the pool.

It's Pete, of course: Just hooked up with a group that's doing a super-early ride tomorrow morning through Manhattan. Going to drop them off after dinner.

Ethan's gotten out of the pool and is holding a towel out to me. "Pete wants to bring the kids home," I say.

"Ah, better deal?"

"Basically," I say.

"What did you say?"

"I haven't replied yet." I'm looking up at him for direction. At my core, I am a mother; my instinct is to put on my clothes and race to where they are, to wrap myself around them in case they've picked up on the fact that they've been dumped for a bike ride. I hate the idea that they feel like I always did, like they are his second-choice activity. And yet my skin is wet in the night air and wants to be pressed up against Ethan, feeling his chest against mine. I want his lips on my neck. In this instant I understand want in a way I haven't before, an irrational shedding of all other thoughts besides: *I want that feeling again.* I reach out and rest my hand on his wet chest.

I feel him take a quick breath.

"I have to go," I say.

"Don't," he says, stepping into my hand, increasing the pressure between us.

Leaving is the last thing I want to do, but I pull away because I think of Cliffy walking into the kitchen and expecting me to be there. "So was this our second date?" I ask. "Do people kiss on the second date?"

"Yes, it's a rule," he says. He runs a hand down the length of my waist and I feel it all the way down through my legs. "This was a great date. My fourteen-year-old self can't believe I got Ali Morris half-naked in the pool." He grabs a towel and wraps it tightly around me.

19

I DRIVE HOME IN A DAZE. IT'S A HALF-MILE DRIVE, AND I catch myself raising my fingers to my lips three times.

I walk into the house and they are already there. Cliffy runs into my arms. Pete wants to know why I'm wet. I say something about paddleboarding with Frannie and falling in the sound, and they ask something about paddleboarding at night. None of it makes sense, but that's fine.

It's late and my kids go right to sleep. I get in my bed and he's texted me: When can we do exactly that again?

My smile goes up through my eyes into the top of my head. I am carbonated. Me: Soon?

Ethan: Now would be good

I grin at my phone in the dark. Me: Soon

Ethan: Good night Ali

ON SUNDAY, I take my kids to my dad and Libby's house in Twin Rivers for lunch.

I always bring Libby flowers to make up for the fact that

I don't really have a relationship with her. I hand her the flowers in lieu of a hug, and if there were a card it might read, *Sorry this was never more natural between us.* Libby is a perfectly nice person. She loves my dad. She's sweet to my kids. They met when he was on a sales call in Twin Rivers when I was five. She had twin eleven-year-olds, Marky and Walt, and my dad sort of stepped into a new family the way a favorite TV character suddenly appears in a spin-off. They're the same, but everything around them is different. I never knew how to approach this spin-off dad, suddenly the father of two boys, and part of me felt like getting too close to him would be disloyal to my mom. I suspect that what attracted him to Libby was that she adores him like my mom adored me.

My dad opens the door and my kids throw their arms around him. "Well, if it isn't the Three Stooges!" he says, every single time.

I hug him and he hugs me back. It's a longer hug than is socially acceptable, but it's all we have. I don't really know how to talk to my dad. But when I see him, I count on this long hug to say everything we need it to.

"These are beautiful," Libby says, accepting the mason jar of pink hydrangeas. She has a helmet of blond hair and an admirably light touch with liquid eyeliner. "Come out back. We're barbecuing hamburgers."

We walk through their living room and I count six photos of Libby's grandkids next to the one of us. I look at my kids to see if they're focused on this particular math and realize that I am the only childish one here.

"Everything okay?" my dad asks when we're scraping plates into the garbage.

"Sure," I say. This is as close to my dad asking me how I am as we've come in a long time. I don't know which one of us is more scared of the answer. "Well, I guess I didn't tell you that Pete and I are going to finally file for divorce. We have our second mediation meeting next week. Sort of a formality."

"Ah," he says. He puts two plates in the dishwasher and turns back to me. "Do you need help? A lawyer?"

"No. It's all pretty simple."

"Okay, let me know if that changes," he says. "And there's nothing else going on?"

"No, why?" I do a quick life scan for what he could be noticing. My kids are fine. I washed my hair, but it's not like I'm wearing lip gloss again.

"You checked your phone six times during lunch."

I blush and he sees it, which makes me blush worse.

"Oh," he says. "Got it." And he walks back outside smiling.

WE DRIVE STRAIGHT from lunch to the inn and launch a canoe for our Sunday afternoon ride. For the past few months, I've been making the kids paddle with me, though I do most of the work. This is something Phyllis taught me about parenting, the importance of making kids do small things that you could do faster and better on your own. Just ask a little kid to make his bed and you'll know what she means. One year she let Greer and Iris plant tulip bulbs all over her yard. She gave them small shovels and absolutely no artistic guidance. That spring, the random garden design felt like a miracle. I look at my kids and imagine them grown up and strong. I imagine them being able to carry a canoe into the water by themselves. I want them to be prepared to be thirty-eight.

I check my phone immediately when we're back in the car. Ethan: Can I see you tomorrow?

Me: Free around 12.

And I am carbonated again.

IT'S MONDAY MORNING and I've just made sense of Frannie's books. I order poached eggs and an English muffin at the counter. "Who's doing the inn's books now?" I ask.

"Harold. The beach attendant," she says for emphasis.

"Wow, your parents must have more of a streamlined system than you do."

"They don't," she says. "And it's a total mess over there. My parents have to know that. The only saving grace is that all of our vendors have known us long enough to give us a heads-up before they cut us off."

"I'll stop by this week and see if I can help," I say. The inn is like someone's totally disorganized but gorgeous mudroom that I'd like to get my hands on.

Frannie puts her hands together in prayer and bows her head. "Thank you." She refills my water and narrows her eyes at me. "So what gives?"

She knows. I have kissed her brother and infiltrated the universe with impure thoughts about him ever since. Saturday night I lay in bed and I could still feel the pressure of his lips on mine, his hand on my waist. She has to know.

"Nothing." I shove eggs into my mouth to thwart a confession.

"Ali. Hard pants, clean hair. I swear when you walked in here you were wearing lip gloss. What gives?"

I laugh with relief. "Yes, I made a fresh start today. And it feels pretty good. These jeans even fit. Did you notice that?"

"I did. And if I didn't know better I'd think you were preparing to date a real grown-up man."

"Oh, please," I say.

She walks away because someone's short stack is ready. I'm not going to admit to her that I get to see him at noon today. Last night I got in bed with Iris and Cliffy on either side of me, listening to them disagree about what we were going to read, and rubbed my fingers together to try to re-create the feel of his hands on my skin. I like the way I've contained things. Nothing in public because my kids can't know. And neither should Frannie. No sex because that might put me on a slippery slope emotionally. Just a fun, easy summer where the end takes care of itself. The magic of the summer romance lies in the constraints.

My phone beeps, and it's him: Is it noon yet?

I smile at my phone and my face goes hot.

"What?" asks Frannie as she walks back.

"Nothing. It's just Scooter. He wants me to come help with the house." I busy myself with replying so I don't have to look at her: Be there in 15.

20

FRANNIE PACKS ME A TO-GO LUNCH OF A GIANT TUR-
key sandwich and a garden salad, and I head to Ethan's.
The door is ajar, so I let myself in. The four piles in the living room have grown since Saturday, suggesting a little
progress.

"Ethan?" I call out.

"Up here," he calls from the second floor. I find him in
the master bedroom, lying flat on his back on the king-
size bed.

"You okay?"

He smiles when he sees me and then motions toward the
closet. "I cannot do this."

It feels natural to plop down next to him on the bed,
so I do.

He takes my hand, and I feel relieved. Like I've plugged
back into an energy source. Warmth moves through my
body as our fingers entwine. "So what are we going to do?"
he asks.

"We're going to clean this place out. Frannie made us

lunch, and we get to eat it after we've worked for one hour. I'm going to set a timer on my phone."

He groans and squeezes my hand. "I've been in that closet since eight a.m. Every single article of clothing feels like a relic, like a piece of history. It's like it's alive and someone's asking me to kill it."

It's time for me to exert my forward-moving energy. I have an arsenal of questions that will unstick this stuck homeowner: Do you plan to use these items in the future? Would it be enough to photograph them and put the photos in a book to honor the memory? But I know exactly how he feels, every time I try to sort through our basement to clear space around the washing machine. Little-boy corduroy pants that crawled in the sandbox. Tiny Mary Janes that sashayed in the kindergarten play. I can't let any of it go.

I stand up. "We are going to walk into that closet and choose the ten best costumes, and we are going to respectfully box them up and keep them. Is ten a good number? Can you commit to just ten?"

"I cannot remember ever being this overwhelmed."

"It's a thing," I say. I know this because I feel this way in every room of my house.

"Can we move to the basement?" he says.

"No. One hour in the closet." I let go of his hand and pull up the timer on my phone. "Starts now." I walk into the closet and am hit with a wall of full-length ball gowns. Some of them are hilarious, and some are exquisite. He stands next to me as I pull each one out.

"Donate?" he asks.

"Okay, start a pile there."

I pull out a shimmery silver flapper dress and hold it up to myself. "What about this?" He turns around and looks me over, up and down, and then settles on my face with that look that is absolutely not how Cliffy looks at me.

"Keep," he says, and takes it from me.

WE DO THIS for an hour, until a quarter of the closet is empty and there's one modest donation pile on the floor. He is unable to part with any of the good costumes, and I don't blame him. They have the full cast of *Alice in Wonderland* and theater-quality costumes from *The Wizard of Oz*. There's a dress and a wig for Morticia Addams that I'm dying to put on.

I turn off the alarm on my phone and say, "So that wasn't too bad, was it?"

"It was horrible, I need a nap."

I sort of feel the same way, and I don't know why. This isn't my stuff, but there's something about the careful way their clothes were chosen and stored that makes it all feel so important.

Ethan flops down on his parents' bed. Now his, I guess. He reaches his hand out to me and I take it. He pulls me to lie next to him. We lie there on our backs, looking up at the amber chandelier over the bed, and he keeps holding my hand. "It's like they're dead," he says. "It feels weird to be doing this. What if they come back? What if they get sick of Florida and come back in time for the jack-o'-lantern lighting and there are no orange pants? Where are they going to find orange pants?"

"For a year after my mom died, I dreamed that she came back and was angry at me for cleaning out all of her stuff. She was going to a party and had nothing to wear." I laugh a little to take the heaviness away. It's been two years and I'm still not able to share light thoughts about my mom. *In time, sweetheart.*

Ethan turns to me. "You were able to clean out your mom's stuff, but you can't clean out your own? That seems a lot harder."

"It was pretty horrible. There was so much stuff, both her lifetime and my childhood. But there was no one else to do it. I brought Cliffy with me most days, while the girls were in school, so that kept me from getting too dark about the whole thing. And I actually found treasures in there."

"Like what?"

I shake my bracelet down on my wrist. "She had this made for me when I was eight. She was a jewelry designer. I don't know if you knew that."

He reaches over and touches the little silver soccer ball and his fingers graze the inside of my wrist. "I didn't know that. So did you find jewelry?"

"No, just more hooks. Like the things she'd use to attach a charm to the bracelet." He's waiting for me to go on. "I don't know, it just felt like hope or something, like she thought more things might happen to me."

"Of course more things are going to happen to you." Once he's repeated it back to me, I am aware of the passive voice I've used. I want to correct myself: I might do more things.

"Maybe. So I kept the hooks, hundreds of them, and

the tiny pliers she used to attach them." She gave my girls bracelets too, but only lived long enough to give them a few charms. Soccer balls. A lightning bolt for when Iris finished the Harry Potter series, a gold hoop for when she took Greer to get her ears pierced. I've meant to keep up with it because that's on me now, but I'm not a jewelry designer, and when I try to find similar charms online, it's just sort of depressing. "I probably kept too much of her stuff, but the process was good for me. I guess it was a way of honoring her. Tidying up her life."

"And that's not something you'd do for yourself?" he asks.

Apparently not. I think of the half-unloaded groceries that are waiting for me at home. I don't want to talk about this. "I honor myself plenty. I have enough candles in my bathroom to burn the house down."

He turns onto his side to face me, so I do too. "What now?" he says. His mouth is so close to mine that I can feel his breath on my lips.

"What do you mean?"

He runs a finger down my neck, leaving goose bumps. "Please don't make me go back into that nightmare of a closet."

"Fifteen more minutes," I say. "And then maybe we have our third date."

21

I SEE ETHAN WEDNESDAY AND THURSDAY WHILE MY kids are at camp. "Clean out the house" has become code for "skateboard and make out." I feel like I'm sixteen and I'm riding the wave of something bigger than me. I reach for a roll of packing tape, and the brush of an arm leads to the grip of a neck, and, before I know it, I am up against a refrigerator for twenty minutes. Or maybe it's five. I have all sorts of alarms set on my phone because I lost my mastery of time. Stopping ourselves becomes increasingly difficult, and the kissing-only rule has been loosened. "Any Ali is better than no Ali," he whispers into my neck.

I shouldn't be surprised that there's a small half-pipe in the basement he nearly burned down. He talks me through the fundamentals of skateboarding while also encouraging me to let go of my fear. He wants me to get my head around skating up to the top and then skating back down. It's all physics and gravity, but also a lot of letting go and changing course, which, for me, happens in very small increments.

Friday is our custody mediation session, and I accidentally spend the morning with Harold at the inn. I'd noticed from the dog park that the flag hadn't been raised, and upon closer examination, the garbage hadn't been picked up either. He sort of left me no choice. I was worried I was overstepping, but the moment I walked into his office he pulled out his desk chair for me and said, "Have at it." I put together a detailed to-do list—what to order when, and a checklist for the most important tasks to manage. Making sure the garbage is out on time is top of the list.

When I get home, I am buoyed by the progress at the inn, so I set a timer on my phone and spend ten minutes loading the dishwasher and scrubbing the pots in the sink. This feels a tiny bit like self-care.

I get a text from Ethan: I'll meet you there at eleven. Still working on my costume.

Me: Can't wait to see. What should I wear?

Ethan: Your regular weary housewife clothes are perfect.

Me: Ouch.

I PULL INTO the parking lot behind Lacey's office, and Pete is getting out of the passenger seat of a white Toyota. He leans over the door and gives the driver his best, most nauseating smile before he shuts it. The smile dies when he turns around and sees me standing there.

"What was that?" I say.

"I'm dating," he says.

"A woman?" My brain is catching up to this state of affairs, and not quickly.

"Ali."

"That's fine," I say, and scan the parking lot for Ethan. I just need to get through this meeting.

"You could date too," he says. And before I eke out a sarcastic reply about just how much dating a woman can do between noon and two on Saturdays, Ethan pulls into the parking lot. He steps out in a maroon velour tracksuit. I am now positive that I am losing my mind, because I like the way he looks in it.

"Hey, guys," he says. "Hope I'm not late."

Pete shakes his head and walks into the building.

Ethan gives me his conspiratorial smile, like everything in this world is funny, and offers me his maroon arm to escort me upstairs.

"Nice threads," Lacey says.

"It's athleisure," he says. "My father's."

We sit at the round table, and Lacey says, "Let's look at a monthly calendar and start outlining our expectations."

Pete says, "Well, what we've been doing is the kids live at the house. I take them to soccer Tuesday nights—the days change with the season and league. And then I have them on Saturdays, when we have either practice or a game. And usually for a while after. I coach."

"What we want to nail down," says Ethan, "is the language here. Let's eliminate the word 'usually' and commit to chunks of time."

"With all due respect, Scooter, 'usually' works for us. Sometimes things come up and I need to change plans." Pete is already up for a fight.

"Do things come up for you, Ali?" Ethan asks, and turns his whole body to me, as if to suggest that I now have the floor. I should be used to this, because Ethan is always giving me the floor. He listens to me in a way that makes me want to share everything.

I sit up a little straighter. "No, I am able to plan out my week and keep my commitments, if Pete does the same."

Pete lets out a dramatic breath and leans back in his chair, as if now he's heard everything. "That's Ali. A huge planner. She's the only person I've ever known who's surprised that every twenty-four hours it's time to make dinner again." He laughs at his little joke.

I open my mouth to speak and nothing comes out. I've had nightmares like this where I'm trying to scream but I'm not able. There's just too much anger behind every word. I've kept my mouth shut for so long, it's almost like my body knows that if I start I won't stop.

Ethan leans in. "Lacey, I assume you've been working with families for a while. Do you think it's emotionally helpful for Pete's children to think they're spending Saturday night with him and then get shuttled home because a big bike ride came up?"

"This is bullshit," says Pete.

"It's actually not. I have it in my notes." Ethan flips through the pages of his legal pad at a deliberately slow pace just to irritate Pete. He runs his pen down each page, nodding, before he turns to the next one. "Here it is. Just this past Saturday night. You decided to keep the children overnight and then returned them immediately after dinner?"

"That's none of your goddamn business."

Ethan looks down at his tracksuit, as if it proves that he's actually in business. "I'm pretty sure it is, Pete."

I want to reach across the table and smack Pete. Smack him for being arrogant and smug and totally thoughtless. There's something terrifying underneath all of this anger. I can feel how Pete acting like a jerk makes me miss my mom. And I picture her, with her big smile, saying, "Oh, that's fine. Let him do his bike ride. You know what would be fun?" I'd let it go. My chest is tight with anger at Pete but also with the unfamiliar discomfort of being angry with my mom. She should have let me speak up. It's like she trained me to be mute around Pete.

Lacey speaks before I can. "We find that the more consistent the schedule, the easier it is on the kids. They get anxious if they're not sure about basic things like where they are going to wake up." Lacey is looking at Ethan like she wants to lick him. This is mildly irritating, but it's good to have another person on my side.

Pete's glaring at me, arms crossed over his chest. "Are you going to say anything?"

"Yes." My voice comes out stronger than I expect, like my anger is a weapon I just found in my purse, and I'm going to give it a try. I look directly at him because I want him to see what's brewing behind my eyes. "I think we can stay loose around the weeknights, because the soccer schedule changes. But the weekends need to be consistent."

"Could you commit to having your children from ten a.m. on Saturday morning to ten a.m. on Sunday morning each week?" Ethan asks. His hands are folded, his gaze is steady.

Pete lets out a breath. "That's twenty-four hours."

And I know what he means. He means that's way too much time for him to not be able to do whatever he wants.

I'm guessing Ethan knows this too, but he doubles down. He jots down a few numbers on his legal pad. "Okay, if we let you have them until four on Sunday, that would be thirty hours. Ali, is that okay?" He must be the best poker player in the world. There is no hint of a smile on his face to give him away. Lacey is sitting with her pen at the ready to record the decision.

"Where'd you get that tracksuit?" Pete asks. I'm not sure I've ever seen him so angry.

Ethan runs his hands down the velour. "It belongs to my father. It would be hard to find one like it now, I think. But thank you." He turns to Lacey. "So did we say thirty hours?"

"Twenty-four is fine," Pete says.

"WE ARE GOING to get so fun-tastic tonight," Ethan says when we're outside. Pete stormed out of the office ahead of us, so we're in the parking lot alone.

"Well, thank you for today," I say. It's not enough, but I need to get into my car and talk to my mom. It wasn't okay, her not letting me sort out my marriage. I should have been standing up to Pete all along. I feel tears welling up and I don't want to darken his victorious mood. I turn to go and he grabs my arm.

"Wait, aren't we celebrating? We won. He committed to time and you have a full free day. Every week." His expression is expectant. Like he's waiting for me to get the joke and laugh.

"I know, it's great," I say. And my voice catches. I don't want to be crying in this parking lot.

"Come with me." Ethan leads me to his car. He opens the passenger door and I get in.

"Really, I'm fine," I say when he's in the driver's seat.

"You're not fine. We won and you're about to cry." He's turned toward me, and he's waiting for me to explain.

"It's all of it. The fact that Pete had to be bullied into spending twenty-four hours with his children. The fact that my kids have never been with him for that long, including when we were married. The fact that I haven't had twenty-four hours to myself since my mom died. All of it."

"He's kind of a tool."

"I may have made him that way. I stopped asking him to step up a long time ago. My mom. She sort of covered for him. I turned into this." I gesture at myself.

"What do you mean by 'this'?"

"A weary housewife. This isn't a costume." I'm crying now and reach into my bag for a tissue that isn't there. I find Cliffy's rainbow sweatband and use it to wipe my eyes. "And I'm also sort of afraid of the free time. What if you just bought me twenty-four hours a week and now I have no excuses?"

Ethan puts his key in the ignition. "We need dogs and some fresh air."

22

ETHAN DRIVES TO MY HOUSE, AND I GO INSIDE TO change into shorts and get Ferris. He wants to come in, but he's seen enough of what a mess I am today, and I know for a fact that, even though I loaded the dishwasher, there are two sets of muddy cleats and the rancid shell of a hermit crab in the sink.

We go back to his house to pick up Brenda, and he emerges in his red swim trunks and a white T-shirt with a backpack slung across his shoulder. It's the outfit of a teenage lifeguard, but I'm having a hard time seeing Ethan as anything but the grown-up man who is currently holding me together.

We drive in silence to the dog park, which is honestly not my first choice. I don't really feel like playing referee and making small talk with my mom's friends. When we get out of the car, there's a breeze pushing backlit clouds across the sky. It rustles the giant leaves of the sycamore trees in a way that sounds like distant applause. As if thirty miles away, someone else has finally gotten things right. There's a hint of lavender in the air. Lavender, I think, is a sinister fragrance—it relaxes you while it calls in the bees.

Ethan leads me past the dog park toward the sound. It's low tide and it looks like you could walk halfway to Long Island. Little kids are in the water in front of the inn with buckets and shovels, the water just up to their ankles, and I imagine what it must feel like to be that free in all that space. Like they're walking on water.

There's a path along the seawall that runs the length of the park but eventually dead-ends into private property. We start walking south in silence and I am loving the feel of the wet breeze on my face. I am loving the fact that he's not expecting me to explain any more about why I was crying.

When we've hit the end of the path, we are at a wrought iron gate around the garden of a waterfront home. The Litch-fields used to live here, but I think they moved to Flor-ida too.

Ethan peers through the gate and says, "The Litchfields used to live here."

"I remember," I say. "Sammy used to have the best par-ties. No one ever complained about the noise out here."

Ethan points to a small island a hundred yards out. It's covered with a couple of hardy trees that bend north as if they've been caught in a photograph of a storm. "That's Pelican Island, or at least that's what we used to call it when we were pretending to be pirates. Sammy's brother Jason and I used to swim out there and build tree forts when we were little. In high school we'd hide beer behind those trees."

"Clever."

"Well, it was if it was a day like this. But on several occasions the tide came in and we were left waiting for a case of Bud Light to wash up on the shore." Ethan is smiling at Pelican Island, and I want to feel as light as he does. "Let's take the dogs."

Ethan hops off the seawall onto the beach and reaches up for Brenda and then Ferris. "Come on," he says. "We'll go sit out there for a bit and get a new perspective." He holds up his backpack. "I even have refreshments." We leave our phones inside our shoes on the wall and start walking across the water. The tide is so low that the water barely covers my feet. We've taken Ferris and Brenda off leash and they run wild, hunting scents and crisscrossing the shore. The sand squishes under my feet and I turn my complete attention to the feel of it. Wet sand gathers between my toes and rinses away with each step. It's rhythmic, the sound of my feet splashing toward the island.

Ethan is ahead of me and stops when we are about ten feet from the island. He calls the dogs and scoops them both in his arms as the water gets a bit deeper. The wet dogs soak his shirt and he's submerged to the top of his thighs by the time he gets there. He places the dogs and then his backpack on the rocky shore. "Want me to come back for you? You're going to get soaked."

I can see that I'm going to get wet past my waist if I keep going, but I don't feel like getting rescued again today. The sun is welcoming me out into the water. "I'm good," I say, and keep going.

Pelican Island is bigger than it looks from the shore. You could probably fit my house on it, but nothing more.

Around the two trees there is sand and rock and washed-up shells.

"Turn around," he says.

And I do. There's Beechwood. Where most of my life took place. It looks different while standing still on another piece of dry land. The inn, the clearing of the dog park, the Litchfields' house. Hidden beyond the canopy of trees is the high school where I was the valedictorian, the church where I was married, the house where I tried to be a wife. From a distance, it's just green. I relax not having to look at all the details. The mess.

We sit down under the trees, and he opens his backpack and hands me a beer.

"You really are a great lawyer," I say, and he laughs.

"I also brought pretzels, no extra charge."

"It feels like we're watching the opening scene of a movie about our town, where they pan in on the whole thing before we get to the action."

He nods. "And then what happens?"

I am quiet for a bit, because I don't know. The woman gets divorced. The kids grow up. The dog dies. "I'm having a hard time seeing the happy ending."

"There's no happy ending to an unhappy story."

I give him a little shove and take a sip of my beer. "That's so annoying. You can't keep quoting my own speech back to me." I stretch out my wet legs in front of me and close my eyes as the sun dries them.

"But it's true," he says. "You can't just keep doing what you're doing and wait for it to turn into something happy. You kind of have to look for the happy things along the way."

"I guess." Brenda comes over and sits on Ethan's lap, like she agrees. I turn to him and watch his profile as he concentrates on running his hand along Brenda's spine. He's so in the moment.

"I'm soaked," he says, and takes off his shirt. The sudden sight of so much golden skin makes my breath catch. I want to reach out and run my hands over his shoulders, but I am a little too vulnerable right now. I want to keep this thing with Ethan fun, and right now I feel like I could grab on to it too tight and ruin it.

"So is it your Zen pursuit of happiness that makes you unreliable?"

"Maybe. I kind of move toward what feels good."

"Like what?" I'm looking straight at the Beechwood shoreline, and I can feel him looking at me. My question is loaded as I say it, because it would feel good to have him lying on top of me on this tiny island.

"Sticking it to Pete today felt pretty good," he says.

I laugh. "It did."

"Was there any particular reason you ever dated that guy?"

I laugh the smallest laugh. "Pete just made sense. He felt like he was going to be a partner. I loved how he was so into everything he was into. There was always a frenzy of activity and it felt exciting." I turn to him and his eyes are on me. Like he's recording my words to play them back to himself later. "But then we had kids and my days were full of messy things and joyful surprises, and Pete's life was about all of his activities. I thought it might help to move to Beechwood so my mom could pitch in."

"And did it?"

"Kind of. She sort of slid in to fill the gap between Pete and me, and it worked."

"And then she died."

"And then she died."

"And Pete left," he says.

"And now I'm actually getting divorced and it's fine. I wish we'd broken up years ago." I look down at my feet, now sandy again. "I'm really grateful that you were there to help me today. But I can't believe it's taken me so long to stand up for myself. Pete said I'd disappeared. The night he left. And I felt that today, just how absent I've been."

Ethan puts his arm around me and pulls me toward him. The warmth of his bare arm and his hand on my shoulder spreads throughout my body. I shift closer to him and rest my head on his shoulder. "You're the architect of your own experience, Ali. You've got to get out from under this," he says.

"Under what?"

"I'm not sure. Something's weighing you down though."

Laundry. A mountain of mail. Grief. I lean into him a little closer.

"You okay?" he asks into my hair.

"It just feels really nice to be with you." I wait to feel embarrassed that I've said this, but I don't. Ethan has seen me in my Costco underwear; he's seen me berated by my husband. He's seen me cry. He's felt safe each time.

"See? You move toward what feels good." He tightens his grip and holds me while we watch the water. I concentrate on the feel of his fingers on my arm and then the feel of the salt water drying on my legs. The white noise of the sea breeze mixed with the so-close sound of his breathing.

"It's too bad you're so unreliable," I say, because honestly I would love to just climb into this happy man and stay forever.

"I guess." He's quiet for a while before he goes on. "Catherine mostly left because of the things that make me happy." He releases me and lies back on the sand. I am not ready for him to stop holding me, that is the only thing I am a hundred percent sure of. I lie down next to him so that I can at least feel his arm next to mine. The sky is remarkably blue behind the leaves of this tree.

"Explain," I say.

"I hated growing up here, as you know. I always felt so lost, like I didn't know who I was or how to be. Even in Manhattan when I was this corporate lawyer with a big paycheck, I still didn't know; it was like I was playing a part. When I moved up to Devon, I felt like I mattered. The kids at the skate park rely on me for a lot of things. A few of the older ones have run away from foster homes, and I try to help get them jobs and places to stay. I keep tabs on them. I do the legal work for Rose at the animal shelter and work with the dogs when they need me. My downstairs neighbor Barb calls every time she sees a spider. Lots of things like that. And I love it. I'm this different person up there. Like I'm not useless. Like it's finally okay that I don't play football." He laughs a little. "Anyway, I'm happy being a guy people lean on, and it got on her nerves. I canceled a lot of weekends away. The last one was a trip to Bermuda we were supposed to take with some of her friends. One of the kids from the park got in a fight and broke four ribs the night before we were leaving. I couldn't go."

He turns to me and we are nose to nose. There's a little bit of sand under his eye and I wipe it away. I love that I get to casually touch him. He doesn't even blink. "Those kids think I'm super reliable, which is ironic, I guess."

"They must," I say, and my heart clenches.

"Catherine said I have a hero complex. And I never really understood that. I mean, what kind of complex would I have if I just blew them off?" He shakes his head, like he's shaking away the thought. "Anyways, it's good for me too, because the kids help run the events at the skate park." When my face doesn't register understanding, he goes on. "I own the skate park. It's just an empty lot with some ramps we built, but kids come now and it's a whole thing. I made it because I couldn't find any place to skate up there."

I reach my hand up and cup his cheek, feel the roughness of his stubble. "You're a good guy, Ethan."

"I don't know about that. But it all feels good. It feels good to finally be happy." His eyes go intense, like he has something he's been wanting to say. He reaches over and brushes my hair over my shoulder and runs his hand along my neck. I see him decide not to say whatever it was, and instead he kisses me. It's a whisper of a kiss, more full of reverence than full of desire. I have the sense that he's told me something. We lie like this, on our sides, looking at one another while the water laps the shore and a soft breeze kisses our skin. I run my fingers over his cheekbones and then along his lower lip. I am memorizing him. The soundtrack for this moment is a gull overhead and the intensifying sound of the waves.

Ethan looks over his shoulder. "The tide's coming in."

I jump up and grab Ferris. Being stranded on a deserted island with an attractive man only works if there's a port-a-potty.

He's got his backpack on and is holding Brenda. "Follow me, I think it's just going to be a little deeper than it was on the way in. We won't have to carry the dogs too far."

The water's only up to the top of my waist, but I have to hold Ferris pretty high to keep him from getting soaked. I like wading through the water behind Ethan and the way he keeps turning around to see if I'm okay.

When the water is shallow enough, I put Ferris down and let him run. He and Brenda are ahead of us and I fall into step next to Ethan. We don't speak as we make our way back to our sneakers, phones, and leashes. We've both missed a call from Frannie, and I'm shocked to see that it's 2:55.

"Wow, I really lost track of everything out there," I say.

"Yes," he says, without looking up from his phone.

"Everything okay?" I ask.

"Yeah, sort of. The guys have an event at the skate park tomorrow and the city's pulled their permit. They can go ahead with it if it's never more than thirty people at a time. I'm going to have to go up tomorrow to act as a bouncer." He tosses his phone into his backpack and we start walking back to the car.

"So do you go every time they need something?" I ask.

"Well, usually I'm there when they need something, so it's easier."

"I'm glad. Someone else might just tell them to cancel it."

He stops and smiles at me like I just said Massa-Cheez-Its. "Do you want to come with me tomorrow?"

"To Devon?"

"Yes, full change of scenery. I'll pick you up at 10:05."

23

E THAN PULLS INTO MY DRIVEWAY JUST AS PETE AND the kids are disappearing around the corner. I'm standing outside because I was watching them go. It was so strange to help them pack and watch them load overnight bags into Pete's car. I can't think of the last time I was away from my kids for twenty-four hours.

"You ready for a road trip?" he asks. There's a nervous air about him, like if he were standing up he'd have his hands in his pockets and be studying his shoes. I want us to be like we were on Pelican Island, where he was looking right into my eyes. I want him to touch my hair.

"I am," I say. Ferris hops into the backseat with Brenda.

We head out of Beechwood onto the highway, and we're quiet as we drive north. We both relax, and the silence feels as easy as our conversations do. The trees on either side of us are a deep summer green, and I feel like I'm moving through a tunnel, like a straight shot out of my life. It's strange to have a whole day without drop-offs and pickups looming. I check my phone to see if the girls have texted. They haven't.

Ethan's phone rings and he answers it on speaker. I feel like I'm invading his privacy somehow, so I turn my body toward the window.

"Hey," he says.

"What time are you getting here? People are showing up and we want to start in an hour." It's a young guy.

"You've got to wait till I get there, probably around two thirty. Promise me you'll wait. I really don't want you guys shut down permanently."

"Okay. Promise. Thanks."

He hangs up. "So I thought we could stop for lunch just outside of Devon. Let the dogs out for a bit."

"Is that okay? He sounded like he wanted us to hurry."

"They can skate all afternoon. And it's good for them to have to handle things and wait sometimes."

"They really are like your kids," I say.

He smiles. "I guess."

"That's absolutely exhausting," I say. "Why would you take that on?"

"You'll see," he says.

WE PULL OFF the highway into the dirt parking lot of a roadside café. There's a wheat field out back that waves us in. I stay outside with the dogs while Ethan goes in to order our lunch.

We find two Adirondack chairs on the back deck and let our dogs off leash. I am tucking into a chicken salad sandwich and looking out onto the wheat field. Ethan's looking at me like he's going to say something. Then he's looking at the fields. He turns his body toward me and shifts back straight ahead.

"What's with you?" I say.

"I don't know. I'm not so sure about this."

"Your sandwich? Mine's great." I polish off the first half.

He shakes his head at me like I'm hopeless.

"You're not sure about what?"

"I guess bringing you along. I kind of feel like you're about to see me naked."

I blush like I'm twelve years old. I feel it prickle on my cheeks.

"God, Ali, stop. I don't mean actually naked. I know the rules." He's smiling now. "It's just that you're going to see my actual life, who I am. I don't know what you're going to think."

WHEN WE'RE OFF the highway in Devon, we head through the city. Ethan points out the different neighborhoods, the building where he has an office. We pass his favorite hot dog stand, and the proprietor waves so enthusiastically that we stop.

"This will just take a second," Ethan says. "We can't just drive by Mort."

I get out of the car and follow him to the stand. The delicious salty smell of hot dogs fills the air. It reminds me of the ballpark on our first date.

"I thought you were gone for good," says Mort. He takes Ethan's face in his hands like he's going to give him a giant kiss.

"Never." Ethan laughs.

"In six years I didn't go a week without selling this man a hot dog," he says to me. Then to Ethan, "You've missed the last two games. Lyle said you were leaving the team. But I said, 'Lyle, you're an idiot. Ethan would never abandon the Red Hot Pokers. Not when I still owe him forty bucks.'"

Ethan laughs, "I think it's sixty." He introduces me and buys two hot dogs, seemingly out of habit.

When we're back in the car he breaks up the hot dogs for Brenda and Ferris. "Red Hot Pokers?" I ask.

"It's just poker. But we're definitely a crew."

"Matching T-shirts?"

"Visors," he says with a smile, and starts the car.

We park on the street in a run-down neighborhood where there's a crowd in front of a vacant lot. Halogen lights, identical to the ones at the skate park in Beechwood, mark each corner.

Ethan comes around to help me out of the car and holds on to my hand for a second. "This is so weird that you're here," he says.

"I'm excited to see it," I say.

"We'll see."

We walk toward the crowd, mostly teenagers, and one with long dark hair calls out, "Ethan!" He comes over and they fist-bump.

"Hey. Thanks for waiting. Justin, this is Ali."

"Oh, hi," he says, and shakes my hand. "I've kept the

gate locked and I'm trying to get people to line up. It's been fine I guess, but they've been waiting a long time."

"Okay, get Louie and Michael and I'll let you guys in first. Then we'll deal with the line."

I follow Ethan into the crowd, where everyone knows him. "Dude, where have you been?" they ask. "Finally," someone else says. They are all clamoring to get through the gate into the park. A half-pipe sits in the center, and on it is painted what might be an aerial view of this neighborhood. I want to get closer to look at the details, but Ethan and I are manning the gate.

When he's let exactly thirty kids into the park, he starts to work the line. It surprises me to see how he interacts with these kids. He's both a high school principal dictating where everyone needs to be and a slightly older brother joking around. I stand at the front of the line and watch. He knows everyone, including the uniformed police. He stops to talk with a couple of teenage boys, and he laughs at something they've said. I can't actually hear his laugh, but I see it and hear it in my head. It's the deep, rich laugh he uses when it's just the two of us and he's completely himself.

He feels too far away, immersed in this crowd, and I want to call out to him, to bring him back to me. I am relieved each time he looks up to check that I'm still there. My job is to stand by the gate and let him know if anyone leaves so that he can let the next kids in. The first person in line looks like she's about fourteen. I try to start a conversation. "I like your skateboard." Fun fact: I don't know how to talk to teenagers.

"Thanks," she says.

"Did you do that artwork or did it come like that?"

"I did it."

"Wow, it's cool." "Cool" is not the right thing to say. Never say "cool." I cross my arms over my chest to protect myself from whatever reaction I deserve.

"Thanks," she says. "Are you Ethan's girlfriend?"

"Um, no?" I say, and hope I'm not blushing again. "He's my friend's brother, I'm just here to see the skate park."

"He went to see my brother pitch in Connecticut, because my dad couldn't go and is superstitious about missing games."

"I was there too," I say, connecting the dots. "It was fun."

"Sounded like a total bust. Now my dad's more superstitious than ever. You skate?"

I laugh. "I've had a few lessons, but I have a lot to learn. Just here to watch."

"Ethan taught me and my friends last summer. It used to be like six of us, now it's a whole thing."

"I can tell," I say. Ethan is walking toward us with a little boy on his shoulders. The little boy has his hands in Ethan's hair and is kneading it like it's dough. By the time they reach us, his hair is sticking straight up. If he knows, he doesn't care.

"Hey, Caitlin. You meet Ali?"

"Yep. I think you should teach her to skate."

"I'm working on it. Let's see if we can get you in there." There's no mention of the human being on his shoulders, like he's just an appendage. Ethan waves Justin over. "All okay in there?"

"Yeah, first round is over, so some kids should be leaving," Justin says.

"Nice. Cops are fine. I think you've totally managed this thing."

Justin is beaming, and I have to look away from the intimacy of it. I have the feeling that Ethan has just given him a gift I don't understand. This is Ethan's superpower, I think. His ability to meet people where they are and just hold the space for them to step into their best selves without any expectation of what that might be.

I watch as Ethan gives the little boy on his shoulders back to his mother. He says something that makes her laugh. I imagine that being this man all the time feels very, very good.

There's a feeling in my chest, specifically my heart. It's a little like gliding down the half-pipe after you've let yourself glide up a little bit. It's both a terror and a thrill to know you could fall.

"HUNGRY?" HE ASKS when we've locked up the park at seven. We're alone on the street now and I feel relieved not to have to share him with all those people.

"I am."

"Good," he says. He leads Brenda, Ferris, and me down the street, and he takes my hand. I like being out of Beechwood and in a place where it's okay to look like a couple. I like trying it on, showing off for anyone that passes by: look at me with this wonderful man. "This is going pretty well," he says.

I squeeze his hand. "I'd say so. I like your life."

"That was the tip of the iceberg."

"What else do you do?"

"Well, I run the Halloween dog parade on this street every year." He looks at me out of the corner of his eye.

"Dog parade," I say.

"It's total chaos, but it's great. Barb is making a witch costume for Brenda. Ferris would love it. You should come." *You should come.*

"Sure," I say.

We stop at a small restaurant with a red door and two tables outside. The restaurant itself is faced in stone and occupies the corner of a more modern brick building. He opens the door and I step back in time. It's the smallest restaurant I've ever been in, with only six tables—three occupied—and an old wooden bar with four stools. One waiter seems to be managing all of it. His face lights up when he sees Ethan, a reaction I'm starting to expect in Devon.

"Ethan! You didn't tell me." He places the tray he's carrying on the bar and starts to smooth imaginary wrinkles from his shirt.

"This is Ali," Ethan says. "Ali, this is Jamey. He does everything here but cook."

"It's a beautiful place," I say. "I've never seen anything like it." And I really haven't. It sort of feels like the Hogans' house. Something painstakingly crafted and out-of-date that no one would bother building now.

"It's one of a kind," Jamey says. "And here forever, thanks to Ethan."

I turn to Ethan for an explanation. I get none.

"Can you seat two of us for a quick dinner? Outside?" He gestures to the dogs.

"Sure. But they say it's going to rain."

"They always say that," Ethan says. "We'll take our chances."

Jamey leads us outside, and we sit at a small bistro table. I ask for a glass of pinot noir, and Ethan says, "Water for me, please. I'm her ride back to Beechwood."

"SO," ETHAN SAYS when I have my wine. "That's my life."

"You have a pretty full life."

"Yeah." He looks at me for a few beats, like he's not sure if he wants to go on. "There's a lot to do here, for the kids. And for everybody really. No limit to the problems needing to be solved."

"And you saved this restaurant?"

"Not really. I just filed the paperwork to make it a historic landmark."

"Of course you did."

"It took me an hour."

He leans down and pets Brenda under the table, as if to change the subject. A taxi passes. An older couple stops to say hello. They show us photos of their grandchildren on their phones and ask to see new photos of Theo.

"Do you know everyone in this town?" I ask when they've walked away.

"I know a lot of them. Those two are clients. I helped with their lease. There's one landlord in Devon who is terrified of me, so everyone in his buildings comes to me with their leases and stuff." He smiles. There is no sign of Scooter here; there's no wrinkle in his brow. Everyone in Devon looks at him the way I do.

"How'd you even get here in the first place?"

"I was assigned to defend a big real estate firm that was accused of endangering tenants in Devon. I was making a lot of money in the city, my parents were so happy. I'd been at the law firm in Manhattan for five years. Everything was fine, but that case sort of stopped me in my tracks." He takes a sip of my wine. "I was turning thirty and hanging out with a bunch of people I didn't really connect with. I was questioning things, you know?"

"When I was thirty I had two little kids and was about to get pregnant again." I take my wine back.

"At least there's meaning there. Making people."

"Yes," I say.

"Anyway, I had to come up here a few times to take depositions, and it became pretty clear to me that my client was totally in the wrong." He leans back in his chair and I want him to come close again. "Long story short, we won the case and I quit. I moved up here and started a private practice, and I finally felt at home. For the first time in my life, I felt like myself."

"And you gave the kids a skate park."

"I gave myself a skate park. It was so cheap. No one wanted an empty lot in this neighborhood. And now it's just an investment of time, getting the police on board and getting the rec center involved."

"And is it worth it? I mean, all that time you spend on this stuff blew up your last relationship." I want to take back the word "last" the second I've said it. I've made it seem like I think we're in a relationship, which of course we're not.

"Totally worth it. I'm a person who people turn to here. It feels good. Knowing who I am feels good. That might sound a little crazy." He takes a breath and looks away. He's quiet for another beat, as if he's making a decision. "Ali, I don't think you get how messed up I was in high school."

I don't know what to say to that, so I reach for his hand.

"I hung out with a bunch of kids who were high all the time, and it was fine. I wasn't into sports, and I couldn't really see any place else I might fit in. I think I'd resolved to just ride out high school in a haze. But by the time we were fifteen, they started moving on to harder stuff and I was sort of stuck deciding if I was going to dive in with them or be totally alone. It sounds crazy now, but at the time those really felt like the only choices."

I think of Greer, so close to those teen years. "That must have been scary."

"It was. I was a kid and I wanted to be part of something. I didn't feel like I fit in at home. I was lost. One day— it was April—I was supposed to meet them at the rec and we were going to drive to find some guy one of them had started buying from. I got there early, and there were a bunch of kids at the skate park. I watched for a while, and I knew there was something there that I wanted. I remember thinking they didn't look trapped, you know? The whole scene was totally intimidating, and I would have never walked in, but Mr. Kennedy was there. Do you remember him? The music teacher?"

"I do."

"He waved me in. Asked me to come help him move a cooler of water." He shakes his head. "If he'd asked me if I wanted to try skateboarding, I would have said no and my life would have gone a totally different direction. I think about that all the time. Long story short, I walked into the skate park. My friends showed up and left without me. Nicky Bowler was dead eight months later."

"I remember this," I say. "He was Ryan's little brother."

"Yeah, he was my friend. It was horrible, and it could have been me. I got really lucky. What were the chances Mr. Kennedy would see me there and wave me in?" His gaze is intense as he holds mine.

"So then the skate park kids became your friends?"

"I didn't really fit in there either, actually. But the thing about skateboarding is it takes so much concentration that I would forget that I didn't know what to say or how to act. And I was finally good at something. It helped. Then I went to college and law school and tried to figure out how to turn myself into a success so that my parents would finally see me as a grown-up. And you've seen how well it's going with my parents." He laughs a little, then meets my eye. "I came up here and it felt like it could be a fresh start. I decided to be the architect of my own experience."

I FEEL THE first drop of rain on my wrist, and before I have a chance to wipe it away, the sky has opened up. We grab our dogs by the leashes and race to the tiny awning over the red door. We are surrounded by three walls of water, and I love the way it sounds. I love the way summer rain comes out of nowhere and hits you hard like a love affair. Rain like this couldn't last more than a few minutes.

"I guess they were right about the rain," Ethan shouts.

I laugh and pull my hair over my shoulder and wring out the ends. My T-shirt is soaked, and I cross my arms over my chest. Ethan's soaked too, and he smiles down at me. I like being trapped in this tiny space with him.

"Listen, I know wet socks are kind of our thing," he says, "but I don't think I'm up for a four-hour drive home soaking wet. Let's go get some dry clothes at my apartment."

"Do you want to stay here tonight?" I ask. His eyes catch mine, like I've surprised him.

"We could. Up to you."

He's pulled back the curtain on his life, and I want to see more. I want to see his home, his books, his heart. "Let's stay," I say.

24

ETHAN'S APARTMENT IS ON THE THIRD FLOOR OF AN industrial building on a tree-lined street. There's a stack of mail waiting for him on the table outside his door because the last time he left, he thought he was just visiting his parents for a few days. He opens his door and we walk into a large kitchen with stainless steel counters. There's a single coffee mug by the sink and I resist the urge to race around in search of his mess.

His phone rings as soon as we've closed the door. "Hey, Barb," he says. "Yeah, I've been in Beechwood. I'm just here for the night." He grabs a dish towel and starts drying the dogs off. "For how long? No. Barb. Do not get on a ladder. I'll be right there."

He hangs up and pulls a nine-volt battery out of a tidy kitchen drawer. "I've got to go change the battery on Barb's smoke alarm. It's been chirping for two days, and she's just been waiting to hear me walking around my apartment." He shakes his head. "Let me get you something dry."

"Okay, thanks," I say, and I notice I am clutching my

hands. I don't know how to act, alone in this apartment with this man about whom I have way too many feelings.

He unleashes the dogs, and Brenda follows him into his room. The interior walls of the apartment are exposed brick, and a full wall of windows looks out over the street. His taste is simple: a rust-colored couch, a Lucite coffee table, a plush cream-colored rug. Once again, I try to imagine how this Catherine person ever decided she didn't want to wake up here with this man every single day.

He comes back in sweatpants and a dry T-shirt, the top of his hair still a little wet. He hands me a stack of clothes—plaid pajama bottoms, a blue T-shirt, and thick socks. "Go ahead and change in there. I'll be right back. Leave your stuff, I'll throw it in the dryer." He reaches out, as if he's going to kiss me goodbye, but then doesn't.

I walk into his bedroom and take a deep breath against the closed door. His bed is covered with a dark gray duvet and there's a brown leather chair in the corner with not one piece of laundry on it. I undress in the en suite bathroom and put on his cozy clothes. I towel-dry my hair, roll up the pajamas at the waist to keep them from falling down, and give in to the fact that I'm not going to turn this look into something attractive.

I turn my back on my reflection and whisper, "Mom. I'm sleeping here. With him. Are you following this?" She doesn't reply. I start pacing, one step in each direction. "I'm having feelings, Mom. Feelings!" The least she could do is chime in right now with a little encouragement. But, nothing. "Okay, fine, don't answer. I don't know what's going to happen here. But don't watch." And she laughs, the big

Massa-Cheez-Its laugh, and that makes me laugh too. I roll my wet clothes into a neat pile and carefully conceal my Costco underwear and my beige bra between my shorts and my T-shirt. He doesn't need to see that again.

He's back from Barb's when I walk into the living room. "Gorgeous," he says. I curtsy and hand him my clothes. He disappears through the kitchen. I sit down on the couch and pull my knees up to my chest. I take another deep breath. There is nothing to fear from Ethan. It's the way I am feeling that terrifies me. I am like a live wire. I want to take my just-kissing rule and burn it to the ground.

I watch the tops of the trees dry outside the window. Ferris is sniffing every inch of the apartment, as if maybe he's looking for the mess too. Brenda curls up on a sheepskin dog bed, and Ferris joins her and fills all of the available space. How uncomplicated it is with dogs. They like the smell of each other. They do not perceive a threat. For dogs every moment is just that moment.

I hear the dryer running and Ethan is in the kitchen. "I guess I'll have a glass of wine if we aren't going anywhere," he says. "Want one?"

"Okay, thanks."

He brings me a glass of red wine and sits next to me. The tips of my socked toes are under his pajamaed thigh.

"It's all so grown-up," I say.

"Oh God, not you too. Ali, I'm thirty-six years old. Of course I own a couch."

"I know. I don't mean that. It's just that this place has kind of an eligible-bachelor vibe."

"I guess," he says.

"Do women like this?"

"Do you?" He turns to me, and his face is serious.

"I do. It gives me a good feeling, like you're in total control."

"I'm not," he says, and holds my gaze.

I'm feeling a little out of control myself, and I clutch my wineglass for something to do with my hands. "If that woman with the St. Bernard could see you here, she'd go nuts."

"I'd never let that dog in bed with Brenda," he says.

I take a sip of my wine and look down at Ethan's socks on my feet. "It's weird to think about actual dating," I say.

"What's weird about it?"

"Just being in a whole relationship. Sex. It's been a really long time." I just said "sex." I heard myself say it. It is the word that is bouncing off the walls of my mind, and it just slipped out of my mouth as its own sentence.

"You're the one with the rules, Ali." He's looking right at me, his arm resting on the back of the couch. His body language is casual, but what he's saying is not.

"Yes," I say.

He smiles a half smile and studies his glass for a second. He twirls it around a few times before he speaks. "I've wanted this for a long time. Since I was fourteen, actually. Since the first time I ever cleared your plate at the diner. You were at the back booth with your mom drinking a vanilla milkshake through a straw, and I thought, God, that lucky straw. That's how long I've wanted you."

He breaks eye contact and looks out the window. When he turns back to me, I don't know what to say. I put my wineglass on the coffee table and take his glass from his hands and place it there too. I take one of his hands in mine.

Ethan squeezes my hand. "But I need you to decide what you want."

His eyes are intense with feeling, and I have the sense that I am looking right inside him, like he's shown me his heart. He has made himself more than naked, and he's not shying away from it. He waits, and I look back at our hands. I take a second to enjoy the feel of his hand in mine and the sound of light rain outside the window. The quiet of this room and the space he's giving me to decide how I feel. It's been a long time since a man has worried about what I wanted. And it's been a long time since I've wanted something this much.

I stretch my legs over his and scoot close enough to rest my head on his shoulder. I breathe in his delicious smell, now mixed with summer rain. He holds me there and runs his hand over my hair. I think I should say something, or he should say something, but I just want to feel the motion of his hand along my hair, hear the sound of the breath he takes when my lips brush against his neck.

"Ali," he says. I raise my head from his shoulder and his face is inches from mine. He puts his hand on my cheek and runs his thumb over my cheekbone. "You haven't answered my question," he says.

"Yes," I whisper into his mouth. "I really want this."

He pulls me onto his lap, and his hands tighten on my hips to keep me there. He kisses me, and it's different. It's a runaway-train kind of kiss, and all my self-talk about slowing it down has silenced. I can no longer hear the rain outside or feel the couch below me. The outside world has dissolved into particles so small that they are meaningless.

When his mouth is moving down my neck and I am clutching the top of his sweatpants, he says, "Are you sure?"

"Sure," I say, and move to kiss him again.

"Sure's not yes," he says, pulling back.

"What are you talking about?"

He takes both of my hands in his. "I just— I don't want you waking up with regret, like we got ahead of ourselves and then things are weird. I really want this, but I'm not moving backward from here." He gives my hands a squeeze. Like our entwined hands are the "here" to which he refers. A new place.

My body is on overdrive, but he's being serious. I look down at our hands together and then back into his eyes. I have seen him today, and he is so much more than I thought.

"I won't regret it," I say. There's no part of my body that agrees with stopping.

"You don't know that." He leans back and runs his hands through his hair in a way that's really not helping me want this less. I put a hand on his chest, and he catches it. "We're in sort of a fantasy here. This isn't your life, we're two hundred and fifty miles away from your reality. You've had two glasses of wine." He brings my hand to his lips. "If you still want this tomorrow, when we're back in Beechwood in the light of day, then I'm all in."

"I'm a hundred percent sure I will." Negotiating for sex was not on my bingo card for this trip to Devon.

He shakes his head, like he has more to say but thinks better of it. He stands and offers me his hand. "My fourteen-year-old self is literally screaming at me, but I'm going to tuck you in and then take the dogs out one last time."

"In the rain?" I get up, reluctantly. I can't believe this.

"Yes, this is my final act of chivalry of the day," he says, leading me by the hand to his room.

He pulls back the covers of his bed and I climb in. He covers me up and leans down to kiss me again. His lips are soft, like they're promising me something. I want whatever that promise holds, and as I feel him pull away, I raise myself up to keep it going.

He rests his forehead on mine. "I must really, really like you," he says. *I hope so*, I think.

"You could stay in here, with me," I say, one last plea. How delicious it would be to spend the night in his arms and wake up to the warm smell of him, already close.

"I don't have that kind of restraint," he says, and squeezes my hands. He gets up, turns out the light, and shuts the door. I hear him take the dogs out. I place my fingers on my mouth and replay the day, his face in the rain, and then replay my entire life from when I was sixteen and drinking a milkshake, totally unaware that I'd just set Future Me up for the way I'm feeling right now. I hear him come back inside and go to the living room. He has not changed his mind. I roll onto my side and imagine tomorrow, the possibility of the two of us picking this back up in Beechwood.

Oh my God, my kids. I sit straight up. This is another nightmare I have, of course, where I'm far away and can't get to them. The car won't start, I can't make the phone work. But this is real. I am four hours from home in another state, and Pete's bringing them home at ten tomorrow morning. I text Ethan: You still awake?

Ethan: Yes

Me: I just remembered I'm a person. What's our plan for getting back to Beechwood?

Ethan: I set my alarm for 4:30, we'll leave by 5, get you there by 9

I can't believe anyone ever tried to tell me this man is unreliable. Me: Oh okay, thanks

Ethan: Are you freaking out yet?

I smile at my phone. Me: just about my kids

Ethan: I'll get you there on time. Good night

Against all odds, I fall asleep.

25

I'VE ALSO SET MY ALARM FOR FOUR THIRTY BECAUSE I'm the mother and the person with the responsibility to get home. When it goes off, it's still dark out, and I briefly don't know where I am. I get up and find my way to the bathroom. I splash water on my face and finger-comb my hair.

When I come out of the bathroom, my dry clothes are waiting, folded on the made bed. He's left me a toothbrush and I am oddly moved by this, another adult thinking of my needs and comfort. I hold the toothbrush in my hand like it's an engagement ring.

I get dressed and find Ethan in the kitchen. He's sitting at the counter, drinking coffee and opening his mail, and I don't know how to approach him. Can I walk right over to him and put my arms around him, riding the momentum of last night? He looks up from his mail and smiles. "Hey," he says, and I get a melty feeling all over.

"Hey," I say, and don't move.

"There's coffee, but no milk," he says.

"That's fine." Coffee gives me a reason to move my feet.

I pour myself half a cup and stand on the other side of the kitchen island. There are three feet between us, but it feels like more.

"Thank you for drying my clothes," I say, finally. "I left yours on the bed."

He smiles at me, so comfortable here in his body, his home, his town. "Come here." I don't know why I need the invitation, but I do. He pulls me into a hug and it feels dangerously good. He kisses my hair and then takes a big breath. "I need to get you home, and for some reason I'm super worried about your kids seeing me drop you off, walk-of-shame style. So let's get moving."

"YOU CAN FALL asleep," he says once we're on the highway.

"I would never. That's such bad passenger etiquette."

"Okay, good, then tell me some things."

"I feel like you know all my things. You're my fake lawyer and I cry in front of you all the time."

"True." He's quiet and I watch him watch the road. He catches me looking and smiles. "I promise I'm going to get you home on time."

I like that he's worried about it. There's no traffic and we should get home with enough time to spare that I can shower and change and get myself back to normal. But I have a feeling there's no getting back to normal.

As we drive in the dark, dogs snoring in the back, the sun rises slowly over the long ribbon of highway. I feel like we are sealed in our own world, and things are easy between us again. In the same way that I talk to my mom, I just say things to Ethan. I tell him about my mom's illness and how badly I handled everything. I tell him that I knew my marriage was over before I was pregnant with Cliffy, but I wasn't ready to know it. We talk about Frannie. He says he's grateful that she wants to run the diner because he never would. He confesses that he's never liked her signature sandwich, ham on a biscuit.

What we don't talk about is last night. Something monumental inside of me has cracked open, and he's the only other person who knows. I want to say, *Wow. So, last night was kind of intense, right?* and have him agree with me that taking this to the next level is a great idea. I want him to hold my hand while he drives.

Instead, I say, "You're really going to sell the house?"

"I am," he says.

"You never feel like you want to be a Hogan and live in the center of town and pick up where your parents left off?" Last night I fell asleep imagining waking up in that house with Ethan. And going to bed in that house with Ethan.

"Exactly never."

"Huh." I turn my body completely toward him. "Why not? You're all grown up now, and you know who you are."

He hesitates before he speaks, concentrating on the road. "Devon feels like solid ground. Back in Beechwood, I feel like I'm in quicksand."

"You feel pretty solid to me."

"With you, yes. For sure." He takes my hand and turns back to the road. "But I finally have a life that I feel good about. I'm not going to walk away from it to run the inn or whatever."

"Do they want you to run the inn?"

"Oh my God, are you kidding? Besides me being a high school quarterback, that's pretty much always been their big dream. Bigger than the corporate law job and the two point five kids. Frannie at the diner, me at the inn. The thought of it makes me feel like I'm disappearing." He laughs.

I sit with this for a second. I try to imagine being Ethan and living in Beechwood and finally giving in to his parents' vision of his life.

"Is that so weird it's made you go mute?" he asks.

"No. I get it. You have a life up there that's your own. And if you stayed in Beechwood, you'd lose that part of yourself."

IT'S NINE FIFTEEN when we pull into my driveway. I want to invite him in, which is ridiculous because my kids could be home at any time. I turn to him and try to think of something to say, because I don't want to get out of the car.

"You should go in," he says.

"I guess." He should kiss me now. We are at that part of the movie. Overnight date and a kiss goodbye. I don't like thinking there's a possibility that he's watching a different movie than I am.

"Thanks for coming with me," he says.

"You have a good life up there."

"I'm glad you saw that, thanks. Sometimes I think my family thinks I'm crazy."

"They definitely think you're crazy."

He laughs, and then we're just sitting there looking at

each other. It's like when you're a teenager talking on the phone with your boyfriend in the dark and neither of you wants to hang up.

"You should go in," he says again. He leans in and kisses me softly, just the press of his lips against mine. It's a we-have-all-the-time-in-the-world kiss, but I am aching for all of it, the rest of it, right now.

"Of course," I say, and undo my seat belt. "Thanks again. And for dinner." I reach into the backseat to grab Ferris, and Ethan walks around to open my door and help us out.

As I walk into my house, there's a knowing coming at me all at once, and I don't really want to take it in. This is not going to be a lighthearted summer romance where we ride bikes with ice cream cones in our hands. It's going to be the kind where the waves crash over us as we feverishly make love on the sand. It has a different soundtrack, but it ends the same.

26

I AM SO HAPPY TO SEE MY KIDS WHEN PETE DROPS them off at 9:50 that I forget to be tired. I try to modulate my enthusiasm so they will know I missed them but that I wasn't miserable without them. And, of course, I wasn't. Even putting this huge leap forward with Ethan aside, I enjoyed the break and the chance to move in the world as just myself. I loved walking around in his world and having a backstage pass to his heart. Ferris, however, does not keep his cool and runs shamelessly around the three of them.

They have a lot to say about Pete's new apartment and their rooms there. Greer and Iris have twin beds and bean-bag chairs, and Cliffy's room looks out onto the train station.

Pete hugs them goodbye and makes a big show of making them promise not to tell me what they had for dinner last night. I let him have his secret.

"Can I have cereal?" Cliffy asks when Pete's gone.

"Didn't you guys have breakfast?" I ask.

Iris is first to defend her dad. "We slept kind of late and Dad said you needed us back by ten."

"That's fine," I say into the refrigerator as I'm discovering we are out of milk. "Want to go get pancakes at the diner?"

They're ecstatic, which is fun. I say, "Okay, five minutes; let me get dressed and check on Phyllis real quick."

"Dressed to go to the diner?" asks Iris.

"I've promised Frannie she'll never see me in these sweats again," I lie. "I'll be quick."

I find a black T-shirt dress that looks pretty good with some sandals. I brush my hair and put on lip gloss. I will never admit this to Frannie, but that took less time than staying in my sweats and looking for my Birkenstocks.

"You look better," Phyllis says when I'm clearing yesterday's glasses to the kitchen.

"Thank you," I say.

"I thought he was handsome, the man who brought you home this morning."

I blush and turn toward the kitchen. "He is," I say.

"It wouldn't kill you to have a romance," she calls over my running water.

"It might," I call back. I scramble her eggs and mentally relive the entire night with Ethan. I let myself step back into yesterday.

"What are you so afraid of?" Phyllis asks when her eggs are on her TV tray.

"He's leaving at the end of the summer."

"Those are the best kind of love affairs. The great love of my life was a summer romance."

"Then what happened?"

"He came back the next summer, we got married and

bought a fairy-tale house." The twinkle in her eye makes me feel like he's still here.

"Well, that's one in a million."

Phyllis shakes her head. "Nonsense. Happens all the time."

"I've had a summer romance. But he's . . . he's something more. If you actually fall for someone who's leaving, it's as crazy as getting a dog."

Phyllis looks confused.

I explain. "You get a dog and you know two things— you're going to fall in love with it and it's going to die one day. You knowingly walk headfirst into a heartbreak. That's the basic madness of dog ownership."

"You're really too young to be so dark," she says.

I don't say anything.

"Alice, besides you and my girls, everyone I know is dead. I've buried them all. Do you think I wish I'd never met them?" She focuses on getting a bite of eggs on her fork and without looking up says, "Do you wish you never met me?"

"Of course not." I am so uncomfortable talking about this. I do not want to talk about her dying. I do not want to engage with death in any way. I can't believe I brought this up.

She smiles at me. "You got a dog. You're a proven risk taker."

WHEN WE WALK into the diner, he's at the counter, just like he was in my daydream. He looks up from his coffee and smiles at me and then at all of us. "Here for French toast?"

"Pancakes," I say, and move my hair behind my ear in a way I don't think I've done since college.

"Ali!" Frannie calls as she brings Ethan his omelet. "You guys want to sit at the bar or at a table?"

I want to sit on that stool right next to Ethan, but Greer says, "Table, please."

"Okay, take that back booth in the corner," she says, and Ethan shoots me a look that makes me go liquid. Frannie hands me a stack of menus. "Are you guys free for dinner tonight? At Scooter's?"

"Will it be fun-tastic?" asks Cliffy.

"Of course," Ethan says. "Come at six. Frannie's requesting no themes, which, come on. And I'm responsible for the meats. Any requests? For meats or themes?"

"What about a luau?" Iris asks. "You can cook whatever you want and we can wear grass skirts. Mom has tiki torches."

"I do," I say, and catch his eye. There's so much in his eyes that I have to look away.

"Perfect," he says. "And I have so many grass skirts. Plastic, silver, some made of actual grass. It's a whole cupboard we could clear out."

We get back home and the kitchen looks happy. We didn't make a mess at breakfast, and before we left I cut some black-eyed Susans from my garden and put them in a jelly jar by the sink. The feeling I'm having walking back into my sort-of-clean kitchen makes me think that cutting flowers might be self-care.

Greer puts her arm around my waist. It's nothing really, my own child giving me half of a hug. But right now it's everything. There was a time when Greer was Velcroed to my side. She cried when I dropped her off at preschool, and I promised that I'd sit outside the whole time. For a while she wanted to sleep in our bed, which was strangely a hard limit for me. I let her sleep on the floor of our room in a sleeping bag until she got over it. What I wouldn't give to have her fall asleep in my arms and tell her that it's all going to be okay. That she'll figure out algebra, that her friends are going to be mean and then they're not. That she'll fall in love and it will last, and that I'll never leave her.

We go for our Sunday canoe adventure and talk about the luau the whole time.

"Are the tiki torches in the garage?" Greer asks over the waves.

"I think. What else should we bring?"

"What's a luau?" asks Cliffy.

"A Hawaiian party. Flowers and pineapple, I think," says Iris. "We should have flowers in our hair."

"Yes!" shouts Cliffy.

"It should really be hibiscus," I say. "But the gerbera daisies in the yard would be good too. Let's do pink."

"Fun-tastic!" says Cliffy.

27

WE ARRIVE AT ETHAN'S AND PILE OUT OF THE CAR with tiki torches, oatmeal cookies, and Ferris. Cliffy had a brief meltdown when Iris told him he only needed to bring enough daisies for the girls, but I assured him that the men would want them too. We ring the doorbell and he clutches the tote bag in which they are likely wilting. This has been a source of bickering in the car for the half-mile drive. Greer is firmly in the camp that Cliffy is killing them by shoving them in a bag, while I insist that gerbera daisies are a sturdy flower.

Ethan opens the door and I forget which side of that fight I'm on. He's in a green and white Hawaiian shirt that brings out green specks in the gold of his eyes. But it's not just that, it's the way he's looking at me.

"We brought flowers," says Cliffy, and I come to.

"Yes, for everyone's hair," I say.

"Great," says Ethan. "Let me take those torches. The grass skirts are out back." Iris hands them over and we make our way past the living room with its giant donation pile in the center, through the kitchen that we haven't even started on, to the backyard.

Frannie and Marco are already there with Theo, and Cliffy gives them each a flower for their hair. Ethan squats down so that Cliffy can put his in the exact right spot behind his ear. Ethan looks up at me and I wonder if all men should always wear a large pink flower.

"I found some luau music," Ethan says to my kids. They follow him over to the bar, where he's set up an actual record player and a stack of LPs. There really is a lot of stuff to clean out of this house. Cliffy chooses a Don Ho album and Ethan shows him how to work the record player. Ethan gives them each a grass skirt and Cliffy tries some hula moves. Greer's pulled up what must be a hula-dancing video on her phone and they're all trying to keep serious faces while he imitates the dance. I want Ethan to keep talking with my kids forever so that I can keep looking his way. He's a beautiful man, I noticed that the first day, but there's something now that makes me feel like my heart is racing out of my body to get to him.

When the kids are in the pool, the tiki torches are lit, and the dogs are chasing each other around the yard, Frannie and I face each other in the armchairs. I luxuriate in the feeling of holding Theo while he sleeps. Two days ago, I sat right smack in the middle of what was wrong with my marriage. I soaked in it. Yesterday Ethan started a fire in my body that has yet to be put out. Currently I'm wearing a grass skirt over my shorts, and I have the sense that I have been through the full range of human emotions.

"What's with you?" asks Frannie.

"It's been a big couple of days."

"Sounds like things went well with Pete."

"Well, yesterday Pete actually took the kids for twenty-four hours in a row."

"That's great for all of you," she says. "Even Pete. Like he can rise to the occasion and you get a break."

"It seems like they had a great time. I actually went up to Devon with Ethan for the day."

"You had your first day off ever and you drove all the way up to Devon and back?"

"I know, not exactly a spa day. But it was fun." I busy myself with straightening Theo's sock because I don't want to look at her.

"Careful with that."

"With what?"

"You know with what." She motions to Ethan with her eyes. "As much as it creeps me out, it's clear there's something brewing. Marco thinks it's already happened."

"Oh my God, stop."

"Okay, okay."

Ethan looks over his shoulder at me. He's still talking to Marco but it's like he's tracking me with his eyes. "He's a very good guy," I say.

"He can be," she says. "But he'll never ever leave Devon."

"Of course," I say, and my voice is too high. Mercifully, Theo wakes up and starts to cry.

Ethan calls over to Frannie, "Can you get me some tinfoil?"

"I'll get it," I say, and hand the baby to Frannie. The kitchen has been redone to look like it could be original, if people had huge marble-topped islands and walk-in pantries a hundred years ago. The door to the pantry is open. It's the size of a small closet with shelves painted a high-gloss royal blue. I decide we'll start here tomorrow. Things are placed on the shelves randomly, and I move the oatmeal so it's next to the Bisquick. Then I line up a box of Cheerios next to it, along with a glass jar of granola. This feels like a breakfast section now, but I want to move it all to the left so that it's the first thing you see when you walk in. I like a pantry that moves with the day. In the middle should be peanut butter and jelly, maybe cans of tuna fish.

"What are you doing?" Ethan is right behind me.

I turn around, and the sight of him with that pink flower behind his ear makes me smile. "I couldn't help myself. Can we start here tomorrow?"

"Sure," he says, and takes a step closer to me. He takes the flower from behind my ear and moves my hair behind my shoulders. He places it behind my other ear. "Perfect."

I can't look away from him as he leans down to where his lips are nearly touching mine. "This is so complicated," I whisper.

"I'm terrified of it," he says, and kisses just my lower lip.

I wrap my arms around his neck and kiss him back. "I want this," I say. "For the record, in the light of day. I'm not going to regret it." He kicks the pantry door shut and his mouth completely takes me in. His hands are on my hips pulling me toward him, and I am in a state of wanting that alarms me.

From a million miles away, I hear Frannie's voice. "Scooter?"

Ethan groans. "I forgot where we were."

I kiss him again because I can't not kiss him again. I've been kissing him for weeks, but it's different now, soaked in meaning and intent. "Okay, go."

"In here," he says, and opens the door. "Where does Mom keep the tinfoil anyway?"

Frannie's standing there, hands on hips, staring at us. "Knew it." She reaches past us, and I avoid her eyes as she grabs the tinfoil off the shelf and leaves.

"Sorry about that," Ethan says. "I mean I'm not. I'm actually really happy." He runs his fingers through his hair, like that's going to smooth out his thoughts.

"We should get back, you go first," I say.

"Okay," he says, but doesn't go.

"Go," I say. I give his chest a push, and he catches my hand and holds it there.

"We'll start in the pantry tomorrow," he says.

28

S TOP IT, THAT'S SO GROSS," GREER IS SAYING ON THE drive home. This is really happening between Ethan and me.

"Mom, make him stop," Iris says. Cliffy laughs. The taste of Ethan is narcotic, and I wonder if that's a thing, if people actually get hooked on another person.

"Mom!" Iris says, and whacks me on the shoulder.

"What? Sorry. I was thinking about something," I say.

"Cliffy's being so gross," Iris says. "He keeps trying to lick my elbow."

"Stop it, Cliffy," I say as I pull into the garage. I put the car in park and turn to them; I'm almost surprised to see them sitting there with me. "That was fun tonight. It was, right?"

"Fun-tastic," says Cliffy, and Iris tells him to shut up.

HE TEXTS ME an hour later: I have a lot to say that I won't say in text in case I need to deny it later

I'm smiling at my phone. A rush of carbonation comes over me. Me: Yeah, me too

Ethan: Let's tackle the pantry at 9

HE'S THE FIRST thing I think of when I open my eyes. I close them again and conjure the smell of him. I open my eyes again—this is not normal. This isn't a want like when I want to buy a sweater. This is a want like I don't know how I'm going to get through the next three hours until I see him again. I grab my phone to review the text from last night. He said nine. I just have to get my kids to camp, walk Ferris, and go to Phyllis's.

I shower and shave my legs with my reading glasses on to make sure I haven't missed anything. I try on a white skirt with a navy top and decide I look like a flight attendant. I try on a floral dress that made sense at Theo's christening but doesn't make sense for pretending to clean out a pantry. I am working myself into a frenzy and I collapse onto my bed. This is not a man I need to pretend for. He is the impossible thing, the one who wants me more when I'm myself.

I put on my favorite yellow shorts and a white T-shirt. I drop my kids at camp, give Ferris a quick run, and stop by Phyllis's. Her daughter Sandy is there and I pretend that I remembered it was Monday and that she was coming. She normally comes from Manhattan on Saturdays, but this week she switched to Monday because of a cough. We had a long conversation about this. I pretend that I'm there to borrow *Portnoy's Complaint*, which is the first spine that catches my eye.

Of course it's Monday. I text Frannie: Sorry, I'm not going to make it this morning. I'll swing by tomorrow

Frannie: I never thought I'd ever find anyone making out with my little brother in the pantry

It's a statement, not a question. I don't want to get into this with her. I mostly just want to get to where he is. Me: And yet here we are. See you tomorrow

When I've sent the text, I look up and his car is in my driveway. He's standing there, and Brenda's in the window. I don't want to go to the dog park. I want to be in his pantry, pressed too close together. As I get closer to him, I see that he doesn't seem light.

"Hey," I say. "Wasn't I coming to you?"

He takes my hand. "Yeah. But I got a call that we're due in court tomorrow morning on this case I've been working on forever. I need to get back to Devon to prep my client."

"Today?" I say. It comes out so small, like I've choked up this tiny, heartbreaking word.

He looks behind me at Phyllis's house. "Can we go inside?"

"Sure," I say. "No."

"No?"

"It's kind of a mess." I'm kind of a mess. It's strange that I want to get completely naked with this man, but I can't handle the idea of his seeing my kitchen. "When are you coming back?"

"As soon as I can. Friday the latest." That's four whole days.

"Oh, okay," I say. I don't want him to see how disappointed I am.

He's holding both of my hands now. "So I'll call you later?"

"Sure," I say.

"Sure's not yes."

I look up at him and smile. "Yes," I say. "Call me."

He looks over my shoulder again and I am a hundred percent sure Phyllis is watching through the window. I don't really care; this is probably making her day. I lead him by the hand to the side of my house, past our kitchen windows, and around back. And I'm up against my back door with his mouth on mine and his hands in my hair before I've had the chance to think another thought about Phyllis. When I have been adequately kissed goodbye, he gives both of my hands a squeeze. "This is torture," he says.

29

PETE WALKS THROUGH THE FRONT DOOR ON TUES-
day at six and stops in the dining room to admire the
mountain of unread mail I've moved there. "You really run
a tight ship," he says. I've just refereed a fight between
Greer and Iris over who owns the guitar that my dad gave
them for Christmas. It deteriorated into one of them saying
the other had ugly fat hands, and there were tears. I'm not
in the mood to take it from Pete.

"Well, it's my ship for the next fourteen years," I say.
"So please ring the bell when you come." I haven't raised
my voice; I just said the words. These words are true and
right and perfectly reflect my reaction to him in this moment. I should have been doing this all along, and that makes
me angrier.

"God, Ali. What's your problem?"

"I'm angry," I say. Again, completely true.

"Well that's new," he says.

I stop and stare at him. Is it new? He'd know, as he's
actually the only other person in our almost-over marriage.

Well, besides my mom. "I think I was always a little angry, Pete. It just never had a chance to boil over," I say. "Maybe today I've gotten angry enough." Now that I've said this I know it's true. When we were married, I never got angry enough. I was appeased and distracted, and it was always easier to just let it go. But now here we are, just the two of us, and I'm angry.

He does not apologize. He does not change his tone. He rolls his eyes and brushes past me toward the kitchen. I grab his arm and turn him back to me. "I don't want you talking to me like that anymore. I'm done listening to it. So from now on, choose your words carefully or you'll be picking the kids up from the street. This is my house."

WHEN THEY'RE GONE, I feel like standing up to Pete has cleared my vision. I sit at my kitchen counter amid the wreckage of the day, the week, possibly several years. It feels like if you woke up one day and noticed you were drowning in credit card debt. How did I let this happen?

"Mom," I say to the puddle of syrup by my left hand. It's impossible that this is my house.

Oh, Alice.

There is so much in front of me to do. I cannot get up to rinse and load. "Mom, I wish you'd just let me figure it out." She doesn't reply.

The bright red wing of a cardinal passes in my peripheral vision, as so often happens when I think of my mom. I turn to look and it's not a cardinal. It's just more of my mess. I've left the cabinet by the window open and what's caught my eye is a red poppy painted on the side of the soup tureen my mother gave me at my bridal shower. It's huge and takes up the length of an entire shelf. I drag myself off my stool and walk over to close the cupboard so I don't have to look at it. But instead, I pull it off the shelf and open it. I gaze at the red poppies painted on the inside. Those poppies have never been covered by soup. Not once in thirteen years. Even resting on the counter, that tureen feels heavy in my hands. Heavy with my mother's idea of what my life might be like. Maybe a life that involved inviting people over for soup. A life where we didn't just stand around the kitchen serving ourselves off the stove. I have never hosted a dinner party with a soup course, and I have no intention of starting. I don't even have six soup bowls that match. This tureen is heavy with unmet expectations.

I think of Ethan telling me to move toward things that make me happy. I run my hands over the poppies painted on the lid, and I feel bad. I was raising kids and trying to force Pete and me into the shape of a happy couple. When was I supposed to be making soup? When was I going to be so in control of things that I would have time to transfer soup to a tureen before serving it just seconds later while it was still hot? I do not need to hold this soup tureen to my heart to know that it's the embodiment of all the ways I am a disappointment.

Honestly, Alice. This is a bit much.

I smile at the sound of her voice and lift the tureen off the counter. I lug it into the garage and place it along the far wall. It's the first item to leave my kitchen in a long time, and I feel a release when I put it down. "It just wasn't a good marriage, Mom. Things were never going to be right." I sit for a few minutes in the silence of my garage waiting for a response. *I know.*

I have tears in my eyes, but I am lighter when I go back into the kitchen and am welcomed by that entirely empty shelf. I wet a washcloth and wipe it with reverence.

This lightness starts to move throughout my body. My eyes clock the breakfast dishes and my feet move me to where they are. I load them into the dishwasher and wipe the counters. I want to see clear spaces, and I start to talk to myself out loud in my professional organizer voice. "When was the last time you used this? Is it something you need to have within reaching distance or can we put it on a high shelf?" I take a garbage bag and toss in the plastic containers that may or may not be killing me. Either way, if I think about dying every time I pick one up, they're probably not doing me any good. I move two weeks' worth of newspapers to the recycling. I carry the laundry basket into the basement and start a load of whites.

With no paper or dirty dishes in my line of sight, I see what is left. I am my own client, moving through my kitchen objectively as if I'm staging it to sell to myself. Everything that meets my line of sight should please me. The platform with a hook for decoratively hanging bananas—gone. The Costco-sized Palmolive dish soap—stashed under the counter. Three of the four rolls of paper towels I currently have in use, to the basement. I work until my coffeemaker is the only appliance I can see. I like it where it is, next to my mother's jar of coins.

I decide to make two areas in the garage—one for the

Salvation Army, and one for things that Pete might want. I will give Pete time to go through it tonight, and then it's all going to be gone.

I pile mismatched dishes and souvenir coffee mugs into crates along with Pete's abandoned juicer. I find a device that turns potatoes into waffle fries, and I deposit it in the garage, where it will eventually find its way to a person who thinks that's a good use of time. I toss spices that expired before Cliffy was born. I toss a broken pie plate and three dried-out bottles of glue. Broken pencils, years-old school directories, lids to things I no longer own. I want to play music but I don't dare interrupt my momentum. The movement of things into my garage feels like its own symphony.

It takes nearly two hours to clear out my kitchen. I sit at the counter and take it in, my geraniums nodding their approval from outside. I could have done this years ago. I stop and wonder if this would have made the difference, if I'd still be married to Pete if I'd just cleaned up. I imagine Pete walking through the door and looking around appreciatively, smelling the dinner warming in the oven. I try to imagine it again with me hopping up to welcome him and asking for the details of his day. Neither rings true. It wasn't just the house getting out of control, or even me going quiet. I resented that he got to go to work, and he resented that I didn't. He was hurt because I disappeared; I was hurt because he let me. It was never right. I don't think love is supposed to be transactional.

I must give myself a break; those are the rules. But I don't want to. This is the best I've felt in years. I am infinitely more relaxed than I am after taking a candlelit bath.

I have a little time before Pete will be back with the kids, and I make myself a cup of ginger tea and pick up the crossword puzzle.

THEY WALK INTO the kitchen and Greer is the first to speak. "Were we robbed?" I think she's kidding.

"I got inspired. Looks great, right?"

Iris runs her hands over the kitchen counter. "We should pick flowers."

"Yes," I say.

Cliffy gives me a hug. "I love it, Mom."

Pete is frozen in the doorway. "It looks like it did when we moved in."

He's somber about it and I don't want him to be. "I know. A life accumulates a lot of stuff, and I guess you need to pare it down more than every ten years." Iris is sliding off her shin guards but is also listening.

"I don't understand," Pete says.

"Come into the garage," I say. I am aware of how neutral I am feeling toward him. I don't feel angry or awkward or any of the things I usually feel. It's like I actually cleared the air. "I made two piles. Stuff neither of us wants, and stuff you might want. Take what you like and I'll donate the rest." I have a bit of showman energy about me. Like I am the Wizard of Oz or a game show host, inviting him to behold the museum of discarded items in my garage.

Pete picks up his juicer. I don't tell him that it's got seventeen pieces that all need to be hand washed after every use. He takes a World's Best Dad mug and a few kitchen towels. It's sad watching him do this and I usher the kids back into the kitchen. I want to move toward the happy thing.

Pete puts his stuff in the car and comes back to say goodbye to the kids. "Really looks great, Ali," he says.

"Thank you," I say. And I feel it again, that certainty that this wouldn't have made any difference. And if it would have, that's not love anyway. Love is not *If you clean up, I'll help you through your grief.* I'm not sure what love is, but I think it's something different from that.

30

I WAKE UP WEDNESDAY MORNING TO A TEXT FROM
Ethan: Hey

Me: How was court

Ethan: Fine. I think Brenda misses you

I am smiling at my phone like a teenager. Me: I miss her
too. Court today?

Ethan: Probably tomorrow too. But I've got to put you
back to work

Me: I actually worked for myself yesterday. Looks pretty
good

Ethan: Can't wait to see

Carbonated again, I get up and start making pancakes.
After camp drop-off, Phyllis tells me that I am different.

"I'm the same," I say, and replace the plastic liner in her
garbage bag.

"You're light," she says, an accusation.

"I cleaned out my kitchen. And Pete took a bunch more
of his stuff."

"Ah." She smiles. "Lots of room now for something
new. But please, have something with that nice young man.

Don't meet someone on the Internet—before you know it they've taken two hundred thousand dollars."

"Was that Dr. Phil yesterday?"

"Dr. Phil most days. Also, crystal meth. Don't do that."

ETHAN TEXTS AT ten p.m.: How's it going?

I sit up in bed but don't turn on the light. Me: Pretty great. Tackled Carla Garcia's attic and my own family room today. Court again tomorrow?

Ethan: Yeah, I won't be back till Friday afternoon

I have too many replies that want to shoot out of my fingers. I just want him back now. Me: Bummer

Ethan: I don't think people say that anymore

I smile because I can hear him saying that in my head. Me: They totally do

Ethan: Don't think so. Pretty sure it's just you

I am trying to think of something to say. I like having him right here with me. He texts again: I also wanted to tell you I've been thinking about you a lot

My fingers can't type fast enough: Me too

Ethan: Good. Okay I think if I say more I might go too far. So just good night

I feel these words in my heart. It's like there's a hope there, born of the fact that Ethan might have to hold back his feelings. Me: Bummer. Good night.

THURSDAY I CLEAN out my bedroom and actually get Marco to come over and help me carry the old treadmill that haunts my bedside to the garage. Pete can have it, or I'll give it away. Heck, maybe I'll even use it. Strange things are happening around here at a pace I can barely keep up with.

When my kids are home from camp, I sit them down in the very tidy family room. I feel like our house is suddenly bigger by half. "So we don't have anything this afternoon, but lucky for you I've hired you the services of a professional organizer until five o'clock."

"For what?" asks Greer.

"Let's go upstairs and I'll show you."

By the time it's five, they are starving and exhausted but kind of excited about the way their rooms look. Cliffy's created a reading nook in the corner of his tiny room with pillows and exactly six stuffed animals. We ceremonially bring two bags of stuffed animals to the garage.

FRIDAY MORNING IS light work in my bathroom. Everything but shampoo and a bar of soap must go, so there isn't a lot of self-talk to wade through. I keep the candles because I wonder if they'll actually be relaxing in a clean bathroom. Also, they cost thirty dollars.

I nearly throw my back out organizing Serena Howe's garage early that afternoon and mentally recommit to updating my résumé. Two days of work per week are not enough, though hauling gardening equipment to a shed feels like a bit too much.

Ethan texts at four: Stopped for gas. I'll be back in an hour. Too late to see you today right?

Me: Oh good! But no I've got my kids here

Ethan: Ok, maybe see you tomorrow?

I stare at the words "maybe" and "tomorrow." I don't like either of those words and am overwhelmed by how much I want to see him. I want to invite him to dinner. I try to picture this in my mind, Cliffy thinking it's fun and the girls being politely cautious. He's a family friend, and they've met him already. Also, I really want to see him. I text: I'm barbecuing chicken later. Want to come? Like at 6?

Ethan replies immediately: Fun-tastic! See you then

"What?" Iris asks. I'm smiling at my phone.

"Nothing. Scooter. He's on his way back from Devon. He's coming for dinner."

Iris seems confused. "Here?"

"Yes."

"Is Frannie coming?"

"No, just Scooter."

"And Brenda?" Cliffy asks.

"I'll ask." I text him: Kids want to know if you're bringing Brenda. We'd love it

Ethan: I'll see if she has plans

31

WE MOVE A FOLDING TABLE FROM THE GARAGE TO the backyard and cover it with a blue and white tablecloth. Cliffy cuts a few hot-pink hydrangeas and arranges them in my mother's cobalt-blue vase. We are having one person and a dog over for dinner, but we are all acting like it's a big occasion. I try to think of the last time we used a tablecloth.

It's five o'clock and I have potatoes and carrots roasting in the oven. The chicken is ready to grill and I have corn on the cob to cook at the end. It's five o'clock and dinner is all organized. Literally everything has changed. The TV is off; this is rare. Greer has a friend over; rarer still. I can hear them upstairs laughing in her bedroom. Cliffy's brought all of his trucks outside and there is a happy amount of zooming in the mud.

Greer comes downstairs with her friend and says, "Oh, we're just having some friends over later," like we are the coolest family in the world.

Ethan rings the bell at six o'clock. I'm carbonated again, so I ask Iris to get the door. He says something that makes her laugh and then there he is, standing in my kitchen, with a cold bottle of white wine, a box of chocolate-covered pretzels, and a dog. These are three of my favorite things, and I briefly wonder if I mentioned it in my graduation speech.

"Hi," I say, and don't move toward him. I am at a total loss as to how to proceed. I want to run into his arms, but my children are standing here. I need to act casual, and that doesn't appear to be in my arsenal right now. He's in a white button-down shirt and navy blue linen shorts, and his shoulders look like something I need to look away from. I'm just standing there, carbonated.

"Where's your mess?" he asks. "I thought you said the cobbler's children have no shoes."

"We have shoes," says Cliffy.

"It's been a really productive week," I say. "I can't even explain it, and if you saw all the stuff in my garage, you'd flip."

"Come see my room," Cliffy says, and leads him by the hand upstairs.

I'm a little relieved when he's gone. I need a second to regroup. Brenda's staring up at me. Greer has taken a seat at the counter and is looking at me too. "You look nice, Mom," she says.

"Thank you," I say, and know that I need to start acting like a normal person. I open the bottle of wine and take out two glasses. I pour myself a half glass. "Let's go check on the grill."

When Ethan and Cliffy join us outside, Cliffy is beaming. "This kid's got a lot of talent," Ethan says. "Did you see
what he made today?"

Cliffy holds out a folded piece of paper with a bunch of
separate drawings on it. "I drew a book," he says.

I take it from him and sit at the table to look at the se-
quential drawings. Two people meet, they play catch, they
fight, they walk away, and then they sit at a table to draw. "I
like this story," I say, and pull him onto my lap. Cliffy has
an understanding of how things are supposed to go. And I
know he feels the transactional nature of the love Pete offers
him. Cliffy's not going to play ball, not on any level. And
he's going to be just fine.

Cliffy gives me a squeeze and gets up to organize his
trucks. I look up and Ethan is watching me.

"I didn't get you any wine," I say, and walk back into the
house.

DINNER IS FUN and easy. *See?* my mother whispers from the
geraniums. Iris talks nonstop and asks Ethan questions
about the X Games. Greer suggests Iris not talk so much.
Cliffy performs a song about farts that he learned at camp,
and the dogs fall asleep under the table.

After dinner, the girls go to their rooms, and I take
Cliffy up to bed. "I'll just be a minute," I say as we go upstairs. I read him the last chapter of Cam Jansen and go
back down to find Ethan sitting on the sofa outside. I sit
down next to him, and he hands me a glass of wine.

"So," he says.

"So," I say. And we are smiling at each other the smallest bit.

He takes my hand, and I love the feel of it. I don't know what's coming next, but whatever it is, I hope I can keep holding his hand. "How did it go with your client?" I ask.

"Fine," he says. "Well, I think really good. Find out next week."

"Ah," I say. Now I have my other hand over his and I'm exploring a scar along his thumb.

"I also need to figure out what happened with the kids' permit last weekend. And I have a new client with an asbestos complaint." He's quiet for a second and we listen to the crickets along the creek. "Anyway, that's all boring. I had a lot of stuff I wanted to say."

I look up at him but don't say anything. I'm not really sure what I want him to say.

"What's happened to you?" he asks. My hand flies up to my hair for some reason. "You seem lighter."

I smile. "I don't know. I had some space. I was ready. I cleaned up."

"Oh my God, I'm freaking Prince Charming," he says.

"Are not." I laugh.

"No, I totally am. I kissed you and you're not a frog anymore."

"First of all, your knowledge of fairy tales is sad. And it wasn't just that." I look down to where I'm still holding his hand. "It's all of it." I don't dare look back up, but he squeezes my hand.

"I guess what I wanted to say is that I really like you." I look up at him to see if he's being casual or intense. "I am very afraid that you're going to break my heart. And I think it's worth it." Intense.

"I don't want to break your heart," I say.

"Okay, then don't." And he leans in and kisses me.

32

OPEN MY EYES SATURDAY MORNING TO A TEXT: I'LL pick you and Ferris up at 10:05. I want my kitchen looking like yours

I don't reply because I'm hearing his voice say those words. I want him to type something else so I can hear it again, but it's my turn. Me: See you then

I head downstairs to make coffee with the sound of his voice still in my head. I pour myself a cup, take Ferris out back, and count the number of things I need to do before I get to see him. Feed and pack the kids; Phyllis. But also pluck my eyebrows and blow-dry my hair. I think it's too late to be a person who wears perfume. I'm in the shower, shaving with my glasses on, when Iris comes in and tells me she can't find her soccer jersey, which opens the door to the Lost Item Rabbit Hole™. We spend the next two and a half hours pawing through the basement laundry, emptying every gym bag, and calling each of her teammates because she thinks she may have taken it off on the field last weekend. We drive to the rec center and go through their lost and found and then drive home and find that it's in the backseat of my car. This is not an entirely unusual occurrence, but today that lost time feels like a catastrophe. I make the eggs and bring Phyllis a to-go serving with minutes to spare before Pete shows up.

Ethan pulls into my driveway right after they've left, and I'm a little frazzled getting into the car. I don't know whether he's going to act intense or casual. I put Ferris on the backseat with Brenda, and he hands me a paper cup of coffee. "Thank you," I say, and that doesn't really cover it. Bringing another person a cup of coffee says *I'm thinking about how your day is going to go.* Or at a minimum, *I want you to also have this thing that I'm going to enjoy.* I am weirdly moved by this.

We start driving the half mile to his house in silence. "It's cooled down a little," I say. "I mean the weather."

He smiles at me. "That's true. What else can you tell me about the weather?"

I smack him on the shoulder and look out the window. "I don't know what we're supposed to be talking about."

"Well my house is a mess and yours is not. So now that I know what you're capable of, I own you."

Ah, casual. I take a sip of my coffee—milk, no sugar—and relax. "We could finish the kitchen in one day, if we really focused."

He gives me a side glance that is not at all casual. "Let's see how that goes."

WE PULL INTO the driveway and take the dogs through the house and into the backyard. I start to open his cabinets.

"Now, the idea here," I say, "is to clean this kitchen out in such a way that it looks like we didn't clean it out. You'll walk in and think: Wow, this is such a huge kitchen, it has room for all of this stuff and then some. But really, we will have thrown out half the stuff."

"Tricky," he says. He's right behind me and he's said it into my ear. The feel of his breath there and the too-close sound of his voice send heat throughout my body. I think he knows this because he keeps talking, right into my ear. "Where do we start?"

His hands are on my hips and his mouth is on my neck. I turn around and his lips catch mine. He lifts me onto the counter. I run my fingers through his hair and wrap my legs around his back to bring him closer. I have the sense that the world has shrunk, and the space where his mouth is on mine is my only point of awareness. I hear a voice speak from far away.

"What?" he says, barely breaking the kiss.

I kiss him again. "What, what?"

"You said something about not the kitchen."

"Out loud?" I am delirious. "Yes. Someplace else," I say, and kiss him again.

He kisses me for so long that I almost forget we are making a location change. "Okay," he says.

He pulls me off the counter and leads me by the hand to a downstairs guest room. Really, this is an unusually large house. The curtains are pulled and, happily, he makes no move to turn on the lights. The reality of this situation—naked in daylight—is threatening to ruin the perfection of this situation, and I try to quiet the thoughts that are bubbling up. Mainly, *how did I not take five minutes to choose better underwear before jumping into Iris's jersey hunt? How am I standing here in my Costco underwear—the dowdy blue ones!*—on this particular day. Note to self: better underwear is self-care.

"You okay?" he asks, taking my other hand.

And I kiss him again, which is the answer. As long as I am surrounded by the taste and smell of him, the feel of him running his hands over my back, everything feels natural. There is nothing in this moment that can stop me from undressing him and pulling him on top of me on the bed.

"Costco?" he says into my neck.

"What?" I am so breathless that nothing is making sense.

"Ali, you literally just said something about Costco. Out loud." He's lying on top of me but has pulled away so that I can see him smile. "You are some kind of freaky woman."

I want to explain, but the last thing I want here is an intermission. "Forget it. It's my underwear. I'll tell you later."

I pull my T-shirt over my head and he stills. He looks at me like I'm art, like I'm made of something so beautiful that it's going to take his breath away. I pull him back down on top of me, because I want to feel the weight of him, his skin on mine. He kisses me and whispers "Ali" into my mouth, "Ali" into my neck. The sound of his voice and the feel of his hands running down my sides, down my hips, have me desperate. Everything about us together feels so right that I'm glad we've waited to be back in my reality, in the light of day. I would not want to miss a second of this.

"Please don't change your mind," I hear myself say.

"It's too late for that," he says. "No turning back."

Ever since I met him he has been calling me back to my-self, reminding me that I matter. He's that way now, but with his body, listening, responding, following up. I wind my arms and legs around him, and I have this feeling as we make love that I am being discovered. Maybe more than discovered—I am unearthed. I am no longer weighed down; I am no longer on this earth.

IT'S THREE O'CLOCK and we have not gotten out of bed except to get water and to open the curtains so we could see the dogs lazing by the pool. I am collapsed on his chest and he is stroking my hair. There is nothing between our bod-ies, as if we've burned through whatever membrane was de-vised to separate people. "I can't believe I get to spend the whole day with you," he says. "I don't know what I did to deserve this."

"You did plenty," I say, breathless.

And he laughs.

My head is on his chest and I'm running my hand along the ridges of his stomach.

I have never felt like this before. Not even close. Not with Pete, not with Jimmy Craddock. Never. I don't think I could have stayed married to Pete for one week if I'd known this existed, a person who was clearly designed specifically for me.

We lie in this perfect space for a while, until I am fight-ing sleep. I don't want to stop feeling the way his arm circles my back and holds me to him. Like I'm a precious thing worth keeping. I stroke my hand across his chest, memoriz-ing its contours, and he examines the charms on my bracelet.

"Let me guess, you were into fairies?"

"School play. Third grade."

"Ah. I remember the soccer. What's the ship? A cruise?"

"No. When I was ten my mom surprised me by pulling me out of school and taking me to see *Titanic*. It was a good movie, kind of long I remember, but we had a really fun day. So she designed this charm as a Christmas gift."

"She designed all of these?"

"She did. She was a little over-the-top about everything in my life. It all mattered. Like she was so focused on all the little moments. Maybe because she was older, or maybe because it was just me."

He's holding the wedding dress charm. "Can we take this one off?"

"Nope. It's part of the story." I roll onto his chest so I can look at him. He doesn't seem to mind what I said. "I'm glad she lived long enough to see my life play out."

"Well, it's not over," he says. "There's room for more." I look at the empty links between the baby boy charm and the clasp. Wide open space.

I rest my chin on my hands and we are nose to nose. "We didn't get any work done today," I say.

"You're fired," he says, and tucks my hair behind my ear. "I'll give you another chance if you spend the night."

I kiss him again, because I cannot stop.

"WE NEED FOOD," Ethan says at five.

"And maybe a little daylight," I say.

"How's this? I'll get up and go forage for food in town if you promise you'll spend the night."

"Of course I'm spending the night," I say.

He pulls me close and kisses my neck. "Thank God."

WHEN HE'S GONE out for food, I acclimate myself in the giant kitchen. I run my hands over the cabinetry and the smooth marble countertops. I open and close both dishwashers and check the wine refrigerator to see what's in there. There's a separate refrigerated drawer that just keeps sodas cold. It's a lot of house. I let myself imagine living here with Ethan. I like the guest room more than that overwhelming master bedroom. We'd live down here and my kids would be upstairs. At night we'd swim and cook outside, and my kids could walk to school. I'd like to plant blue hydrangeas in the garden beyond the pool. While I'm engaging in this daydream, I've taken all of the glasses out of the cupboard and rearranged them the way I like. Juice glasses to the left and then water and then wine. The way the clock goes.

I don't hear Ethan come in, and he's standing there with a grocery bag, watching me. "Are we working?"

"A little," I say. He comes and puts his arms around me and it feels like he's been gone forever.

"What do you want to do first? Eat or swim?" he asks.

"Eat," I say.

We eat outside, plates on the coffee table by our two armchairs. Same spot, and everything's different.

33

ETHAN SHOWS UP AT MY HOUSE ON MONDAY MORN-ing when I'm back from camp drop-off. He's standing at the kitchen door backlit by the sun. Dog on a leash, two coffees in hand. He takes my breath away. In one movement he puts the coffees down, drops the leash, and pulls me into his arms.

"Today we do no work," he says with his arms around my waist and his lips hovering over mine.

"I'm pretty sure we did no work on Saturday," I say, and kiss him.

"See? And I loved Saturday." We're interrupted by a text. It's Phyllis: It's time I met him.

Me: Who?

Phyllis: Don't be coy

"Any chance you want to come with me to check on my neighbor? She needs eggs and is a little nosy."

"Sure," he says, and kisses me again. I could spend the

entire day this way, just standing here in my doorway kissing Ethan.

I grab two eggs from my refrigerator and we walk over
to her house. I let us in with my key and call, "Hi, Phyllis!"

"In here," she calls from the sitting room, unnecessarily.

We walk through the front parlor and I see she's put on
lipstick. "Phyllis, this is Ethan Hogan."

"Charlie's son?" she asks.

"Yes, ma'am," he says.

"I knew your grandfather," she says. "William. He was
in my fourth-grade class. Got better looking as he got older."

"A lot of us are late bloomers," he says.

"I'm very hungry," she says to me, which is a lie because
she's never very hungry. I have to sit and watch her eat half
a plate of eggs each day just so I know she's eaten something. But, okay. I pick up a few glasses and head into the
kitchen, trying to make out their conversation as I go.

When I return with the eggs, Ethan is sitting in the
chair next to hers. She pats his hand and says, "He's a lovely
young man."

"Yes," I say.

I sit on the sofa across the room and watch them talk
while Phyllis eats. She remembers William's wedding reception in the backyard of the house. Her husband was
from Illinois but made friends with William because he
liked to eat breakfast at the inn. See, Phyllis never liked
cooking breakfast, which is why we're all sitting here.

When she's done eating, Ethan helps her up and she
goes in for her shower. "What now?" he asks.

"I just putter around here a bit until she's out of the shower and dressed." We go into the kitchen, which is original to the house. Wooden countertops tell the story of a million chopped onions.

"This house is amazing," he says.

"Yeah, it's always been my favorite. Like since I was little. So when my house came on the market I figured it was as close as I'd get. And it's pretty close." I gesture to my kitchen window right outside of hers. "I want to talk with her daughters about it, like what's going to happen." My voice catches. I hate talking about this. The thought of Phyllis dying feels like a punch in the arm right where you already have a bruise.

Ethan puts his arms around me. "She's really lovely," he says. "Do we come back at lunchtime?"

This makes me smile. "No. She eats vanilla pudding for lunch, and I pretend not to know."

My phone beeps with a text from Frannie: Just a friendly reminder that it's Monday.

I am truly living in one long Saturday. "I have to go to the diner for a bit," I say. "Want to come? And then we can go back to your house and do absolutely no packing."

34

A S SOON AS PETE AND THE KIDS LEAVE FOR SOCCER
on Tuesday night, Ethan is at my kitchen door with a
bottle of Sancerre and chocolate pretzels. I love every word
in that sentence. I spent the day cleaning out Deb Parker's
basement and wishing I was in Ethan's pool watching him
swim toward me underwater, waiting for him to pull me
under with him. We've both already eaten dinner, so we sit
outside with wine and dessert and listen to the creek. He
tells me that Rose just got a big shipment of recalled dog
food for the shelter, and he laughs because Brenda hates the
new designer kibble he bought in town.

I've draped my legs over his and he puts his arms around
me. It feels like we've been doing this for years. "I can't wait
to get you divorced," he says into my hair.

"Me too," I say.

"Want to get all your information together tomorrow?
We could do it together during camp."

I look up at his face and see it's a sincere offer. I suspect
that's the only kind of offer Ethan makes. "Thanks, but I

feel like I need to tackle it myself. You know I used to be a pro."

"There's really nothing sexier than an accountant," he says, pulling me onto his lap and dipping his head to mine.

HE LEAVES THIRTY minutes before my kids could possibly be home and I kiss him by his car. I think of Phyllis and kiss him anyway. When they're home, Greer tries to be cool telling me that Caroline Shaw invited her to sleep over on Friday night, but I can tell she thinks it's a major win. They all shower and Cliffy wants to read Captain Underpants, so I get in bed next to him while he giggles and turns pages. When he's sleepy, I go down to the basement and put the wet clothes in the dryer. I haven't cleared this space yet, and I'm sort of looking forward to it. But I know I have to go through the paper first. We are meeting with Pete on Friday to decide on a budget. That's only three days away.

I go to the dining room and flip on the lights. The paper pile has grown. In the dead of night I can hear it breathing. There are actually two stacks of paper and I fight the urge to measure them. Measuring your paper piles is an exquisite form of procrastination, and I won't allow it. I do, however, take my laptop, which I happen to know is thirteen inches wide, and hold it vertically against the piles. Yes, they are each over a foot tall. Earlier today I ironed my pajama bottoms, mainly because I was waiting for the girls' soccer stuff to dry. I look down at them now and they remind me of a crisp summer suit. They trigger a memory, and I follow it back upstairs to my closet.

My closet is a terrible double-barred thing where any-thing that's longer than half your body sort of lounges in a mess over the bar below. I hunt around through blouses and skirts and the dress I wore to my rehearsal dinner until I find my navy blue suit. I pull it out and there's dust on the shoulders. It's been neglected since before Greer was born, but it's still in pretty good shape. The skirt is too short, but the blazer is sublime, with its three gold buttons and the tag right inside the collar, brandishing those two beautiful words: **ANN TAYLOR.** I pull it off the hanger and put it on over my T-shirt. It fits perfectly. I dust off my shoulders and button just the top button. It's a pantsuit now over my ironed paja-mas. Somewhere, the *Rocky* theme song starts to play.

I race back to the living room and set a timer on my phone. I open my laptop and start a brand-new spreadsheet. The white of the background and all of those tiny rectangles give me the chills. I type EXPENSES at the top and take a deep breath.

The first envelope I open is the hardest. I feel the old overwhelm creep up, like the sheer volume of paper in front of me is going to suffocate me. It's my utility bill, $257 for the month of June. I decide to just track the single expense and I search through the pile for other utility bills so that I can come up with an average. I am both ashamed and de-lighted to find that I have data going back to November because it's been so long since I dealt with the paper. I esti-mate the earlier fall bills by googling historical weather, and I have a number.

I do the same with the credit card bills. They are basi-cally food, clothing, and general household expenses like haircuts and plants. There's a separate bill for club soccer that I find astounding. Summer camp isn't that cheap either. The mortgage, the life insurance, health care copays. There's the servicing of our boiler and, of course, cable and mobile phone charges.

When I have a number for the average minimum amount of money we need to sustain life around here, I lean back in my chair. I didn't have an expectation of the number so I can't say if it's high or low, but I like knowing what it is. There was nothing in this pile of paper that was going to take me down. In fact, the order created by these little rect-angles emboldens me. I remember my onetime dream of a spreadsheet that would monitor my many accounts. When this is settled, I am going to figure out the next steps to get me there.

I sort the bills in piles and three-hole-punch them into a binder. A binder! I print out overviews for each category and then a summary page for the front. I format my spread-sheet with thick lines between categories and then change it into Times New Roman font. I reprint, re-three-hole. It's two a.m. before I head back upstairs, hang up my blazer, and go to bed.

35

FRIDAY MORNING I FIND A PAIR OF NAVY PANTS AND A short-sleeved white blouse in the back of my closet. At the last minute I add a belt. I could wear my navy blazer, but it's August now and I have enough reasons to sweat. My kids won't be up for a while, and neither will Phyllis. So it's just Ferris and me in the backyard watching the sky brighten over the creek. The air feels wet from the dew coming off the grass. My coffee is warm in my hands.

I have been feeling so good lately that I am letting myself be hyperaware of how I am actually feeling. When I was married I learned that all of my feelings were wrong. I should have felt grateful, not overwhelmed, to be home with three kids. I should have felt relieved, not mournful, that I didn't have to go to work anymore. My mom in particular painted a picture of my life that I felt guilty not embracing. I had everything she'd ever wanted. I think for a long time I just sat in that disconnect. What was wrong with me that I wasn't ecstatic? I adore my children with a ferocity that astounds me. But I did not love Pete. And I missed my job. My mom saw me so clearly; she had to have seen that.

"I don't want Ethan to leave," I tell her. I say it so quietly that the geraniums almost miss it. This is a thing I cannot unknow. *What else?* she asks me. And I sit in the silence of that question for a minute. I feel the hard edges of the binder I've been clutching since I got up this morning. I open it and run my finger over the columns of numbers, left justified. "I want to work," I whisper. Unless they build fifty new exceptionally messy houses in Beechwood, my organizing business is going to dry up. I'm definitely going to need more income, but I also want to be that person again. *What else?* I want a job with a desk and endless spreadsheets. In the same way I don't know how I'm going to have a relationship with Ethan when he lives four hours away, I also don't know how I'm going to find meaningful work in a small town while being the mostly-sole parent for my kids. But this morning, that's okay. It just feels good to sit here and know what I want.

Ethan texts: Can't believe we're almost done with Pete

I smile at my phone. Me: Same

Ethan: I'm going to meet you there, if that's okay. I have a call at 9

Me: Take your time, I can totally handle this

Ethan: Wow, okay

Me: Seriously, I've got spreadsheets. And a belt

Ethan: A belt? Pete's not going to know what hit him

After I get my kids to camp and make Phyllis's eggs, I take my laptop and my three-ring binder and head for Lacey's office. I am aware that it's not confidence that's holding me up right now. It's information. For sure, being prepared is self-care.

I sit in the parking lot for a second to take a few breaths. "I'm going in," I say. *You're going to knock 'em dead.*

I walk into the office and Pete and Lacey are waiting. I say hello and catch Lacey looking over my shoulder for my attorney.

"He's coming," I say. "But it's fine. I have what I need." I gesture with my binder and sit down.

"What's that?" Pete asks.

"Our bills, a list of expenses. That's what we're going through today, right?"

"Yes," says Lacey. "Let's get started. Pete made copies of your household's expenses and has made a preliminary offer of support." She hands me a spreadsheet.

I look over it, line by line. "You left out cable and home maintenance," I say without looking up. I refer to my binder and add the numbers in the margin.

Lacey looks at her copy and says to Pete, "That makes sense to add. Do you agree?"

"What are you trying to pull, Ali?" Pete's leaning forward.

I fold my hands on the round table. I lean in. "I'm trying to make sure the kids and I have enough to get by. And I don't think you want our house falling apart, since it's half yours." I'm being even, and I love the evenness in my voice. I love my binder. I look back to his spreadsheet and compare it to mine. "You've estimated utilities by annualizing the May bill, which, as you know, is the lowest of the year. I have the winter bills going back to November." I pass my open binder across the table to him.

Lacey makes a note. Pete is silent.

"Hey, sorry I'm late." Ethan is standing in the doorway. He's in a dark blue suit and a crisp white shirt, and he looks breathtakingly handsome. I like that today is the day to drop the costumes. He takes the seat next to me and places his legal pad and pen on the table. I squeeze my hands together because I am afraid I am going to reach out and touch him.

"We just started," I say, and try to refocus.

"That's fine," Lacey says for me. "We are just adding a few of Ali's line items to the monthly expenses."

Pete's leaning back in his chair, and I know he sees something between us. I say, "Okay, let me see if there's anything else." I take my binder back from Pete and run through my summary page. I tick off line items as they match.

"She used to be an accountant," Ethan tells Lacey. They're quiet as I go line by line and then replace Pete's numbers with mine and add up a new total.

"This is the right number," I say, and slide the paper back to Pete.

"Is that your dad's suit too?" he asks Ethan.

Ethan smiles. "No, it's mine. Kind of a bore, I know." He holds Pete's gaze.

"You're a weird guy," says Pete.

"For sure," says Ethan.

Lacey steps in. "Pete, can you agree to that number? Because if you can, we can move on to formal paperwork and I can get the divorce agreement filed."

"Fine," he says.

36

E THAN AND I WALK DOWN TO THE STREET AND INTO the parking lot, and he leads me to his car. Pete is right behind us, so we're quiet. Pete's Honda is parked next to Ethan, and we stand there and watch him root through his briefcase for his keys.

"See you tomorrow," Pete says.

"Yes," I say.

He looks at us over the hood of his car. He's about to say something but just shakes his head and gets in.

When he's gone, Ethan takes me in his arms and I rest my head on the lapel of his beautiful suit. "Do you feel good?" he asks.

I check myself for how I really feel. "I feel great," I say.

"You were amazing. Like if the person you were in high school grew up to have superpowers."

Yes, I think. *That's how I feel. I am Super Me.*

"Let's go celebrate," he says.

"The diner?"

"Nope. Get in."

We drive to the inn and walk through the lobby, but before we get to the deck, we turn into a long hallway that leads up a flight of stairs to a locked door. Ethan opens it and we are in a suite. It has a beautifully furnished living room, all blue and white fabrics against lemon-yellow wallpaper. There's an antique writing desk and a wall of hardcover books. I stand there for a moment taking it in, the fact that I am the sort of woman that a man would bring to a secret suite for sex in the afternoon.

"It's my grandparents' apartment," Ethan says. Okay, not exactly a secret sex suite. He walks through to the kitchen and pulls a tray of sliced chicken and Caesar salad from the refrigerator.

"Grab that?" he says, and eyes the bottle of champagne chilling on the shelf.

I grab it and follow him through the living room onto the terrace. We're at the corner of the inn, looking out over the water toward the end of Beechwood Point. A dining table has been set for lunch, champagne glasses included. I take this in, the fact that I am the sort of woman a man would plan a surprise for.

I reach for his hand. "I can't believe you did this."

"We have a lot to celebrate," he says. "Sit."

When we're seated and we each have a glass, he raises his. "I'm just so happy you're single. And that Ferris peed on me."

"Cheers to wet socks."

Ethan clinks my glass and laughs. Then he looks out at the water, sort of smiling at his own thought. "Do you know how many entries they get for the Sunbelt National Sweep-stakes?"

"I don't."

"I was thinking about this the other day and I looked it up. Nine hundred thirty-six thousand entries."

"That's a lot." My salad is delicious.

"So I called my mom and asked her how many times she entered, just to see what her chances were." He's looking at me like what he's about to say is going to blow my mind. "Once."

"Wow."

"Right? A one in nine hundred thirty-six thousand chance. One in nine hundred thirty-six thousand chance they'd win that thing, decide to move to Florida, and make me come down here that day that I ran into you."

I smile and reach for his hand. "You might have been here anyway."

"No. Not a chance. I never come down here except for holidays, and that was the first time I'd ever been to the dog park. My dog before Brenda, Sharon, was totally antisocial."

"Sharon?"

"You'd understand if you met her. She was a total Sharon." He pours me a little more champagne. "Anyway, what I'm saying is that this was totally meant to be. One in almost a million."

He sits back and smiles at me, delighted by the statistical unlikelihood of our meet cute, unaware of how ridiculous his dogs' names are, and I feel a warmth in my chest. I picture him stopping to buy hot dogs that he doesn't want from an old man. I see him standing up to Pete. I feel him holding my hand as I step onto a skateboard, steadying me just enough to prove I can balance, all on my own. I see him ahead of me at low tide, looking over his shoulder to check that I'm okay. Ethan shows up, every time, in the best possible way. And there it is, right in front of me—I am in love with him. The realization makes me catch my breath. I am at once surprised and not surprised; he's impossible not to love. Of course I'm in love with him. And of course there's a world of pain waiting on the other side of these feelings.

He reaches for my hand. "You okay?"

Maybe, I think. Because I'm Super Me now. I love the person I am with him. I love how there's no hiding or ducking or making myself small. Maybe I can handle this. "I am," I say. "This is such a fun surprise."

I get up and sit on his lap. I wind my arms around his neck, and I want to say all of it. It's as if I've completely unlearned how to push my feelings away. I want to believe he's looking at me like he loves me too.

"Let's be done with lunch," he says, and kisses me.

"Okay," I say, and kiss him back. I run my hands inside the collar of his crisp shirt and then my hands are unbuttoning it, all on their own. He gets up, barely breaking the kiss, and leads me into the bedroom.

WE LIE IN his grandparents' bed. There's a balcony and we have the curtains open so that we can see all the way out to Long Island from the bed. A sailboat goes by and I track it with my eyes as Ethan runs his fingertips up and down my arm. He asks if I want him to bring me my glass of champagne. I say no; I already feel as if I could float away.

"I'm going to have to go get my kids soon," I say into his neck.

"I won't allow it." He pulls me in closer. "What if we call Frannie and ask her to get them? Doesn't she owe us some babysitting?"

I imagine Frannie at camp pickup trying to explain to my kids that their mother's in bed celebrating her divorce. "I don't think that'll work," I say. "Also, Greer has a very important sleepover tonight, like maybe the most critical make-or-break sleepover of all time, so I'm going to need to be there to get her ready and out the door."

"Sounds like high stakes," he says.

She's lost her grandmother, her parents have divorced, and now she's tiptoeing toward the minefield of seventh grade. The stakes could not be higher. "I've been training for this my whole life," I say.

And I have. Here I am, weirdly, inexplicably in love with this man who has cracked me open and helped me feel things again. I am in possession of a clean kitchen, a binder full of power, and a man who wants to surprise me with champagne. I can handle whatever Greer's about to walk into.

37

I T'S SATURDAY MORNING AND PETE'S PICKING GREER UP from Caroline's house to take her directly to soccer. I did everything I could. You never, ever want to be the first one to leave the sleepover. Your departure opens the circle, and when it tightens and closes again, the new, smaller circle will gossip about you. These are the rules. I could not make Pete understand these rules. He actually said, "You sound a little crazy, Ali."

I text her at eleven: How was the sleepover

Greer: Fine

Me: Oh, great!

Greer: Not great, fine

Me: Sorry, are you ok?

Greer: I'm fine

I send a heart, she doesn't reply, and that's the end of it.

Ethan and I spend that day like a regular couple. I love having him in my house and seeing him interact with my things and my space. At his house, I sort of feel like we're house-sitting for his parents. Plus, there are all the boxes, though honestly we haven't done much packing and he's sort of stopped talking about the Realtor. At my house, I feel like he's stepped into my life.

It's my dad's birthday tomorrow night and I'm hosting Sunday dinner in his honor. I haven't had my dad here in a few years because I didn't really have the bandwidth for it, and also because I thought it might sting too much to see him see me in my swirling mess. I am excited to show them my newly revamped home—the lanterns in the yard, the flowers in every vase. The empty spaces where you can rest your eyes and hear yourself think.

I invited Frannie and Marco. My dad knows Frannie from my kids' birthday parties, so there's that, and also the extra nonrelated guests distract from the fact that I don't know how to talk to him. I try to explain this to Frannie, who always says, "But he's your dad." I can see why she wouldn't understand; there's an intimacy between Frannie and her dad, like she could cry in front of him or tell him something embarrassing. I never got there with my dad; there was always a gap between us that I couldn't cross. It's almost like we've been trying out for a play about a daughter and her father; we get the words right but can't quite deliver them in a natural way.

I've also invited Ethan, who is all in on this party. He's been to the grocery store with me and is outside sweeping my patio when my dad calls to see if Libby can bring tuna casserole from Stop & Shop (no, thank you). I mention that Frannie's brother is in town and I might invite him. "You know I love a full table," he says.

"Oh good, he's a nice guy," I say.

"Oh?" And I have the feeling that he is onto me.

"Not 'oh,'" I say. I don't know what to say next.

"Ali, it's fine for him to be a nice guy. You deserve a nice guy."

I feel tears welling up. I never would have told him, but it feels so good that he knows. "Thanks, Dad. He is a great guy, actually." I look out the kitchen window to where he's dumping leaves in the creek.

"You deserve it, angel," he says.

It lands right in my heart. He used to call me "angel" when I was really little and stopped at some point, maybe when he got so involved with Libby's kids. I'll never forget the first time I heard him call me Ali, like he was one of my friends. "Thank you for saying that," I say.

"It's true. You deserve your own happiness." He doesn't add, "separate from your mom," but I know he means it.

THE NEXT NIGHT my dining room table is set for nine, plus a high chair for Theo, and it looks beautiful. My mother would say it sparkles. I have the sense that I have stepped into my very best self. I feel warm and generous, as if the love I'm letting myself feel is touching everything around me. My dad and Libby arrive fifteen minutes early. Libby has brought a macaroni salad from Stop & Shop.

Iris and Cliffy are all over my dad, and they take Libby and him out back to show them the frogs in the creek. I call upstairs to Greer that the party's started, and she calls back that she's coming but doesn't come. When she got home from Pete's this morning, I asked again about the sleepover in my too-chipper voice. To reiterate, it was "fine."

Frannie, Marco, Theo, and Ethan arrive together.

"Does your dad read? I don't know how I don't know this, but I got him a book," Frannie says, laying flowers and the birthday cake on my kitchen counter. "What happened to this place?"

Ethan crosses the room and puts his arm around me. "I kissed her, and now she's no longer a frog." I give him a nudge and he holds me closer.

"They're coming," Marco says, and Ethan releases me.

My dad and Libby walk into the kitchen, and hugs and hellos are exchanged. He reaches out his hand to Ethan. "Nice to meet you, I hear you're a great guy," he says.

I have never seen Ethan so caught off guard. "Thank you," he says.

"And I like your parents," my dad goes on.

"Thank you," Ethan says again. "I like your daughter."

DINNER IS LIVELY. We eat a New York strip roast with whipped horseradish sauce, roasted potatoes, and green beans. There's an endive salad, and the popovers turned out great because I cleaned my oven. The food, the laughter, and maybe the distance from her phone have perked Greer up. My dad wants the report on the Hogans' relocation to Florida and wants to know why Ethan lives in Devon instead of Beechwood when his nephew lives here.

"It's sort of a long story," he says. I wait for him to

elaborate on the long story. I want to jump in and explain about the dog parade. "I like my work," is all he says.

"Life isn't all about work," Libby says. I am starting to be embarrassed. Like they spent the whole drive here plotting how they could lasso me a guy.

Cliffy saves me. "There's also skateboarding."

Ethan gives him a side glance. "Yep. And Cliffy and I are starting tomorrow after camp in the high school parking lot." I haven't heard anything about this, and the thought of Cliffy skateboarding terrifies me. But I do love that they've made plans and the happy way I imagine this makes Cliffy feel.

Frannie rolls her eyes. "You were always so embarrassing riding that thing around like it was attached to you."

Ethan says to Cliffy, "It really takes some women a long time to realize what's cool."

38

I 'M NOT GOING TO *NOT* LET HIM GO. IT'S IMPORTANT that Cliffy try things and build his confidence, though Cliffy on a skateboard sounds like the fast track to a broken arm. But I thought I was going to crash and burn the first time I tried, and I didn't. In fact, I am starting to understand the lightness that comes from focusing so hard on a single thing. Without all the distractions, it's almost as if you could fly.

Iris isn't really interested in skateboarding but brings a soccer ball. Greer comes under duress. She was still low before camp this morning, quieter than usual and epically preoccupied with her phone. I want to grab her and pull her back from this psychic ledge, but my efforts seem to backfire every time. So, when in doubt, fresh air.

Ethan meets us at the high school at three. He's brought a small skateboard for Cliffy and one for himself. He's trying to get Cliffy to be easy about it, but Cliffy seems scared. Ethan leans down and tells him something and Cliffy shakes his head. Ethan goes to his car and retrieves two baseball caps. When he's back to Cliffy, he makes a big show of placing it on his own head and turning it around backward. This makes me smile so much that I have to put my hand over my face.

He hands the other hat to Cliffy, and Cliffy places it on his head and carefully swings it around. Ethan approves and they high-five. Soon Cliffy is standing on the board. Ethan holds his hand and gets him to bend his knees a little. Cliffy is concentrating so hard as Ethan starts to ride him around the parking lot slowly. They go back and forth, and I am mesmerized. Everything in my life has changed since the night he did this with me.

"This is so boring," Iris says, abandoning her soccer ball and plopping down next to Greer and me on the blacktop. "Can we go canoeing?"

"Yes," I say without really thinking. I do not want to be inside today.

Greer's scrolling through her phone with a blank expression on her face. I know this expression because I've felt it on my own face. You scroll through the photos of all of your friends who are having better, more meaningful lives than yours until the only thing you remember about your own life is that you're not living your best one. Instagram knows this because it sends me commercial breaks from this NumbScroll™ to suggest how I could get that best life. This usually strikes me as funny, or at least ironic, but it's not funny when I see it on Greer's face. There's an emptiness there that makes me ache.

Ethan gets Cliffy to put his right foot down and push off

a bit. It's a slow start but he does it. Ethan picks him up off the board and spins him around. And the lesson is over.

"Is that it?" Iris asks.

"Yep, you've got to stop while it's still fun."

"It was fun," Cliffy agrees, and falls into my lap.

"You were great," I say, and smooth his sweaty hair off his forehead.

"Come on, Ali, your turn," Ethan says, reaching out his hand to pull me up.

"Mom? You're going to try?" Greer asks. It might be the first thing I've heard her say today, and I have an urge to be brave for her. To show her something that's not on her phone. I get up without taking his hand. I don't know how to touch him in a way that looks platonic.

"Sure," I say. "Scooter's given me a couple of lessons. I think I've got it." I take Cliffy's hat and put it on and turn it backward. He gives me a thumbs-up and Ethan hands me his board. They're all watching me and I know that I could fall flat on my face, but I want to trust this thing, this piece of wood with wheels. I want to trust myself to stay in balance.

I push off with my left foot. The parking lot is flat so I only get as much speed as I try for. I lean a little and turn and feel the way I've controlled the board. Just a slight lean in, almost imperceptible, makes all the difference. I turn as I go, showing off now. *Who's more unstuck than me*, I think. I make a sharp turn at the end of the lot but can't quite stay on my board. I get back on, and I can feel how little is weighing me down. I imagine myself going up the half-pipe and turning in the air the way Ethan does. I imagine Greer dropping her phone to cheer. I skate back to them and Ethan and Cliffy are beaming. Greer rolls her eyes.

"Can we go canoeing now?" Iris asks. Before I can answer, she says, "Scooter, you can come too. My mom is so fast."

"I've heard," he says. "Let's do it." And he's so comfortable. Like of course we should all go out in the canoe—it's a beautiful day. He doesn't know how loaded that canoe is in my head. Ethan in my canoe sounds absolutely perfect.

LINDA HAS A big smile for my kids. "Two days in a row! What a fun surprise!"

"Cliffy was learning to skateboard and it was hot and boring so we came here," says Iris.

"That's pretty much it," I say. "Linda, this is Ethan."

Ethan reaches out his hand to shake. "Hi, Mrs. Bronstein."

She pulls him into a hug. "Scooter Hogan. US history. I cannot believe it. I ask Frannie about you all the time, and she tells me about your life up in Devon. I can't believe you're all grown up."

"I get that a lot," he says, and hands Cliffy a set of oars.

THE PADDLING IS so easy. I can't remember when it was this easy. My muscles are sore because yesterday was our Sunday ride, and this feels restorative rather than taxing. We are in a rhythm, and, as usual, Greer and Iris take it very seriously and Cliffy takes lots of breaks.

"Let's stop at Pelican Island," Ethan shouts. It's just ahead of us, and it's high tide, so it's smaller than it was when we were there together.

Cliffy perks up and shouts, "Yes! Is that it?"

We slow down as we approach and Ethan jumps out to pull the canoe on shore. We get out without getting wet, and it feels like a luxury. "This would be fun in pirate costumes," Ethan says to nobody in particular.

Cliffy jumps on this. "Can we do that next time? I like the big hat with the three corners."

Iris is listening and I see her teetering between wanting to join in with abandon and thinking maybe this is babyish.

"I have that hat, and I now have a striped shirt with a stuffed parrot that sits right on the shoulder," Ethan says like it's the most normal thing in the world. "And a treasure chest full of stuff you guys might like."

"Okay," Iris says. "And an eye patch?"

"I have a bunch of those," he says. And to me, "Good thing we're so slow about throwing stuff out. I even have a Jolly Roger flag we could hang off the back of the canoe, to make it sort of foreboding."

Cliffy hugs Ethan so spontaneously that I think I notice it before he does. "I'm going exploring," Cliffy says, and leads Iris between the trees to see what may be lurking on the other side of the island.

Greer has taken her phone out and is taking a picture of Beechwood in the distance. I'm annoyed because I just want her to enjoy the new perspective and the sound of the water lapping up against the rocks from every angle. I don't want her seeing this as another opportunity to gain footing with her friends.

"Can I see?" Ethan asks.

She looks surprised but says, "Sure." She hands him her phone, and I nearly faint.

"It's a good photo," he says. "I like the way you kept the inn to the left so that it's mostly the unbroken tree line." He hands the phone back to her.

She looks at the photo again and almost smiles. "I'm going to go find Iris," she says, and takes off behind the trees.

"What was that?" I ask.

"What?"

"Like, you just communicated with my daughter? She let you touch her phone and accepted a compliment. What kind of sorcery is this?"

He laughs. "I don't think you realize how much time I spend with teenagers. I'll give you pointers." He takes a step toward me and I am afraid that if I take even one step toward him, I won't be able to keep my hands to myself.

"Everything I say is wrong."

He squeezes my hand and lets go. "It's sort of a subtle thing, I guess. But you have to meet them where they are. I talk about skateboarding with kids so that eventually they'll take my advice about other stuff. If she's into social media, meet her there."

This is right, of course. "I'm not sure I know how to do that."

"Just in little steps, I think. Teenagers need a little room." He looks back at the shore, hands on hips. "I used to love looking at Beechwood from here because it made me feel like I left it. Like I could enjoy the town from a distance, when it wasn't smothering me."

I look at him and wonder what it would take for this place to stop smothering him.

"Anyway, this is definitely more fun with kids. And I guarantee the next time we do this, we'll be in costume. Even Greer."

"I'm in," I say.

"And Iris feels like a natural on the water. Have you noticed that?"

"I have," I say. "She's strong."

He turns back toward me and I can't help but touch the front pocket of his shorts. "Do we have the day together tomorrow?" he asks. His voice is husky, as if it's holding back an avalanche of emotions.

"Yes. Starting at nine. And it's Tuesday, so the evening too," I say. This morning, I actually sat down and made a grocery list for the entire week, went shopping, and picked up Greer's contact lens prescription—all so that I would be able to spend more time the rest of the week with Ethan. It's funny what you'll do when properly motivated. "Do you want to come with me to Phyllis's again?"

"Yes. In my perfect world, I would be with you all the time, no breaks," he says.

I look up at him to see if he means it. He does.

CLIFFY HAS LIBERATED a dozen rocks from Pelican Island, and we paddle back to the boathouse. Iris is chanting, "Yo ho ho and a bottle of rum," which isn't quite wholesome, but it's happy.

When we are pulling the boat onto the shore, Ethan says to Greer, "Have you seen your mom's Instagram account? Storage something?" I'm not sure, but he might have rolled his eyes.

"Do you mean 'coat rack goals'?" she says, and laughs.

"What?" I say. "Was that lame?"

Ethan makes a yikes face and my kids laugh. "You could use some help, Ali."

Greer lays her paddle in the canoe and looks at me with something close to interest. "Would you help me, Greer?" I ask. "I really don't know what I'm doing, and half the time I don't remember to post anyway."

"Yes," she says, and that's it. She turns away and I'm not going to get any more, but Ethan is smiling to himself and I see what he's done. He's opened a door for me.

I lead the way as we carry the canoe up the beach, which is why I see Pete first. He's walking through the dog park gate toward the boathouse when he looks up and sees us. We're clearly both headed to the same place so I can't act like I didn't see him. I wave with my free arm and he walks over.

"Daddy!" Iris and Cliffy drop the tail end of the canoe and run over to him. Greer hangs back.

"We're pirates!" Cliffy says.

"Well that's fun," says Pete, with his arms around each of them. "Bringing your lawyer in case there's any trouble?" he asks me.

"Scooter was giving Cliffy a skateboarding lesson," I

say as if that explains everything. Naturally, if you give someone a skateboarding lesson the next step would be to usurp their father's spot in the family boat.

Pete's looking at the five of us, beyond windswept, like he's about to take our photograph. "Skateboarding, huh?" And then to Cliffy, "How'd it go?"

"Good, once I got my hat on." Cliffy smiles at Ethan. "And you should see Mom, she's practically a pro."

"On a skateboard?" Pete is incredulous.

"Yes, on a skateboard," I say. "And I am getting quite good." Pete is looking from Ethan to me, and I know that me skateboarding is pretty damning evidence of how much time we've been spending together. But it's also evidence of Super Me—balanced, steady, and gleefully unstuck. "Quite good," I repeat.

Pete gives me a long look. "Well, I got out of work early, so I was going to take a scull out for a while. Mix things up."

Linda is visibly uncomfortable behind him. Apparently, Pete didn't get the memo that he lost boating rights in the divorce. Apparently, Linda didn't count on a Hogan showing up when she was handing an expensive piece of equipment over to someone who is not a guest of the inn. I wait for Ethan to react in some way, put Pete in his place. But he doesn't say a word.

As Pete heads to the water in his single scull and we carry the big canoe into the boathouse, I think, *This. This man is right in our canoe. I love this man.*

39

GREER'S TAKEN OVER MY INSTAGRAM ACCOUNT AND her recent post of Carla Garcia's attic got thirty-six likes, more than four times more than I've ever gotten before. Greer and Ethan think something about this is hilarious.

I spend nearly all of the hours that my kids are occupied with Ethan. Our days feel like a honeymoon in five-hour increments. We take out a double kayak and paddle all the way to Connecticut and back. We eat fish tacos on his grandparents' terrace and watch the sailboats from their bed. We break through the Ghost Gate with our dogs and look at the city in the distance. We go to the skate park, where there is no breeze at all, and I master turning around on a flat surface. Once I've done it, I cannot stop doing it. With my weight on my back leg, my hips make the turn happen and propel me forward. Ethan talks me through going back and forth on the mini ramp. It's only three feet high and the trick is to shift my weight and lean into the transition at the top. But I don't get going with enough speed to get there, because I'm afraid I'll go right over the edge. We cool down afterward in his pool and make absolutely no progress on the house. I am happy in a way that I haven't felt since before I was married.

My dad calls when I'm driving to Ethan's, and apparently, he's noticed too. "Hi, Ali," he says, a little hesitant. He doesn't just call me unless it's to discuss specific plans, and we don't have any.

"Hi, Dad. What's going on?"

"Nothing really, was just thinking that Cliffy's going to be tall."

"Oh?"

"Yeah, I saw some other kids his age at the park, and I even asked how old they were. Much shorter. Does his doctor say this?" There is no way this is the reason for his call.

"He's definitely above average," I say. "I'll ask for a percentile next time we're there. So what's going on with you?"

"Nothing, really. Same things." He's quiet for a second. "That Ethan's a nice guy."

Ah. Now I see. "Yes, he really is. And the skateboard lesson went pretty well too." Ethan is basically the only thing in the world I want to talk about, but I don't have enough experience talking with my dad about personal things to feel comfortable in this moment.

"Good. Good. Just wanted to say so. Also, that I liked the way he listened to you."

"Dad, seriously?"

"Yes. I mean, every time you opened your mouth to talk he acted like you were about to perform a never-before-heard Beatles song." He laughs, and I do too. I am so touched that he noticed this. "Pete, I mean, he's fine. But he always did this thing like he was waiting for you to finish talking so he could say something. Even early on. I hate that."

"Thanks, that's nice to hear. About Ethan."

"There's something between you two that's just sort of . . ."

"Right," I say, almost to myself.

"Yes, it seems right. That's exactly it."

"Okay, thanks, Dad." I pull into Ethan's driveway and have the sense that my dad has more to say. I find myself wishing that we'd been having these conversations all along so that this would feel easier. I wish this felt more like sitcom banter and less like each word drops like an anvil.

"Well. Just wanted to say I like this new guy. That's all."

"Thank you," I say. "For calling. It was good to talk to you."

"Yeah, it felt good," he says. And we say goodbye.

I'M A LITTLE raw from this conversation when I walk into Ethan's house. He opens the door and pulls me into his arms like he didn't just see me yesterday.

"Hey," he says, and kisses me. I wrap my arms around his neck and sink into this kiss the way I always do. I will never get used to this. I can't imagine ever just passing Ethan on the way out the door with a peck on the cheek.

He's leaving this morning to go up to Devon to appear in court this afternoon, and Frannie's here sorting through her mother's china cabinet. I didn't want to make any decisions about that stuff in case it's valuable, and Ethan doesn't want to look at it.

"Do you want this silver tea service?" she asks as he's getting ready to leave.

"For what?"

"I don't know. Tea?"

"Not a huge tea guy. You keep it."

"I don't have any place to keep it, but it was Great-Grandma's. Maybe I'll pack it up for Theo for a wedding present someday."

"Perfect," he says. "Then Theo can put it in his attic and give it to his kid."

Frannie laughs. "The Hogan legacy of packing and storing. Love it."

"The Realtor came by Thursday and says she wants me to clear out that kind of stuff anyway, so this place will appeal to young people. I just don't know any young people that are going to want a giant old house in the middle of town."

"The Realtor came by?" I ask. I don't know why this surprises me. The whole point of cleaning this place up has been to get it on the market.

"Yeah, Thursday. It goes on the market in two weeks."

I have a feeling of having woken from a dream. The kind where you wake with a start and that fuzzy world that your mind has created fades away and you're just looking at the clock on your cable box. It's time to get up. The summer is almost over.

"You okay?" Ethan must notice a look on my face.

"Of course, sure," I say. "You should get going."

He crosses the room to me and takes my hand. "See ya, sis," he says to Frannie. "I'm going to let my girlfriend walk me out so you don't have to watch me kiss her goodbye. You're welcome." I want some of this lightness right now.

He grabs his bag with his free hand and leads me out to his car. "Seriously, are you okay? You don't look right."

"I am," I lie. "I think I just got really tired. Maybe I'll go home for a bit."

"Fake cleaning up won't be that much fun without me anyway."

"It won't," I say.

"I'm not going to tell you I'm going to miss you because that would be embarrassing. But I am." He pulls me into a hug and I just want to stay there. In this moment, where my head is in his chest and his arms are around me and he's still here.

40

THAN TEXTS THAT NIGHT: DID YOU GET ANY REST?

    Me: I did

Ethan: Good. I miss you

Me: Me too. How was court

Ethan: It went our way

Me: Congratulations

My phone rings; it's Ethan. "What's going on?"

"Nothing, why?"

"You sound so weird, like a robot."

"Do I?"

"Yes, and you do right now too, so it's not just texting. Like you don't miss me, which makes me a little nuts because I really miss you."

I smile a little. "I miss you. Listen, I've got to go get Cliffy to bed. Let's talk tomorrow." I hang up.

Ethan texts immediately: Okay something's spooked you. Trust me, I've been spooked this whole time

Me: Ok, talk to you tomorrow

Ethan: Robot

I GET MY kids from camp. Iris and Cliffy both want to have a friend over and I say okay. My house is full of people and noise and it's a welcome distraction. I have a man who is actually in love with me, I know this, and there must be a way to make this work. It's too much to walk away from. I feel sick from how much I want to crawl into Ethan's arms and have him love me through this. Feeling your actual feelings isn't always so pleasant.

I abandon the chaos of the double playdate and go into my garage and get in my car. "Mom. What am I doing?" She doesn't say anything. "I love him. This is going to end so badly." The sound of those words surrounds me and I start to cry. *Protecting your heart is self-care.* And I don't know which of our voices that was.

41

I DON'T SLEEP. I TRY TO BEND MY MIND TO SEE HOW I could keep Ethan without compromising who he is and the happy life he's built. I cannot ask him to leave it. I cannot move to Devon. My kids need to be near Pete and in their schools and with their friends. I could go see him one day a week for the next twelve years until Cliffy goes to college. It's an eight-hour drive round trip. None of it makes sense.

I close my eyes and tell my mom, "I am in a knot." I know she knows what I mean. I picture the two of us trying to untangle a tiny gold chain, trying to loosen a knot that is so fine and so tight it will not give. *You're pulling too hard.* I know she's right. We have two more weeks, and I'm racing to the end already.

IT'S FRIDAY, AND Ethan calls. "Ali, I'm losing my mind here. Tell me what's going on."

And it's hard to be distant when his voice is in my ear.

Just the sound of it makes me want to settle in and wrap everything about him around me. All of the thoughts in my head sound crazy, and I know if I share one of them the rest will pour out. "I'm scared," I say.

"That's what happens when something matters. I think it's normal. I'm scared too. Terrified, really. I want to see you."

"When can you get back?"

"Maybe Tuesday." The "maybe" is the worst part of that sentence. "Any chance you can come up here tomorrow? Spend the night?"

A four-hour drive actually feels like nothing. "Okay."

"Okay? Really?" All the well-being in the world rolls over me. He is excited to see me, and this time tomorrow we'll be together.

"Why not? Assuming Pete's on time tomorrow, I can be there by two."

I DROP FERRIS at Frannie's house and try to ignore her concern for me. She's not saying anything in particular, but there's a question mark at the end of all of her comments. *So that's fun? And he's coming back Tuesday?*

As I get on the highway I think about how stuck I was after my mom died. Moving through the fog of grief and overwhelm just to sit and stare at my mess until it was time to panic about dinner. Driving sixty-five miles per hour north and watching the distance shrink on my GPS is the opposite feeling. I am exhilarated moving forward. I'll be there in two hundred miles. Now one hundred seventy-five.

My phone rings, and it's Greer. "Hi, sweetie."

"Mom, can you come get me?" She's crying.

"What's wrong?" A small panic creeps into my chest.

"Everything," she says. And I relax. This is going to be a little melodrama, and then it will be fine.

"How can everything be wrong? What's going on?" I switch lanes to get around a too-slow cement truck.

"Caroline started a new group text without me on it." She's really crying.

"How do you know?" I brace myself. *Ah, seventh grade has finally hit.*

"I've been texting them all morning and no one is responding. It's impossible that all eight of them don't have their phones. So I went online and they were all together last night at Jessica's and today they're at Olivia's pool." She's crying again and I don't know what to say to make her feel better. I know she's right: she's being Seventh-Grade Dumped. I can feel it all come back to me with the sound of her voice. It's as if, at the most terrifying part of your identity creation, your peers gather and declare you worthless. Seventh grade is a social experiment devised by monsters. *This happened to you. We got through it.*

I stall because now I'm only eighty-six miles outside of Devon, which I don't exactly want to tell her. "How do you know there's a new group text?"

"Mom."

"Okay, and how do you know it was Caroline?"

"Of course it was Caroline." And of course. Caroline is the worst. "Can you come get me? I just want to be home with you." I'm eighty-five miles outside of Devon.

"Did you talk to your dad about this?"

She gives me a half laugh. "Mom, come on." Part of me wants to force a situation where Pete has to hear her out, where he has to wade through the volcano of feelings she's having. But he doesn't have those skills. I feel a bubble of anger rise from my chest. Where was he supposed to get those skills? I never asked him to step in and engage with any of us emotionally. I'm the one who taught my kids not to expect anything from Pete.

She's quiet for a while, but I swear I can hear her heart beating and her stomach churning. "Mom, I really need you." *Auntie Mame.*

And it's not even a decision. I put on my turn signal and get in the right lane to get off the highway. I would throw my body onto a mountain of live grenades to protect her from pain.

"Greer, I'm coming. I'm with a client right now, but I can pick you up at Dad's in three hours. I'm not going to tell you this is no big deal. Because I know exactly what this feels like. Why don't you go to soccer practice—that might feel good—and then you and I are going to spend the rest of the day together." I'm off the highway, I turn left to cross the overpass, and I'm back on, headed south. My GPS tells me, "Rerouting." No kidding.

I CALL ETHAN. "Hey," he says. From the background noise, I can tell he's at the skate park. "How close are you?"

My words are stuck in my throat.

"Ali? You there?"

"Yeah. I can't come."

"What? I thought you've been on the road for hours."

"I was, but Greer called. She needs me, and I turned around."

"Is she okay?" And it's worse that he's worried about her rather than being angry that I've ruined our plans. I want to go back to feeling angry at Caroline Shaw rather than sinking into this bottomless pit of sadness.

"She will be. It's middle school girl stuff, and she needs me."

"Oh. Wow, I really wanted to see you."

"Me too. I'm sorry. I'll call you tomorrow."

He's quiet for a while, and the din of the skate park pours through my car speakers. "I hope Greer's okay," he says.

42

GODDAMN IT, MOM." IT FEELS GOOD TO SAY IT. THE
words roll around against the white noise of the engine
and the rumble of the tires against the road. I clutch the
steering wheel and say it again: "Goddamn it." If she hadn't
stepped in all the time, he would have had to lean in a little.
Pete and I were never going to make it. We'd still be getting
divorced, but maybe if Pete had been pitching in all along,
he'd know how to be there for Greer now, and I would still
be heading north.

Tears are running down my face. I have two hands on
the steering wheel and I'm gripping it so hard that I could
break it. I am sinking into a deep well of sadness and anger,
and I don't know who else to blame. "It was my life. Not
yours. And I know you wanted me so much and that you
loved me so much, but that didn't mean my life belonged to
you. It was for me to walk through, and for me to figure out."

Darling.

"Don't darling me! I mean this, Mom. You knew it was
all wrong. You had to have known. You could have just

taken a step back and let me handle things. That marriage was going to end either way. I didn't have to lose myself too." Now I need to mop up my face because I'm having a hard time seeing the road.

I would have thrown my body onto a mountain of live grenades to protect you from pain.

All right, touché.

"This is really hard, Mom."

"HAVE YOU BEEN crying?" Greer asks when she gets in the car.

There's no denying it. I've been ugly crying and talking to my mom for three hours. We actually worked a lot of stuff out. Halfway back to Beechwood, I felt the last threads of anger toward her loosen and give way. She was my mother. Of course she wanted to step in.

"A little," I say. "I was just thinking about Fancy and remembering what it was like to be in your exact same spot."

"It sucks," she says. What I wouldn't give to see my mom's wide smile on her face today.

"It does. Have you had dinner?" I grab her hand, and she lets me.

"No."

"Let's go to Rockport for an early dinner. We can sit right on the water and eat lobster rolls." I know enough to know that she wouldn't want to be caught dead eating with her mother in town today.

"Okay," she says, and gives me half a smile.

"I'm going to need to get gas."

I AM TRYING to be more even-keeled than my mom was in this situation. When this happened to me, we got through that first day, and then my mom immediately suggested I apply to private school. We didn't have the money for private school, but she pretended we did; that's how much she wanted to protect me from Jen Brizbane. I remember how scared it made me to see how upset she was, like she agreed this was the end of the world. As I sit across the table from Greer, who hasn't touched her lobster roll, I can feel all of my mom's feelings. I can feel the fury of a million mothers inside of me, and I want to roar my fiery mother breath on anyone who might steal a moment of my daughter's happiness. I know I need to let her wade through this, but the truth is, if I could step in, I would. If I could snap my fingers and make those girls appear with balloons and apologies, I would. If I could prevent her from ever suffering another loss and growing from it, I might. And it's in this moment that I understand my mother's love for me. I can still feel the intensity of that love and the way she walked into my home, bright as the sun, and blinded me to all the shadows. How lucky I was to be loved like that.

In the end, I did not switch schools. In fact, the social tide shifted before any of the applications arrived in the mail. That's the other part I need to remember—this will pass. My mother taught me how to create a cocoon for Greer, but inside of it I will allow her to feel how she feels.

"Put your phone away," I say.

"What?" Greer looks at me like she's never heard of such a thing.

"They're not texting, right? Because they're horrible seventh-grade girls. But this lobster is delicious and that seagull is eyeballing yours."

She shoves her phone in her pocket and looks out at the water, like she just noticed where we are. "Can we move?" she asks.

"No." I smile at her. My mom would have loved this idea.

"Rockport's nice."

"Middle school girls are awful in Rockport too," I whisper. "It's universal. It's like anthropology or something; girls turning into women fight amongst their own to jockey for power. There's actually a ton of learning that happens along the way."

She's not really buying this. "Name one thing you learned."

"Well, I learned a lot about what I wanted. I mean at first I just wanted to be back in the group, but when they came around and I was suddenly cool again and Hillary Epstein was ostracized, I realized I didn't want friends like that. I learned that I like people who make me feel safe." I hear my own words in my chest, and I want Ethan to call me and tell me he's never leaving.

Greer doesn't say anything, so I go on. "So when you're back with them or when you find a new crew and everything's going your way, you need to remember this and decide who you want to be. You'll have a chance to do this to someone else, and that's when you find out who you are."

"A joke," she says under her breath, like it had to come out, but she didn't know where to direct it.

"A joke? What's a joke?"

She's dismantled her lobster roll without having taken a bite and is now picking at the coleslaw. "Me, Mom."

"Greer." I say her name like a prayer, like it's an affirmation that will steady her. "You are not a joke."

Then she's crying again, and it all comes out. "I just keep thinking of them getting my texts when they're all together and then laughing about it. It's so humiliating. And Fancy's gone. And no one even notices what's happening in my life, and Dad—he only cares about us when we're playing soccer. It's like I'm going to wake up one day and every single thing will be gone. No Fancy, no parents, no friends."

"Of course you still have Dad. And you definitely have me."

She rolls her eyes. "Barely."

"What does that mean?"

She's going to say something but doesn't. She forks a piece of lobster and stares at it. "You're here. And you're happier lately, but for a while it was like you were gone," she says.

This hits me in the chest. "Since Fancy died?" I ask. Because, sort of.

"Well for sure since then. And then Dad left and I thought you'd be sad or angry but you weren't. Like you agreed with him that we weren't worth staying for. And now—" She puts her fork down and looks me right in the eye. "I'm with Dad a lot, and I'm sort of seeing how he is. He talks about you like you're a problem. Like you're a joke. And I think that's how he's always talked to you, and you just took it." Big thick fresh tears pour down her face, like her mother being a doormat is the actual thing that's breaking her heart.

I reach for her hand and she pulls it away. "That's between Dad and me, and I agree I was too quiet for too long. But that's not for you to be sad about."

"Well now that it's my turn to be treated like a joke, I guess I'll just take it. That's what we do, right?" There's an angry bite to this that I've never heard in her voice before. I am horrified to think how long it's been waiting to get out.

"It's not," I say.

There's more, and the words keep pouring out. They confirm every suspicion I've had about how she's been hurting and how deeply I've let her down—including my never setting Pete straight and allowing him to be so absent all these years. I was so worried about what Ethan might think seeing the way Pete treated me. He wasn't the one I should have been worried about.

"Oh, Greer," is all I can say. I want to roar my fiery mother breath on myself.

She mops up her face and takes a bite of her lobster roll. As if releasing that demon has freed up her appetite. I want to believe that the tirade is over, but there's still tension in her face that tells me it's not. *What else?*

"What else?" I ask. "I swear I can take it."

"This summer has been nice, with the house and the flowers and everything. You seem more like you, like the person I think of as my mom."

"Yes," I say. "I do feel more like myself."

"But this thing with Scooter."

It comes out of nowhere, and his name feels like a blow. "What about him?"

"Iris and I both think you have a crush on him. She doesn't really care, but I do. He's not staying, Mom. Just like Dad, just like Fancy. It's going to be the same thing again." She's wiping her eyes with the back of her hand. Her soccer ball charm is wet. "I don't want you to disappear again."

And just like that, in the way only our children can, she has held up a mirror to my biggest fears—that I've set myself up to fall apart again. Ethan is going to be gone and I am going to be in my sweatpants watching the paper pile grow out of the sink. I'm going to let my kids down.

I have been dancing on the edge of this cliff, just a breath away—or eight days, to be exact—from a huge fall. It was a fall I was warned about, big orange cones marking the danger. I climbed up anyway.

"It's been a great summer," I say. "And it's been fun getting to know Scooter, learning to skateboard." The word catches in my throat, and I don't know why. I take a sip of my water to buy myself a second. It's been a summer of learning to take risks and trusting myself not to crash and burn. And yet, as they say, here we are in the flames. "But fall's coming, and I promise you're going to get through this—with or without these girls."

Greer blows her nose into her napkin. "You think I'll have friends again?"

"One hundred percent guarantee," I say. "And, Greer, I promise I am here and I'm not going anywhere. Neither of

us is a joke." She smiles at me, the smallest smile, and I see
my mom for a second. I am flooded with the relief that
comes from forgiveness, both the giving and the receiving.
And I know that if I had to choose between the love of my
life or the well-being of my kids, I would always choose this.

WHEN WE'RE HOME, we watch *Auntie Mame* under the yellow blanket and eat popcorn. I have no idea why that movie
is so soothing.

Greer seems to feel better for having unloaded her painful thoughts. Greer feeling better goes a long way toward
making me feel better, but I am now the keeper of Greer's
painful thoughts. Phyllis has always told me that Dr. Phil
says that I am the primary role model for my same-sex children. So, in addition to staying off crystal meth and not
being catfished, I am supposed to be showing my girls how
to be strong women. Instead, I have shown them how to
let life take you by the tail and swing you around until one
day you wake up with four boxes of cornstarch and a husband who belittles you in front of your children. I can't even
think about what Cliffy is learning about being a man.

I GET INTO bed that night and text Ethan: I'm upset because this is going to be over.

I erase it and try again: Why are we doing this if you're
just leaving as soon as you sell the house?

I don't send that either. I finally text: I've seen you
naked

Ethan: Wait is this phone sex? Because I don't really get how that works

I smile the saddest smile. It feels like it's my very last one. I call him. "You told me you'd never move here. You told me from the very beginning. But I jumped into this anyway, the way you go ahead and get a dog even though you know it's going to die. You hide from the reality of it, because you really want a dog. I really wanted to believe this was going to last more than another few weeks."

"I'm not going to argue the dog thing with you. Plus they live like sixteen years. I know you're scared. I am too, but we can figure this out. I'm a problem solver, remember? Would you ever come live up here?"

"Ethan, I have kids."

He's quiet for a second. "I kinda do too."

"I know," I say. "And I've seen it. You've got kids and friends and clients and a dog parade. In Devon you're the person you're meant to be. If you walked away from that you'd lose yourself. And you'd resent me." As soon as I say this, I know it's true. He'd walk away from his life and resent me the way I resented Pete all those years.

"So that's just it? We're giving up? We're the architects of our own experience, for chrissake."

I'm quiet on the phone. That stupid speech. "I don't know what to say."

"Tell me what you want. Really."

"I want you," I say.

"Done."

"I want two of you. I want you to be a person with no past so that you can be the person you are in Devon in

Beechwood. I want you to pick up your entire community and bring them here so that I can go to sleep next to you every single night. I want all of it. That's the problem."

"Okay, I'll see what I can do," he says.

"Come on."

"If you give up, you're going to break my heart. You promised, Ali."

"This isn't going to work." Quiet tears are running down my face.

"Of course it's going to work. We'll figure it out."

"Tell me you're willing to leave Devon."

He's quiet on the phone.

I can hear him breathing. I picture him standing by the window, looking at the tops of the trees. I imagine Barb downstairs, comforted by the sound of his feet. He's exactly where he should be.

"I drove six hours today. This is actually impossible. We need to stop." My heart is racing like I lit a match under my curtains and I am waiting for my whole house to go up in flames.

"No. Absolutely not. Is this about dogs dying?"

Yes. It's exactly that. "This was great. You're great. Let's just cut our losses." This is too flippant, and I know I'm hurting him. There's no way out of this without a world of hurt.

"Who are you? You don't even sound like you right now."

I don't say anything. I'm a mom. And a joke and a terrible role model. I have a daughter who's never seen her mother stick up for herself. "I'm sorry. I think I've been living in a fantasy where the summer would never end."

He doesn't say anything. He always says something. "This is ridiculous," he says finally. "I can make this work."

"This isn't a problem you can solve. To make this work, you'd have to alter the whole space-time continuum."

"Then that's what I'll do," he says.

And I want to tell him to grow up. You can't just have what you want all the time. This was fun and easy for the summer. Now it's painful and hard.

"It's not going to work," I say. "It was a summer romance, and it's run its course. Maybe I'll see you when you come to close on the house."

He doesn't say anything. My chest aches like I'm tied to train tracks and someone's placed a boulder on me. We sit in silence for a few beats. I can hear him breathe and I want to go back to yesterday. I want to go back to any time before this.

"Don't do this, Ali," he says, and I hang up.

43

I MOVE THROUGH SUNDAY LIKE I'M MOVING THROUGH Vaseline, slow and murky. There's a heaviness to every step I take; I am the opposite of carbonated. Flat.

We go to my dad and Libby's for lunch, and he knows the minute he sees me. I go in for the long hug and wish I knew him well enough that I could cry. This is a whole new kind of grief, something beautiful that had to be killed.

"JUST THE FOUR of you?" Linda asks when we get to the boathouse for our canoe trip. I'm not sure what she sees on my face, but she backpedals. "Well, great! Let's get you guys out there!"

Greer steps forward and takes her paddle and mine.

"Come on, Mom, it'll be fun," says Iris.

"Of course!" I say. "Let's go!" Exclamation points are false enthusiasm, but I'm taking my cue from Linda. Today they're the only enthusiasm I have. We paddle out, and I am on autopilot. I say all the things I always say. I comment about the light breeze. I smile at Iris when she makes a joke about Cliffy's flip-flops, even though I'm not sure it was nice.

"Mom, you look like you've gotten a little tan," Iris says.

"Yeah, looks good," agrees Greer.

"Thank you," I say, and keep rowing. I'm trying not to look at the inn as we go. I don't want to look up at the widow's walk where I might as well be confined to pacing for the rest of my life, a newly tragic figure gazing at the horizon. All the times I looked up there and felt my own longing, I really had no idea what love could be. And now I can never unknow the truest true thing—the intensity of the love you feel will match the intensity of its loss. This is practically physics.

"Mom," Cliffy's saying. "Want to do Fancy's crazy dinner tonight? What's the game called?"

"Mystery Dinner," says Greer. "No. Let's barbecue a pizza. I saw it on YouTube."

"It's too late to make a crust," I say, watching Pelican Island appear behind her head.

"I'll ride my bike to get one when we get home," says Iris. All of my alarm bells go off. My children are complimenting me and offering to do errands. My poor kids.

"That sounds great," I say. "Let's eat it down by the creek! Cliffy, we need to work on your footbridge."

CAMP'S OVER SO the girls sleep late on Monday. I leave them a note and take Cliffy to the diner for pancakes before

I do the books. Marco walks out from the kitchen with Theo on his hip.

"How are you cooking back there with a baby in your arms?" I ask.

"It's not easy and probably not entirely safe," he says. "I have the playpen, but he lost his mind when Frannie left."

"Where'd she go?" I ask.

"She had to go to the inn. Again. Harold forgot to schedule the laundry service, so there are no clean towels."

I reach my arms out and he hands Theo to me. I balance him on my lap and he grabs Cliffy's nose. The laundry service is on the checklist I sent him. "Frannie thinks they should sell," he says. "The Beekman offer is still good."

"No." It comes out of my mouth so fast and so emphatically that I feel my face go hot. I don't want someone to buy it and change it or, God forbid, tear it down. But more than that, it's an open door for Ethan to walk through, a reason for him to come back here. I try to change course. "Sounds like a mess."

"Speaking of a mess," he says, "I talked to Scooter this morning." My stomach clenches. I want to hear every word that's about to come out of his mouth. And also I don't. I'm not sure I can temper my reaction in front of Cliffy.

I nod my head toward Cliffy to caution Marco against saying too much. "Oh?"

"Is he coming back?" asks Cliffy. "I still have his skateboard and we were going to do pirate things."

"Yes," Marco says. "And he says he's called you a few times?"

"I've been busy," I say.

"Doing what?" Cliffy asks.

"I don't know," I say. I've been trying to refocus on the reality I had before I met him. My kids, my dog, and Phyllis. I've been compulsively deadheading the geraniums in my backyard to summon my mother's comfort. "The usual stuff."

44

I CAN'T GET FOOD OR GAS WITHOUT GOING TO TOWN, and I can't go to town without seeing Ethan's house. It's been nine days since I told him it was over, and today the **FOR SALE** sign appeared. It feels like an assault.

His car has been in the driveway on and off. He must have finished getting the house ready on his own, and I feel guilty about this. I owed him a lot of hours. He texted me that he missed me two days ago. Me: Me too, but I can't do this. So he backed off, and I haven't heard from him since. I pushed him away, and I deserve the silent treatment. Also, I was right.

I dread going to the diner in particular, but it's Monday again. I sit at the counter and order poached eggs before I get to work. "You look terrible," Frannie tells me.

"I don't really sleep."

"Have you talked to him at all?"

"He's texted a few times. I just have to move on."

Frannie puts the coffeepot on the warmer and comes back. "I think you should give him a chance."

"A chance to what? Live in a town he always wanted to escape?"

"He could be happy here—he's just stubborn," she says, rolling her eyes.

"Don't do that," I say.

"What?"

"Roll your eyes about him. And he's not being stubborn. He's happy up there, completely at peace."

"Huh." I have Frannie's full attention, and I think we both know that I know her brother better than she does. "How do you know?"

"You know that thing he does with his face? Sort of like a wince?"

"The Scooter face? Yes." She starts to roll her eyes but catches herself.

"He doesn't do that in Devon. Ever."

She's quiet for a second, considering this. "I haven't seen him do it at all since he's been with you."

"Yeah," I say. I don't want to tell Frannie what it was like when we were alone together, partly because I don't know if I could describe it, and partly because it will make me cry.

"You're good for him," she says. "The whole thing is so weird, but I loved seeing him so happy. I've been worried about Scooter my whole life. He was always getting into trouble and being an idiot."

"That's part of the problem. Worrying about someone is sort of like expecting them to fail. He hates that you guys worry, like he can't convince you that the life he loves is good enough. Or that he's smart enough to decide for him-self what he wants."

Frannie looks away and takes a breath. "That's kind of harsh. We adore him."

"If I walked in here and said, 'Frannie, I'm so worried about you,' how would you feel?"

She lets out a little laugh. "Defensive."

"Exactly, because what I'd be saying is, 'Frannie, I don't think you can handle the life you built.' Or, worse, 'I have a better idea of how your life should go than you do.' Which I never would because you are so good at life, but if I said it, it might shake your confidence. My mom worried that I couldn't handle my marriage, until I actually couldn't. I think we kind of need to trust that people can figure their lives out. And Ethan's life is incredible." My voice falters, and I look down at my coffee.

"You love him," she says.

I look up with the intention of protesting. But of course I love him, and it doesn't matter that she knows anyway. "That's why I'd never let him come here and lose all that."

My phone buzzes with a text from Phyllis. It says "Come" followed by the laugh-till-you-cry emoji.

I AM IN my car speeding home, and I know there is nothing to laugh about. I find her sitting in her armchair with the remote control on the TV tray and a glass of iced tea spilled on the floor.

"Phyllis," I say. "What's going on?"

"Sit."

I do. "Do you need an ambulance?"

She looks at me sideways. There's a DNR on her refrigerator specifying that there will be no ambulances. No surgeries, no drama.

"Tell me," I say.

"I'm slowing," she says. "It started last night, and I want to get in bed, but I can't get up."

"Slowing?" I ask, and my voice cracks.

She takes my hand. "This is not the time for you to be afraid. I'm the one dying. You get to stay here with the cute boyfriend." She smiles at me, a mischievous smile. The generosity of that smile in this moment grips my heart. Also, the fact that I haven't told her that it's over between us. I know she'd think I was being a coward.

"Let's get you to bed," I say. I help her up and drape her arm over my shoulder. She's so light that I imagine she's already gone. We walk slowly down the hall to her room past the photos of Sandy and Camille in front of birthday cakes. *So many cakes in a lifetime,* I think. *And also, there are never enough cakes.* Neither of us is in any hurry, and I know this is the last time I'm going to see her out of bed. I've done this before. I am not ready to lose her, but I'm not going to say so.

I pull back her covers and help her sit. I cradle her legs under one arm and her head under another and lay her down. I cover her up to her shoulders and sit on the bed next to her. "Should I call Sandy?" I ask.

"Yes," she says, and takes my hand. Her hand is warm, her skin paper-thin. Her platinum wedding band is loose on her finger. "You are going to be fine. I've lost all of my friends by now, but it was worth having had them. I hope you feel that way about me."

"Of course I do," I say, and my voice betrays how afraid I am.

"Oh, Alice. Come on." She's smiling again, like this isn't the scariest thing in the world. "Hand me my water." I hold it against her lips, and she takes a sip. "And call Sandy."

I call Sandy from the kitchen and tell her that it's time to come. I don't say much more than that, but I'm certain that the tone of my voice conveys how urgent it is.

When I'm back in her room, her eyes are closed. Without thinking about it, I walk around to the other side of the bed and climb in. I know from experience that in the weeks to come I will be longing to be close to her, to feel her still-alive presence next to me. I scoot in next to her and take her in my arms.

"Sweet Alice," she says, and pats my hand. "I've lived alone for thirty years, and I always knew I wouldn't die alone."

"Of course not," I say. "We're the Sisters. I'm always right here."

She doesn't say anything for a while. My mind races to calculate how long it's going to take Sandy to get here and I worry that I didn't remind her to call Camille. Of course she called Camille. I try to quiet my mind and calibrate my breathing to Phyllis's. I think of the chaos around my mom's last hours and how I was racing around looking for nurses and calling her friends. I almost missed her last moments because I was filling out a form.

"You know you walked right into this," she says. She's startled me.

"Into what?"

"You befriended an eighty-six-year-old woman. That's how old I was when we met. I could have hired someone all these years, but instead we had this life together with our flowers and our eggs."

"It was the best part of my day on a lot of days."

She squeezes my hand. "Life's going to do what life's going to do, Alice. You might as well have a dog."

45

I SPEAK AT THE FUNERAL. I AM RAW STANDING AT THE altar delivering a eulogy for the second time in two years. I talk about what Phyllis meant to me—our talks, our passion for her weeping willow, her complicated relationship with Dr. Phil. I am about to land a joke about Phyllis's fear of my being catfished, when I see him. He's in the fifth row on the aisle. In his divorce-day suit and a powder-blue tie. I stumble over the joke, but a few people laugh.

I look back at my notes to regroup, but when I continue speaking, I am a bit out of my body. I watch myself give this eulogy, and the watcher remembers a younger me going on about how I am the architect of my own experience. And I guess it's true: I have created this moment. I am here because I befriended an elderly lady. I stepped into all of that beauty of my own accord. I made my own decisions about leaving my job and hiding from my marriage. I am also the architect of the wall I built between myself and my happy ending. I could have been brave enough to try. I panicked because I was about to get hurt, and I decimated myself in the process. I'm teaching my kids to act out of fear, to run away from the happy thing.

His eyes are on me as I talk about Phyllis's too-short fairy-tale romance. All eyes are on me, actually, because I'm the only thing happening in the church, but his are the ones I can feel. And I can still feel how just a look from him could make me happy and excited about my life. It's unfathomable that I walked away from that. I let my fantasy about a life in Beechwood with him keep me from having any kind of life with him at all. I catch his eye and think, *Any Ethan is better than no Ethan.* I need to tell him.

ETHAN'S STANDING OUTSIDE the church with Frannie, Marco, my dad, and my kids. He's talking to Cliffy and Iris in a natural, casual way. Greer stands back. My dad says something to Ethan and then shoves his hands in the pockets of his suit and turns back to Frannie. I approach them with complete uncertainty. I do not know how to say hello to Ethan.

My dad hugs me, which feels good and buys me time. I turn to Ethan, and he makes no move toward me. "Thank you for coming," I say.

"Of course," he says. "I know this is really hard." For a second, I feel it, the beautiful weight of his gaze. But then he looks away, like maybe I don't deserve it.

"Thank you," I say, and the world's most deafening silence falls over us. An avalanche of words waits to spill out. But I am surrounded by my kids and my dad. Frannie is trying to catch my eye, maybe just to tell me to let it go. The last thing I want to do is let it go.

"Well, I have to get going," Ethan says. He shakes my dad's hand, reaches to touch Theo's head in the stroller, and walks off.

My unspoken words retreat and weigh heavy on my chest. *Stay* and *Can we talk?* settle rotten on my heart, like love withheld.

Before I can go after him, Sandy and Camille join us. I do not know what to say or how to approach their grief. They're a lot older than I was when I lost my mom, but I can see in their eyes that there's no such thing as being ready to lose your mom.

My dad steps in. "I am so sorry. I know how hard this is. Ali lost her mother two years ago. Her name was Nancy, they were very close." And a mountain is moved by those words. He hasn't mentioned her in so long. Just his saying her name shifts my heart. There's a sprinkle of grace here, and sometimes that's all it takes.

I take his hand and say to Phyllis's daughters, "Your mom told me this pain is worth all the fun we had. And I believe her." I need to go find Ethan.

46

I HAVE SOMETHING I NEED TO DO REAL QUICK," I SAY to my kids and my dad. "Can I meet you at the inn in a bit?"

"I left my purse in the church," Greer says.

"Okay, Grandpa will wait," I say. I need to go to Ethan's house. I need to take him to our chairs by the pool and tell him that I was wrong. That I don't give up, that I want more, whatever that looks like.

"No, could you help me find it?" she asks.

Something's up. "Sure," I say, and we walk back in through the big double doors. I start up the aisle to where we were sitting, and Greer takes my hand to stop me.

"I didn't bring a purse."

I turn and look at her.

"I was really upset," she says. "About my friends. And I guess I've been upset about everything else too."

"I know that. And you have every right to be," I say, and squeeze her hand.

She drops mine and fiddles with the strap on her sundress. "But I didn't mean that about you disappearing. I don't think you're going to. I know you've been sad, but I know you're here for me."

"Thank you, it feels good not disappearing," I say. Super Me in a world of pain is still Super Me.

"And maybe that thing with Scooter was a good thing. He's cool," she says. "Like, he's so easy to be around."

"Yeah," I say.

"Fancy would have liked him." She smiles my mom's smile.

"Yes." I'm pretty sure Fancy sent him. I pull her into a hug. How complicated it is to be a daughter and a person. "One time when he was teaching me to skateboard, I was trying to learn how to go up the ramp with the right amount of speed, you know? I went up, and when I was coming back down, I could feel my balance go off. I could feel myself start to fall. And the funny thing was that as I was falling I thought, this was really fun and totally worth it."

She smiles up at me. "Did you get hurt?"

"No," I say. "He caught me. Just like Fancy would have. And I'll always catch you too."

MY DAD TAKES my kids to the reception at the inn. I don't need to tell him where I'm going. He knows.

I'm going to tell Ethan that I'm sorry, that it's not over. I'm going to tell him that I know who he is, and that I know he can be that person anywhere, that we'll figure it out. I don't know why I never told him I loved him. In the agony of the past two weeks, the one thing I've been sure of is that

I will never feel this way about another person again. He was it. When I'm Phyllis's age I will remember this summer and the way it changed my heart. And if he doesn't want to believe me, it's fine. I just need to tell him.

I pull up in front of Ethan's house and his car is not in the driveway. There are two other cars, and a guy is standing on a ladder looking at the gutters. A woman in a sensible suit is checking things off a list. The **FOR SALE** sign is gone. I catch my breath and rest my head on my steering wheel. *It's just a house,* I tell myself. But it's an ending. It's the end of the summer I've just spent there and the end of Ethan coming back here. Even when he visits his parents for the holidays, he'll be going to Florida. Frannie's the last Hogan in Beechwood.

I wipe the tears off my cheeks with the back of my hand and make my way toward the inn. I slow down as I pass the skate park, delusional that I'll find him there on the half-pipe in his divorce-day suit. The inn is the last possible place he could be, unless he's left town already. The thought gives me an empty, sick feeling in my stomach. I picture Ethan driving home to Devon to get back to his actual life. In a different life, I would be getting on the highway with him.

I park at the dog park rather than at the inn because I don't want to get blocked in, and I could use a little fresh air. I walk across the park in my sandals and feel the dry grass of summer's end brush against my feet. I pass the spot where Ferris picked Ethan for me, and I tell myself it was worth it. I wouldn't go back and unlove Ethan in order to not be feeling the broken way I'm feeling right now. I'd do it again.

I get to the end of the dog park and walk through the gate to the inn. It's hot, and I could really use a breeze. Even the flag that usually flaps over the inn droops in the thick, still air. To its right I see something hanging over the railing of the widow's walk. I think it's a blanket, but when my eyes focus, I see it's a suit jacket. Next to it are two forearms resting on the rail, clutching a beer. I would know those golden forearms anywhere. I race behind the inn and around to the side where the narrow stairwell has been bolted shut forever, and the door is open. I climb the steps more slowly than I want to because of my shoes and take them off halfway and run. When I throw open the door to the landing, he's there looking out at the water.

We are very high up. Of course I knew this, but I've never been up here to get a real sense of it. There's no breeze at all, and everything seems perfectly still. In front of me, I can see all the way to Long Island. Behind me, I can see all the way to the end of town. In this stillness, I am feeling clear on everything.

He turns and sees me holding my shoes. "Hey," he says.

I walk over to him, but I don't touch him. We both turn back to the railing and watch the tide roll out as I catch my breath.

"It was a nice funeral," he says.

"Yes."

"It's going to be hard for you without her. She was a big part of your life."

"Yes," I say again. But it was worth it. I'd make eggs for Phyllis and sneak vanilla pudding into her refrigerator all over again, knowing I'd miss her like this today. Because that's what life is—joy peppered by loss. It's why you get a dog. And then you get another dog. Madness repeating itself just to get another taste of joy. I turn to him and don't say any of this. "It's weird there's no breeze up here."

"Yeah. Everything feels kind of stuck."

"Yeah." Someone goes by on a kayak. There are sailboats out in the distance. I want to ask him if I can touch his hand. Or if we could take a walk. I want to know if I could spend one more day with him before he goes because there's value in a single good day.

"You're really great at talking about the weather," he says finally.

"It's a gift," I say.

He looks out at the water.

"I'm sorry. I was wrong," I say.

"No kidding." He takes a sip of his beer. I want him to turn to me, to invite me in.

"This has been really hard," I say.

We watch the water. A pair of paddleboarders are passing Pelican Island. "Did you really think I was just going to let this go?" he asks.

"You didn't really have a choice."

"You always have a choice, Ali. You broke your promise."

"I know," I say. "I broke my own heart too."

I'm looking for some way back in. Like some sign that he'll give me today, or this week, or the rest of the summer. But he's not reaching out to me. His body language is closed. He stares at the water, and I feel shut out.

Desperate, I ask, "How long will you be here?"

"How long do you want me to be here?"

"As long as possible."

He doesn't say anything.

I try again. "I thought it would be too painful to say goodbye to you. And I was right, by the way. I can't do it." I want to tell him I've changed my mind about the dog thing, but I'm sick of talking in circles. I take a breath and just say it. "I love you."

He turns to me, finally, and I go on. "I know that's a big thing to say, but I do. Can we just have more time? I can't handle the idea that this is over. I'm not going to feel this way again."

There are tears in his eyes. He pulls me into his arms and I rest my head on that spot on his chest where I could stay forever. It would be nice if he said he loves me too. My words are just hanging there, but I guess that's okay. Not everything balances.

I pull away because I might as well say the thing. "I think what I wanted to say to you, besides that, is that I think you'd be the most important part of any community you lived in. I don't think you'd lose yourself if you left Devon. You are so strong and sure that you make other people strong too. I'm not saying move here, I'm just saying you're loved here too. And if moving is impossible, then that's fine too. I could drive to Devon every week. I would totally do that."

"Ali," he says. He takes both of my hands. The shock of the feel of his hands in mine temporarily removes me from this conversation. Yes, I just told him I loved him. But God, do his hands feel good. "I'm staying here, in Beechwood."

"No, you can't do that," I say. I'm looking right into his

eyes and I know for sure that no one, including me, tells Ethan what he can or cannot do.

"Don't make me say the whole architect thing." He pulls me closer. "I made kind of a big decision. You might not actually like it. I don't know. I did it for myself, but also hopefully for us."

I don't say anything. I'm mesmerized by the word "us."

"I gave the house away. I donated it to the city."

I come to. "What?"

"I was wandering around Devon trying to get it to feel like home again, trying to get back to being the person I was before you. And it just felt empty. I moved there because it felt good. I realized that what felt good there was that it was a place where I could belong. But that's not enough anymore. I belong with you."

My heart stops and I don't even blink. I want to make sure I heard him right. "Really?" I wrap my arms around his neck.

"Really," he says. He kisses me, and the salty taste of him is my first clue that I'm crying. Relief washes over me, just being this close to him. He rests his forehead on mine and wipes my tears with his thumbs. I have this funny feeling that neither of us has the upper hand; I can feel both of our hearts reaching out for one another.

"But what about everyone in Devon?"

"That's sort of complicated. I mean, Barb can find a guy to change her alarm batteries, and I can do legal work remotely, but the kids at the skate park still need me. They've got my number, and I'm going to go back to Devon once a week. But I'm also setting up my parents' house as a place for kids to come when they've aged out of the system. Michael and Louie are the first two who are coming down. I have a social worker involved, and Frannie's going to give them temporary work at the diner. We always need people at the inn in the summer."

"Frannie knows this?"

"Yes, she's been very cool the past few days, actually, and she's been begging me to tell you, but it wasn't settled until this morning. And I wasn't sure what you'd think."

"It's an amazing thing to do."

"And, honestly, Ali, it's not like no one needs me here. I've been coming back here like a teenager, sort of regressing to what they expect of me. But my parents do need help, with the inn and everything. Theo needs me; you know they're never going to let that kid learn to walk."

"True." I laugh. "And you thought I wasn't going to like this?" I run my hands over the sleeves of his crisp white shirt.

"Well, maybe. You love that house. Maybe you pictured a different kind of future. But it feels right. And all the rest of it, I can figure out." He smiles at me, and I feel like I want to spend the rest of my life in that smile.

"You are honestly the best person I've ever met." I wrap my arms around his neck.

"I doubt that. But I love you, Ali, like in a way that's so intense I don't think I could even explain it to you. So I'm staying." He kisses me again, more deeply, and I feel myself melt into him in that way I never thought I would again. "I love you," he says into my mouth. "I love you so much, Ali." In the irony of my lifetime, everything I have ever yearned for has materialized on the widow's walk.

Ethan cups my face in his hands and presses his forehead to mine. "No more goodbyes, okay?" I nod and kiss him again. It's a promise. The wind picks up out of nowhere and I feel the breeze skim my cheek. A flash of red catches the corner of my eye as the flag waves at us. *This sparkles for sure*, she says.

The sun is getting low over the town behind us, but I don't want to turn away from him to watch it set. I want to stay in his arms, where I am somehow completely protected and completely free. The impossible thing. "Where are you going to live?" I ask into his neck.

"I don't know. Maybe I'll stay at the house for a bit. Just to make sure things get off to a good start. I'll find a place, and in the meantime I can always stay here, at the inn." He looks around. "We should get some furniture up here, just for us. I'm the only person in the world with a key. I found it in my dad's office."

"I can't believe you did this."

"I can't believe you didn't think of it. Weren't you the valedictorian?"

"I never in a million years thought someone would completely change their life for me."

"I never in a million years thought I'd want to." He kisses me again, and I want to stay here forever.

"Wait, do your parents know?"

"Yes, I put together a whole pitch to explain it to them, how it would work legally as a nonprofit and with the city.

All they focused on was you. Of all the things, I think you're the thing they're finally proud of me about. They asked about a hundred times if we're getting married. They wanted to know what your kids think about step-grandparents."

I am smiling at this possibility. More grandparents, more family, more Ethan. "Thank you for doing this. For everybody."

"I did it mostly for myself."

47

WE MAKE OUR WAY DOWN THE NARROW STAIRS AND across the terrace to the inn's waterfront restaurant. People are still milling around and eating mini versions of Frannie's signature sandwich. I am different and there is no way to conceal it from the people who love me. My dad sees it first and puts his hand over his heart, as if to tell it to be still. A smile takes over Frannie's face, and she elbows Marco too hard.

Greer narrows her eyes at me, and I see the realization that something good is happening move across her face. Iris wheels Theo's stroller through the crowd to where we are talking with Sandy and Camille. Their grief is temporarily lifted and they seem like they're just at a party. I know this is a trap in the same way I know they'll eventually be okay. Cliffy's at my side with his arms around my waist. I squeeze him back and feel Ethan watching us. In this moment I am nothing but my heart.

After everyone's left, and I've said goodbye to my dad, I find Ethan on the terrace holding Theo by the hand and talking with my kids. I don't know who I want to touch first. *You can have all of it,* my mother says in the wind.

"I guess we'd better get home," I say.

"Yes," Ethan says. "It's been a big day."

Greer crosses her arms. Iris looks like she might be holding her breath. "Come on, Scooter," she says.

"Really?" he asks.

Cliffy lets out his breath. "Don't chicken out."

Ethan turns to me, and he's overly formal in a way that makes me want to laugh. "These three have given me permission to ask you on a date."

I try to contain my smile. "Is that true?" I ask them.

"Yes," says Iris. "And he said a real restaurant. Maybe even here."

"Well, that sounds nice," I say. "I accept."

"Good," says Iris. "Because Grandpa and Libby are coming to babysit tomorrow at six."

48

WE DON'T GO TO THE INN AFTER ALL BECAUSE HAR-old's had a mix-up with the fishmonger and all they're serving is chicken. Instead we go to a bistro in Rock-port and eat mussels and flagrantly hold hands.

He has me home by eleven after our date and furiously kisses me good night by the front door. We can't go to his house because it's being painted inside. We can't go inside my house because my dad's inside. I feel like I'm sixteen.

When it's finally Saturday and we are alone in my very own house in my newly clean bedroom, I lie in his arms and let all of the feelings wash over me. Ethan is something I never thought possible—a partner with whom I am totally free to be myself. A summer romance that doesn't have to end.

"How long do I have to wait to ask your kids if I can marry you?" he asks. He's not being serious, but he is.

"Definitely a few weeks," I say.

His phone buzzes, and I don't want him to move. "Don't get that," I say, and drape my leg over his to trap him.

"I have kids," he says. "I always have to get it." I lie next to him as he answers questions about an event at the skate park today.

I get a text from Sandy: I don't know how you ever did this. It's brutal

She and Camille are next door cleaning out Phyllis's house. They really only have the weekend to get through it together because Camille is going back to San Francisco on Monday. After that it's all on Sandy. And me, of course.

When Ethan's off the phone, he pulls me close and says, "I never want to get out of this bed."

"Same," I say. Tomorrow my kids will be home, and he won't be here. I remind myself that he's just down the street, and that's so much better than Devon. "But we may need to go over and help Sandy and Camille for a bit."

Ethan covers his face with a pillow. "All those books."

"It's a lot. But it's a lot more for them than it would be for us. Let's give them two hours of help. I'll set a timer. And we can come right back here."

I CAN TELL Sandy's a wreck the minute we walk through the door. And that's before she starts to cry. "All of these photos. And the letters my dad wrote to her after their first summer together. I could do this for months and not be through it all."

I give her a hug. "We're going to help. And you can use my garage for the give-away pile."

Camille comes out of the bedroom carrying stacks of clothing. "Oh, thank God you're here."

"Give-away, right? Take that to my garage."

"And thank God your garage is so close," she says. "We only have to move a thousand more loads before this place goes on the market."

Ethan is in the living room, running his hands over the stone fireplace. "She took really good care of this house," he says.

Sandy nods. "She thought of her life as a fairy tale. This house was part of the romance, even after my dad was gone."

"I love that," he says. He opens a corner cabinet full of books and teacups. "Mind if I go upstairs?"

Sandy nods again. "Knock yourself out. And maybe bring the old coats down from the closet at the top of the stairs?"

Camille is back from my garage, and I start putting boxes together for things they may want to keep. "Let's call this box 'treasures.' We'll put the love letters and the old photos in here and move it immediately into your car. Then we'll clear out the books. I suggest you each pick ten, and then we can have Mr. Tripodi from the library come take what he wants. Then tomorrow we'll tackle the kitchen."

Ethan comes back down with a pile of coats. "Garage?" he asks. I get the door for him and lead him the ten feet across the lawn. He drops the coats and takes my hand. "So you love me?"

I smile. I am not tired of talking about this. "I do."

"Like for the rest of the summer? Or longer? Like if you had to guess."

I put my arms around his waist. I have never felt like

this before and I have never wanted forever more in my life. "Longer."

"Would it spook you if I moved into that house?"

I check his face to see if he is serious. He's looking down at me with a certainty that I'm getting used to. Ethan is a person who knows exactly what he wants.

"I would love that," I say. "I would actually love that." I cannot stop smiling. Ethan is here, right here.

49

B Y MID-OCTOBER, THE PURCHASE IS COMPLETE AND Ethan has moved into Phyllis's house. He's kept some of her furniture but has made it his own. He sleeps in an upstairs bedroom that faces mine, and to be honest, there's a lot of sneaking around. He goes up to Devon once a week if he needs to be in court and to check in with the kids and the skate park, and when he comes back it's as if he's been away for a month.

Ethan's devised a system for keeping tabs on Devon. Barb now calls her downstairs neighbor for quick emergencies, but she still calls Ethan a few times a week to talk, which may have been the point all along. He's hired a guy from the YMCA to manage the skate park and Mort keeps an eye on the kids too. He has a ridiculous text thread with the Red Hot Pokers, which amounts to a bunch of old guys telling him he's whipped. He still does the legal work for Rose at the animal shelter, and we're all going up for the dog parade. Barb's making Ferris a monkey costume. I have concerns.

Ethan's been learning to garden on YouTube, and with what I remember from Phyllis's routine we have kept things alive pretty well. Soon we'll wrap the rosebushes in burlap for the winter. I don't know why we do this, but it's what we've always done. In the spring we will unwrap them, and they'll thank us by blooming. We buy dozens of tulip bulbs from the local nursery and lie on a blanket under the weeping willow while my kids plant them around the yard and along the bank of the creek. I have never in my life had so much to look forward to.

THE FIVE OF us have been trying to keep the feeling of summer alive by having dinner in my backyard most nights, and Ethan brought over a small fire pit to keep off the chill. Tonight I've grilled steaks and asparagus, and the heat coming off the grill helps. The creek is raging with water from a recent storm and the gate on the fence between our houses has come unlatched and is banging in the wind.

"Why do we even need that fence?" asks Greer. She's cut her hair short in an unexpected burst of confidence. Seventh grade seems to be agreeing with her. She made the school's modified soccer team, which has had the surprise benefit of the company of a totally different group of girls. I noticed when she sat down that she left her phone inside the house again. It's been a month since Caroline texted her that she missed her so so much (sad emoji, of course) and asked her to come to a sleepover. That text has been sitting on her phone, un-replied-to, for one solid month. I think Greer is starting to understand the nature of power.

"Let's get rid of it," says Iris. "We'd have so much space."

"And we could see all the way down the creek to Phyllis's tree," Cliffy says, and climbs into Ethan's lap. Ethan lets him cut his steak and catches my eye. I don't remember when this started happening.

"Fine with me," I say.

"Let's do it," says Ethan. "I love the idea of two houses with one yard." I love the idea of all of us in one house, but it's too soon for that. Besides, being in this super-close relationship while also having my own space with my kids feels exactly right.

Ethan's phone rings, and it's his parents on FaceTime. "Hi, sweetie," his mom says. Ethan holds the phone up to me and then to Cliffy on his lap.

"We're just having dinner at Ali's," he says. "Tomorrow we're taking the fence down."

"Oh, just marry her already," his dad says in the background. Mrs. Hogan shushes him. Greer and Iris exchange looks. Cliffy smiles the smile of a six-year-old boy who thinks this is the best idea in the world.

"I'm sorry to interrupt dinner," she says. "But I wanted to let you know we're coming up for Thanksgiving."

"That's great," Ethan says. "We're going to cook here. Frannie and fam are coming. Ali's dad and Libby. You can stay with me."

"That sounds so lovely, sweetie," his mother says.

"Just tell them," Mr. Hogan says. We see nothing but a ceiling fan for a few seconds, and when they're back, it's Mr. Hogan. "We're coming for Thanksgiving and staying. We can't live here all year. I'm sunburned as hell and we feel too far away."

"Theo walked," Mrs. Hogan says, taking the phone back. "And we missed it. By the time they get down here to visit, he'll be running. I can't take it. Our whole life is there."

"Wow, that's great," Ethan says. "But you know the house isn't ours anymore, right?"

"It's fine," she says. "We're moving into the inn. Your grandparents' apartment. It's perfect for us. And they can cook all our meals when we're old."

Ethan looks at me for a reaction. I have none to give except that I'm excited there will be two more people at the table, all the time.

"When we called Harold this morning to tell him we were coming back, he asked for his old job back and we agreed. But the truth is we don't want to manage that place. Frannie's frantic to find someone new, because she doesn't want it to fall on her."

"I want the job," I say. It comes out a little aggressively, which I'm not going to apologize for because my tone matches just how badly I want this job.

"Let me talk to her," Mr. Hogan says, and Ethan hands me the phone.

"Hi," I say. "I want that job. I've been sort of coaching Harold about things for a while, but major changes need to be made. The billing should be automated, the garbage con-tract should be totally renegotiated. The winter menu is too broad, and the linens should be dealt with on Mondays, not Fridays. I can totally do this."

He smiles. "Well that's . . . that's an idea."

Mrs. Hogan grabs the phone. "It's the perfect idea. But please promise me the stress won't make you dump Scooter."

Ethan just shakes his head. They really do talk about him like he's still in middle school. "I don't think that's something you should be worried about," I say, and he takes my hand.

"You can work out of your house if you want," Mrs. Hogan says.

"I'd like to go to the office." I surprise myself by saying it. I am also surprised by the way my heart races a little at the thought of an office of my own, seven pencils in a cup, and a whole mess to set right. I know exactly what I'm going to wear.

"Okay, done," Mr. Hogan says like he's just won the lottery. "I'll send a salary number over in the morning, as well as a full job description."

"Thank you," I say. "This is wonderful." Ethan puts his arm around me and kisses me on the forehead.

"Enough business," Mrs. Hogan says. "Frannie tells me she's bringing all the pies to Thanksgiving dinner. Can I bring mashed potatoes and a salad?"

"Salad?" Iris and Greer say at the same time. Ethan hands them the phone and wraps his arms around me while his parents argue the merits of salad at Thanksgiving dinner.

"Ali Morris, running my family's business," he says.

"It's sort of my dream job," I say. I feel a jolt of adrenaline from the leap I just took. And for a second I understand what it would feel like to race up the half-pipe, turn in the air, and land exactly where you want to.

"Just wait till I negotiate your salary," he says, and laughs.

He pulls me close and we watch my kids laugh with his parents. I feel all of it. The love for my kids that sometimes feels like it could engulf me in flames. The burning love I can still feel coming from my mom, like it's something alive inside of me. And the way Ethan feels like a thing I have been waiting for my entire life.

"WHAT DO YOU think Pete's going to say about you running the inn? I'm guessing Cliffy will tell him immediately when he comes for them tomorrow." The kids have gone to bed and we're sitting in the backyard listening to the water rush through the creek. The forsythias that line the path to the creek have turned their dark fall yellow. The hydrangea blooms are long gone, as are most of their leaves, leaving bunches of lifeless sticks all over my yard. A younger me would have thought those plants were dead, but Phyllis taught me otherwise.

I cover his legs with mine, and he covers us both with a blanket, as is our habit.

I am so happy that tomorrow is Saturday that I almost miss Ethan's question. "I don't think it really matters. Pete can think whatever he wants."

"Good. I don't even care if he calls me Scooter forever. I kind of like it when your kids do, actually."

This makes me smile, Ethan finally letting Scooter be happy here. "Can we try the half-pipe again tomorrow?" I ask.

"I'd love to." He pulls me close, and the wind rattles the

old fence. "I didn't expect it, but this is kind of a big night—your new job and the death of that ugly fence." He reaches into his jacket pocket and pulls out a little box. "I got you something, a while back. This feels like a good time."

I hesitate, because a little box from the man you love could mean forever. But I can tell from the look on his face that it's not a ring, and that somehow it still means forever. I open it, and inside is a tiny silver charm, a heart. I run my finger over its smooth surface, rounded in the middle with a sharp point at the bottom. "I can't believe it," I say.

I have tears in my eyes and he's smiling at me. "What can't you believe?"

The answers chase each other around my head. That I didn't already have a heart on my bracelet. That in the hieroglyphics of my life story, my marriage was marked by a dress, not love. That I never thought there would be another charm for this bracelet. "That there are going to be more things, and it's starting with this."

I rest my head on his shoulder and silently thank myself for putting my heart on the line. It's madness loving someone like this; I must be a natural born risk taker. In fact, it's possible that I am just foolhardy enough to be happy. Spring is always coming, and I know for sure that I will always have a dog.

AUTHOR'S NOTE

When my mother passed away in 2009, my sister received an email from Sister Maureen Murray, who had been my mother's teacher at Marymount High School in Los Angeles. Sister Maureen remembered my mother as "the instigator of many pranks," which did not surprise me at all. She ended the email with these words: "Remember she is as close as your breath."

I have turned that sentence around in my mind for years. I originally took it to mean that she would come from the beyond and stay right next to me throughout my life. Her spirit would wrap itself around me when I needed her. And, maybe. I feel her presence all the time. She has the habit of leaving hearts in the bottom of my coffee cup and sending cardinals into my line of sight when I'm thinking of her. But what I've come to understand is that the love we receive, especially from our parents, becomes a part of us. We internalize the ways they showed their love, the things they always said. Their comfort becomes self-comfort. And that love, like our breath, is inside of us and outside of us all at once.

Which is all to say, I don't want you to worry that I am hearing voices. I do talk to my mother in the car. I ask her for advice all the time, and I usually get something, not because she's talking to me but because her voice is inside of me—I know exactly what she would have said. After all these years, her words of affirmation, her encouragement, and her humor are truly as close as my breath.

ACKNOWLEDGMENTS

This book feels especially personal to me. The grief, the soft pants, the socially awkward dog, the pantry. Certainly my mother's oatmeal cookies. The professional organizer part, not so much. I am not organized, even on the amateur level.

Biggest thanks to my brilliant, kind, and patient editor, Tara Singh Carlson. Remember in *She's All That* when Freddie Prinze Jr. turns his attention on Laney Boggs and suddenly she has a better haircut and a happier future? Tara is my Freddie Prinze Jr.

Thank you to my wonderful agent Marly Rusoff, who takes such care with me and whose handwritten notes make me feel like all is right in the world. And thank you to Kathie Bennett at Magic Time Literary for creating opportunities for me to meet so many new readers.

Thank you to my team at G. P. Putnam's Sons—Aranya Jain, Katie McKee, Nicole Biton, Jazmin Miller, and Molly Pieper. Your enthusiasm for my books and the way you move mountains to make sure people know about them feel like a daily gift. Extra special thanks to the Penguin Random House sales force for the herculean effort they make to get me on the shelves. Thank you to Sally Kim for all of it, but mostly for sharing my books with her mother. That may have been the happiest part of my year.

Thank you to the super-talented cover designer Sanny Chiu for the vibrant way she brings my stories to life. Thank you to Aja Pollock, my eagle-eyed copy editor, Claire Winecoff, my wonderful production editor, and to Ashley Tucker, the interior designer who made this book feel so visually crisp.

I am so grateful to Jane Rosenstadt for talking me through the basics of divorce mediation. Even the simplest divorce is complicated, but I boiled it down to the easiest possible scenario because I didn't want to stay in that room for too long. Any oversimplification is on me, not her. Thank you to Ann Franciskovich for sharing with me her mother's appreciation for the champagne day.

Thank you, always, to my writing friends—those I've known for years and those I only know online. Thank you for reading my work and for letting me read yours. Thank you for sharing your ideas, frustrations, and collective fear of looking dumb on TikTok, and for always cheering each other on. I feel so lucky to be part of this community.

The book world is a happy world because of the people who care so much about connecting readers with stories. Thank you to the independent booksellers, the librarians, the Instagrammers, the TikTokers, and the book reviewers for all you do to connect readers to the right book. I have had a blast with book clubs—in person and online this year—and I'm starting to think book clubs might be the current hotbed of creativity.

I can't say enough about how grateful I am to every reader who has embraced my books, showed up at an event, told their sister about it, and emailed me to say a nice thing. Meeting readers is the joyful fuel that keeps me typing. Extra credit and extra thanks if you're Annissa Armstrong and you show up to five events in a row. With snacks.

To my children, Dain, Tommy, and Quinn, who at this printing will all be adults: thank you for everything you've taught me about Right Amount Parenting™. I haven't always gotten it right, it's been trial and error, but seeing the wonderful young men you are makes me think that good enough is good enough. I am so incredibly proud of you guys. This is probably a good time to mention that there will be a special consideration in my will just for Tommy, who read this book multiple times from the earliest version and texted copious notes from Singapore. Hope that's okay.

Tom, I am so happy that you are the person I get to walk around with. You are the best part of my day every day. I have more to say about this, but I need to run out and get a box of cornstarch. I think we're out?

SUMMER Romance

ANNABEL MONAGHAN

A Conversation with Annabel Monaghan

Discussion Guide

Excerpt from Nora Goes Off Script *by Annabel Monaghan*

A CONVERSATION WITH ANNABEL MONAGHAN

What inspired you to write *Summer Romance*?
Summer Romance started out as a story about a woman who is trying to lighten up. She's weighed down by grief, longing, and her cluttered house. I wanted to write about the finite (and light) nature of the summer romance, and how it can be something you dive into without caution because you don't need to plan past Labor Day. I wanted her to get back in touch with her fun self and move through her grief around losing her mother and the adjustment to being a single mom.

Now that it's done, I see in Ali and her relationship to her mother and her relationship to her children that a lot of this novel is inspired by my experience as a parent, particularly the tightrope I walk between not doing enough and doing too much. When my kids were little, they used to ask me to put the ketchup on their hamburgers because, apparently, I have a unique skill for squeezing out the exact right amount. As a result, my kids call me Right Amount Monaghan. This is something that's rolled around my head a lot as they've grown up—ketchup is easy, but when it comes to mothering, what's the right amount? When do you step in and when do you stand back and let them learn?

Ali's grief over her mother is such a central part of

the narrative. Did you always know Ali was going to be grieving her mother? Did you model Ali's grieving process after your own or someone else's?

My mother was the first person I ever really grieved. For one solid year, I lost my sense of humor. I had a hard time socializing with people and listening to them talk about their normal lives that didn't involve losing their mothers. It took time and small steps to move out of that murky gray space.

While my mother wasn't anything like Fancy, there is a big chunk of her heart in this book—her oatmeal chocolate chip cookies, her bright red lips. She was a bit like Ali's neighbor, Phyllis, emotionally hands-on and, otherwise, completely hands-off. She never knew where I was or what kind of trouble I was stirring up, but when we were together, she was present and dialed in to my well-being. For me, this was the right amount of parenting. She thought the best way to parent was to "give birth and get out of the way." I love how courageous that is and how much faith she had in my ability to figure things out.

Like Ali, Nora in your debut, *Nora Goes Off Script*, was also a divorced single mother. What interests you in writing about women with this experience finding love?

There's no quicker way to complicate your life than by having kids. Throw in a mortgage, a job, and an ex-husband, and you have instant drama. I like the kind of chaos that naturally comes with parenting, where you're rowing your own boat but also scrambling to row everyone else's boats. Some days it might feel like life is pelting you with water balloons from the shore. Falling in love and connecting to your romantic self can be challenging with all of that going on, and I like the complexity of that challenge and how it raises the stakes. I also like how a big love affair at that stage of life feels unexpected, like a bonus.

Ali had wonderful traditions with her mother, some of which she carries on with her own children, like greeting the first day of summer at sunrise. Do you have any such traditions with your own children?

I love Sunday dinner. I set the table, I pull something out of the oven, I gather the people. But on Sunday nights during the summer, it all happens outside—my family packs a picnic, and we eat dinner at the beach. We are serious picnickers. We pack bug spray, plastic wineglasses, and a tablecloth that has been washed threadbare. We roll a cooler filled with meats, potatoes, coleslaw, and a hunk of cheese. We sit by the Long Island Sound, close to where Ali might have sat with her kids, and we play cards under a giant oak tree. We're not quite welcoming the summer, just welcoming the week, gathering from where we've been scattered. Sunday dinner feels like a comma, a quick pause between what came before and what's coming next. We usually drink seltzer and white wine, but these are my champagne days.

Ali learns about gardening from her neighbor, Phyllis, and the garden holds quite a bit of symbolism.

Do you garden? If not, are there other outdoor spaces that are symbolic to you?

I am not a gardener, but I love a garden. I am fascinated by both the amount of work people put into caring for a garden and how much of the work the garden does on its own. Ten years ago, I was at Costco (I feel a theme coming on) and made an impulse purchase of a six-dollar peony bulb. I got it home, dug a hole with my hands, and stuck it in the ground. The following year, I had two giant peonies the color of pinot noir. I remember thinking, *Wow, I wonder if this is what God feels like.* By late fall, the whole plant turns to sticks, but it comes back to life again in the spring. Every year it feels like a miracle, and it makes me think of how nature, animals, and people have an innate sense for how to take care of themselves and bloom. This year I had twenty flowers!

Ethan is a skateboarder and you describe the experience of skateboarding well. Have you ever skateboarded? How did you capture the experience of skateboarding on the page?

Me, on a skateboard, is not a great idea. Just the idea of trusting your body to balance like that sends a small panic up my spine, but I have loved learning about how skateboarders master their fears. While writing this book, I listened to a bunch of podcasts about skateboarding and lurked in some online chatrooms where people were sharing their experiences. I watched hours of YouTube videos, and my main takeaway was that skateboarders have convinced themselves that they can fly, so they can. It's all very spiritual actually, the amount of presence it requires to focus and the amount of confidence it takes to let go.

All three of your novels to date have been set in the vicinity of New York City. What draws you to writing about this area? What does New York City represent to you?

I live about forty minutes north of New York City, just south of Connecticut, approximately where Beechwood would be located if it was a real place. I lived in Manhattan for two years as a single person and then returned for eight years when I was married. (I had to leave Manhattan to meet a man. I always suspected that I was too short for a man to see me in a bar.) When I moved out of the city, I realized how much I need space and quiet. I love sitting in my backyard and watching the sunrise over the forest. But I also love knowing that the heartbeat of the city is right there. I love the electric jolt of stimulation I get when I visit, followed by the quiet of coming home. I think this is why I write about quiet places outside of New York City; it feels like the rhythm of my life—fast and slow, noisy and quiet, outside and in.

Without giving anything away, did you always know how the story would end?

I always knew how it would feel and who Ali would become, but, as usual, I didn't know how I was going to get there.

What do you hope readers might take away from *Summer Romance*?

My personal takeaway from this story is that it doesn't take a winning lottery ticket to get you unstuck from grief or sadness or general inertia. We don't need to wait for a lightning bolt to strike from out of the sky. Any small action toward feeling better will lead to another. Make your coffee the way you like it, put on a pair of hard pants, take a walk, call a friend. It takes tiny steps and time.

And I'm serious about the dog thing. I have thought about this for years, watching friends fall in love with their dogs and then bury them. What madness it is to intentionally walk into that kind of pain. But then in 2018, Tom and I went on a thirty-day cleanse (this is not a joke) and felt like Super Us for a minute. The next thing I knew, we'd adopted a dog. Now I am two things: in love with my dog and certain he's going to break my heart by dying. And I get it now: the joy is worth it. This is the nature of the summer romance, the act of throwing yourself all in, even though you know there will be a teary goodbye. The joy is worth it in the moment.

Also, don't go on a cleanse.

What's next for you?

I am hoping to write a bicoastal love story about a studio executive whose career is on the line.

DISCUSSION GUIDE

1. Ali's mother gave her a charm bracelet with charms that represent different milestones in her life. If you were to have such a charm bracelet, what charms would you put on it and why?

2. At one point, Ali says, "I always wanted someone to think of me that way, that I was the one." Do you think a relationship necessitates this feeling?

3. Ali finds organizing to be a deeply peaceful activity. Do you feel similarly about organizing? Is there some other activity that brings you a sense of peace?

4. Have you ever had a summer romance? Did you know the romance would be just for the summer when you began it?

5. Do you think a summer romance is fundamentally different from a relationship that doesn't have an inherent end date?

6. What was your favorite scene, and why?

7. Ethan says he feels more like himself in Devon than in Beechwood. Do you think that where you live can affect who you are? Where is your favorite place that you have ever lived, and why?

8. The Hogans make a drastic decision and then later feel differently. Have you ever made a big change in your life and then reversed it? Or wished that you could have? How do you think the novel might have ended differently if the Hogans didn't change their minds?

9. Over the course of the novel, Ali's understanding of her relationship with her mother changes as she helps her twelve-year-old daughter through a difficult time. What do you think of how Fancy helped Ali throughout her marriage? Are there any instances when help you gave backfired? Or the help someone gave you didn't have the desired result?

10. What did you think of the ending?

Keep reading for an exciting excerpt from

NORA GOES OFF SCRIPT

by Annabel Monaghan

1

HOLLYWOOD'S COMING TODAY.
I'm not going to lose my house.

Those two thoughts surface in the same moment as the sun starts to brighten my room. I've been paid for my screenplay, and the bonus money for letting them film here will hit my bank account at noon. Good-bye unpaid real estate taxes. Good-bye credit card debt. And to think, Ben's saying good-bye to me has made it all possible. I don't know how this day could get any better. I hop out of bed, grab my heaviest morning sweater, and head downstairs. I pour my coffee and go out to the porch to watch the sunrise.

Whoever buys this house from me, I always think, will tear it down. It's over a hundred years old; everything's broken. There's a certain point in January when the wind blows right into the kitchen and we have to duct-tape a fleece blanket over the doorframe. The floorboards droop; there are only two bathrooms and they're both upstairs.

Each bedroom has a closet designed to house six outfits, preferably for very small people. Ben had a list of house complaints he used to like to run through daily, and I could never shake the feeling that he was really complaining about me.

This house is a disaster, sure. But I fell in love with it when I first looked down the long windy path of the driveway. The magnolia trees that line either side touch in the middle, so that now, in April, you drive through a tunnel of pink flowers. When you emerge onto the main road it feels like you've been transported from one world to another, like a bride leaving the church. It feels like a treat going out for milk, and it feels like a treat coming home.

The house was built by a British doctor named George Faircloth who lived in Manhattan and came upstate to Laurel Ridge in the summer, which explains the complete lack of winterization. It was built to be enjoyed on a seventy-eight-degree day and primarily from the outside. I imagine his landscaping this property like a maestro, arranging the magnolias and the forsythia beneath them to announce the beginning of spring. After a long gray winter, these first pink and yellow blooms shout, "Something's happening!" By May they'll have gone green with the rest of the yard, a quiet before the peonies and hydrangea bloom.

I knew I'd do anything to live here when I saw the tea house in the back. It's a one-room structure the doctor had commissioned to honor the ritual of formal tea. Where the main house is flimsy white clapboard with peeling black shutters, the tea house is made of gray stone with a slate roof. It has a small working fireplace and oak-paneled walls. It's as if Dr. Faircloth reached over the pond and plucked it out of the English countryside. I distinctly remember hearing Ben use the word "shed" when we walked into it, and I ignored him the way you do when you're trying to stay married.

The first morning we woke up here, I got up at first light because we didn't have any curtains yet. I took my coffee to the front porch, and the sunrise was the surprise of my life. I'd never seen the house at six A.M. I didn't even know we were facing east. It was like a gift with purchase, a reward for loving this broken place.

I stand on the porch now, taking it in before the movie crew arrives. Pink ribbons, then orange creep up behind the wide-armed oak tree at the end of my lawn. The sun rises behind it differently every day. Some days it's a solid bar of sherbet that rolls up like movie credits and fills the sky. Some days the light dapples through the leaves in a muted gray. The oak won't have leaves for a few weeks, just tiny yellow and white blooms pollinating one another and promising a lawn full of acorns. My lawn is its best self in April, particularly in the morning when it's dew-kissed and catching the light. I don't know the science behind all of it, but I know the rhythm of this property like I know my own body. The sun will rise here every single day.

BY THE TIME I've gotten my kids up and fed and off to school, I've changed my clothes six times. I stand in front of the mirror in the same jeans and T-shirt I started with, and realize the problem is my hair. The frizz isn't as bad as it's going to be in August, but it's still pretty intense. People in Hollywood have tamed hair, or if it's wild, it's been professionally disorganized. I dunk my head in my bathroom sink and then get to work blowing out my hair piece by piece, something I don't think I've done since my wedding day in my childhood bathroom with my brides-maids crammed in behind me.

When my hair is straight, it's still only nine A.M. They're supposed to be here at ten, and I know that if I spend any more time in front of a mirror, I am going to overthink myself into a panic. I decide I look perfectly fine for a thirty-nine-year-old mother of two. And it's not like I'm auditioning for this movie; I wrote it. I decide to go into town and do some non-urgent errands. Maybe I'll get home after they've arrived so I can show up in an oh-hey-I-lost-track-of-time kind of way. I'll walk into the Hollywood version of my real-life drama in full swing, like it's some kind of sick surprise party.

I kill as much time as I can by dropping a pair of boots at the shoe repair and browsing the discount rack at the bookstore. I stop by the hardware store to chat with Mr. Mapleton about his hip surgery and to pick up the stack of crossword puzzles he saves me from his paper each week. By ten o'clock, I run out of things to do, so I know it's time to go home and see exactly what a movie crew looks like and what the consequences will be to my lawn.

I've misjudged, and they're late, so I'm back on the front porch watching their arrival. I grip the railing as the eighteen-wheelers barrel down my dirt driveway, dislodging the lowest magnolia blossoms and darkening the sky with startled birds. For a second, my whole property looks like a Hitchcock movie.

I never saw this coming. I'm as surprised as anybody that *The Tea House* is being made into a real movie. The last movie I wrote was called *Kisses for Christmas*, an eighty-minute TV movie with well-timed breaks in the action to make room for the forty minutes of commercials. The one before that was *Hometown Hearts*, which is pretty much the same story, but it takes place in the fall. My superpower is methodically placing a man and woman in the same shiny town, populated by unusually happy people with maddeningly small problems. They bristle at first and then fall in love. It's all smiles until one of them leaves, but then comes back immediately after the commercial break. Every. Single. Time.

The Tea House is a departure from the formula and is definitely the best thing I've ever written. The first thing my agent, Jackie, said when she'd finished reading it was, "Are you okay?" I laughed because, sure, it did seem like I'd gone dark. The story runs deeper, with heavy doses of anguish and introspection, and for sure the guy doesn't come back at the end. In the months after Ben left, I sold two fun, light scripts to The Romance Channel, but then this darker thing sort of spilled out of me. I'd tried to keep my personal life to myself after Ben left, but I guess some stories just want to be told.

"I mean this is great," she started. "But this is like a big film, not for The Romance Channel. If it's okay with you, I'm going to pitch this to major studios."

"That's going to be a major waste of your time," I said, pulling crabgrass in my front yard. "No one wants to watch two hours of angst and abandonment. I swear I tried to perk it up at the end, but no matter how hard I tried, I just couldn't stomach him walking back through the door."

"Nora. It hasn't even been a year."

"I know. So I need to get back to what I do best. Do whatever you want with this thing; I think maybe I just needed to get it off my chest. Everything okay with your mom?"

"She's fine. Give me a couple of weeks on this. This script is a game changer."

As the first truck stops in front of my house, nine of its eighteen wheels on my grass, I realize that the game has indeed changed. I hold on to the porch railing for support as two more trucks start unloading cameras, lighting, furniture, people.

A pink-haired young woman with a clipboard and a smile approaches me. "Hey, you must be Nora. Don't freak out. Cuz I'd be totally freaking out. I'm Weezie, Leo's assistant."

"Hi. Not freaking out. I can replant the grass." I reach out to shake her free hand.

Another woman, closer to my age in a black jumpsuit, approaches. "I'm Meredith Cohen, executive producer."

"Nora Hamilton, homeowner," I manage, still hanging on to the porch railing. "And writer," I add, because I'm awkward.

"Listen," Meredith says. "We're a lot. Hell, just Leo's a lot these days. We're going to make a lot of noise and a big mess, and then we'll clean it all up and be out of your hair in two days. Three, tops."

"That's fine; it's what I expected. I've never seen a movie shoot before, kind of exciting." A red pickup truck pulls completely onto the grass, towing a silver Airstream trailer. "What's that?"

Weezie turns and laughs. "Oh, here he is. Of course, that's Leo. We're all staying at the Breezeport Hilton; he doesn't stay at Hiltons." She rolls her eyes and smiles again, like it's mildly annoying but also adorable that this guy is wrecking my lawn.

"Leo Vance is going to sleep in that thing? In my front yard?"

"It can't be avoided. He's quirky. But he's got a bathroom in there and we have a honeywagon coming for everyone else. So don't worry about your house."

The Airstream door opens and out steps a forty-year-old, shoeless superstar. His jeans hang too low and his gray T-shirt is torn in two places. His hair needs a trim, and he's way too handsome to play Ben. But then again, Naomi Sanchez is playing me. He squints up at the sky as he gets his bearings, as if he's emerging from the dark after twenty-four hours. It's eleven A.M. and we're only a ninety-minute drive from New York City.

Leo Vance is the highest-paid leading man in Hollywood. I know this because I've been googling him for three days. He has homes in Manhattan, Bel Air, and Cap d'Antibes. He owns a share of an NBA franchise. No kids, never married. A Libra. He's originally from New Jersey and has a brother.

I've seen every one of Leo's movies, which isn't really a credit to him. I've seen a lot of movies. He's a good actor, and he's most famous for his smoldering stare. I have to say, it's a little over the top. In his first film, *Sycamore Nights*, he gave his co-star Aileen Bennett a series of white-hot smolders that got him named Sexiest Man Alive that year. I guess it became his signature move, so he kept it up film after film, even when it was entirely unnecessary. Like in *Battle for the Home Front*, he's telling his newly pregnant wife that he has to go away to war, and he's smoldering. Or in *Class Action*, he's giving a commencement speech at a military academy and smoldering all over everyone's parents and grandparents. And don't get me started on *African Rose*. A refugee center with a wild malaria outbreak is no place to smolder. Leo Vance seems prone to the inappropriate oozing of sex appeal.

When the smolder is turned off, he has an impressive range of smiles that are unique to each film. They range from timid to maniacal, and I've always admired the way he can keep each one consistent throughout an entire film. I'm curious to see what smile he'll invent for *The Tea House*. What smile would he imagine Ben having? I can't even remember the last time I saw Ben smile.

Leo Vance is walking toward my porch, and I brace myself for an introduction. Perfection on the screen, scruffy in real life. He is going to be transformed into a man with a lot of issues who ends up walking away from the woman he built a life with. Leave it to Ben to be maddening enough to make me finally write something worthwhile. I smile at the irony of Ben actually helping out after all.

Leo brushes past me on the porch like I'm not there, then stops and takes a step back. "You're missing a dimple," he says.

"The other one's inside," I say.

He nods and walks into my house like he owns the place. Not much of a meet cute.

MEETING THE DIRECTOR, Martin Cox, is as intimidating as I anticipated. Weezie's gone in after Leo, so he finds Meredith and me on the porch. "You must be Nora." He's not tall but he's big, and I can't decide if he's physically big or if it's his presence that takes up a lot of space.

I shake his hand and try not to say anything else. If I start talking, I'll tell him what I thought of the final scene in *Alabaster* and why I think he was robbed of an Oscar. I'll tell him that the lighting alone in *The Woman Beneath* was sublime. Mainly to avoid using the word "sublime," I keep my mouth shut.

"So, can we see it?" he asks. I lead Meredith and Martin behind my house to where the tea house sits at the entrance to the woods. There is no path to it, just lawn, so that a consequence of visiting the tea house is almost always wet shoes. I'd left the big oak door open, as is my habit, because with the door open, you can see straight through the steel windows on the back wall into the mouth of the forest. It gives me the feeling of endless possibility.

The tea house is a sacred space to me. The space in

which I have been able to preserve myself by writing. And, unlike the main house, it is airtight against the elements. I imagine the Faircloths approaching the tea house as I do, anticipating a fire in the fireplace and a table laid with tea and treats. I imagine lovers meeting here for hushed conversation and first kisses. Ben had always wanted to use it for storage.

It may have come down to that, for all I know. My belief that the last thing the world needs is more storage versus Ben's belief that he needed a third motorcycle. Among the many consolations around his leaving are that he took most of his stuff with him, and he didn't ask for the kids.

The tea house plays prominently in the breakup of our marriage, which is what earned it the title role. Ben resented the time I spent out there; he resented the work I did. He resented the fact that I'd been paying our bills for the past ten years. Which made two of us, actually. The more competent I became at taking care of our family, the more he despised me. The more he despised me, the harder I worked to make things right. Me writing in the tea house was a mirror he didn't want to look into. That's how it goes in the movie. In real life, I don't know, maybe he left because he just wanted more storage. Ben wanted more of just about everything.

Now, as we approach, I hear Martin catch his breath. "It's otherworldly," he says. "The photo doesn't do it justice."

I smile and keep walking. "Well, it's certainly from another time. This is where I write."

It's warm for April, and the slate roof glistens in the

sun from last night's rain. Two giant hydrangea bushes flank the door. They're getting their first leaves now, hopeful celery-colored things, but soon they'll be bursting with cerulean blue blooms the size of my head. "If you could have waited until July, you would have seen these in bloom," I say to no one, because Martin has already walked inside.

"This is absolutely perfect," he says, running his hands over the paneled walls. He pulls out a walkie-talkie. "I'm back in the tea house. Bring the linens for the daybed, I'm going to need three o'clock sunshine coming through the back window. And a mop. Make sure Leo and Naomi are in makeup."

Meredith gives me a little wink, presumably to make me feel better about the mop comment. I give her a shrug, what do I care? "Okay, so I'll get out of your way, let me know if you need anything."

I GO BACK into my house, relieved to find it empty. Outside every window, there is activity—a catering truck, a woman chasing Leo Vance with a spray bottle. From the largest trailer emerges Naomi Sanchez, somehow all legs in a frumpy housedress. I assume she's dressed up as how Martin imagined me. I first saw Naomi Sanchez in *Hustler's Revenge* when she was about twenty-five. There was a scene where she discovered she'd been double-crossed that was shot so tight that her whole face filled the screen. Where are her pores, I'd wondered. At thirty-two, she is still the most beautiful woman I've ever seen.

I text Kate: Leo Vance was in my house. Naomi Sanchez is exquisite.

Kate: Dying.

I'm having a hard time figuring out what I should be doing. I mean I'm inside my house which isn't a writing-working space. Inside my house is a mom-ing space. The kitchen is still a mess from breakfast, and it occurs to me that Leo Vance has seen my pancake spatter and has smelled my bacon grease. I'm mildly agitated that he's been in here as I start to clean. There will have to be boundaries of some sort. I don't want to walk in here to-morrow and find him smoldering at my dishwasher.

I call my sister, and her nanny, Leonora, answers. "She's out with her friends," she says. Penny and her hus-band, Rick, live in Manhattan and East Hampton and are frequently featured in *Town & Country* wearing the right things with the right people. This is the first time in my life I'm doing something cooler than Penny, so I leave a message. "Please tell her I called and that Naomi Sanchez and Leo Vance are in my driveway." Leonora squeals, and I am satisfied.

Once my kitchen is clean, I try to think of what I'd normally be doing. It's Wednesday, and on Wednesdays we eat meatloaf. Of course! I take a pound of ground tur-key out of the freezer and place it on the counter. This doesn't take as long as I'd hoped.

I WATCH THROUGH the corner window in the sunroom. They're filming the scene where I tell Ben that it might help if we both had a steady paycheck. It was the day he lumped me in with all the other people who don't have the vision to believe in his dreams. I was a drone, a robot, a slave to convention. I'm pretty sure it was the last straw. I imagine my words coming out of Naomi's perfect mouth, and I start to think maybe this film was cast all wrong. How is Leo Vance going to be able to be as dismissive as Ben was when he's looking at a woman like that? It seems like people as beautiful as the two of them might have been able to work things out. No man's going to walk away from Naomi Sanchez.

I've been watching the filming for an hour when I realize it's time to go get my kids. I open my garage to find three guys smoking in my driveway. They drop their cigarettes and extinguish them with their shoes and move to the side and wave me out, like I'm in some kind of valet-parking situation. I have no choice but to drive up onto my own grass to get around the trucks and onto the dirt portion of my driveway that takes me to the main road.

It feels good to put the chaos behind me and drive out into Laurel Ridge where nothing ever changes. Ben bought into this town because he was literally out of choices. He wanted a big life in the city—Penny's life, to be exact. But when that proved to be too expensive, he wanted a big house in a commutable suburb. That was impossible too. As I got more and more pregnant with Arthur and it became clear that our walk-up studio apartment would never contain us, we were in a race against the clock. We had twenty thousand dollars to put down on a three-hundred-thousand-dollar house, and a three-hundred-thousand-dollar house was a lot farther from the city than Ben had imagined. -

Ben told his friends that we bought a teardown in the sticks as an investment. It's an up-and-coming town, he told them, which I always thought was funny because this town's motto should be: We Are Neither Up Nor Coming. It's a town that agonizes over progress of any kind, secretly fantasizing that it was the model for Main Street at Disneyland. There's an architectural review board and a planning commission whose sole purpose is to keep people like Ben from making Laurel Ridge less quaint.

We have six or seven shops that have been in Laurel Ridge since the beginning of time. These shop owners enjoy a cultlike loyalty from their patrons. Laurel Ridge is a place where you'll always be able to buy a hammer from a guy you know and a bowl of homemade ice cream scooped by a teenager. A handful of other businesses pop up and collapse as people come from Manhattan to sell us designer vitamins and personalized dog cookies. They rarely last a year.

At the end of town is Laurel Ridge Elementary. I park and find my friends among a group of parents on the playground, like this is just some normal day.

"OMG spill it," says Jenna. She's standing under the basketball hoop with Kate.

"What?" I say, trying to be casual. "Just hanging with Leo and Naomi, whatever."

"Is he cute? Does he give you that look?" Kate asks.

"Yes and no. Absolutely cute and he's barely looked at me."

"So, the hair's a waste?" Jenna's referring to the fact that I've blown out my hair.

"Yeah, that was a little overboard," I admit. "If you saw Naomi Sanchez in person you'd understand why he wasn't so focused on me."

"Hey, Nora." Molly Richter approaches us. "Looking good, nice hair." Molly's that classic bitch you knew in middle school who never snapped out of it. We have to be nice to her because she's head of the PTA and seems to have the authority to randomly assign volunteer positions. We steer clear of Molly Richter like people used to steer clear of the draft.

"I hear you're playing Hollywood this week," she goes on.

"I am." It's important when talking to Molly that you don't offer any additional information or ask any follow-up questions.

"Well, cute. Don't forget that *Oliver Twist* rehearsals are next Wednesday after school and you've signed up to watch the kids backstage."

"How could I forget? It's all Arthur talks about." And I've shown my hand. I should never have blown out my hair. Kate gasps, like I'm sinking into quicksand and she has no rope to throw me.

"Oh, is Arthur interested in a big part?" Molly doesn't give me a chance to respond. "That's great! Because I was going to name you play chairman, and if he's going to be so involved, you'll be there anyway. Perfect." She jots something down in her Columbo-style notebook as she turns on her heel and walks away.

Jenna is laughing. "You're so screwed."

"Yeah, I hate to say it, but you are," Kate says. "If you say no, not that she even gave you a chance, she'll make sure Arthur's a tree or a stone or something." Tryouts were today, so I'm hoping it's too late for Molly to wield her power and blackball my ten-year-old. Arthur is in the middle of another round of spring sports disasters, and this play is a lifeline.

"I know. And it's fine. If Arthur gets a part, I'll get people to help."

"No one wants to help," says Jenna.

"Then I'll do whatever it is. This is literally everything to Arthur. It's the first thing I've seen him excited about since Ben left."

I don't usually mention Ben. Not because it's too painful, but because I almost never think about him. I've created an awkward silence though, and it seems to work to my benefit.

"We'll help," they say.

"You guys are the best." The bell rings and dozens of children pour out of the school. Arthur runs over to us, dumps his backpack at my feet, and chases a bunch of kids to the jungle gym. I'm not sure what this means about how his audition went.

Bernadette, the eight-year-old boss of my family, barrels over to me and slams me with a hug. "Did he say anything about your hair?"

"He did not; I should have worn yours." I smooth my hands over Bernadette's brown curls. They seem straight out of *The Little Rascals*, like old-fashioned hair.

"Let's go," she commands. "They're leaving in three hours."

"They'll be back tomorrow," I say. Bernadette looks at me like I've lost my mind. "Okay, fine." I call to Arthur, and he drags his body across the blacktop.

"Seriously? It's only three-fifteen. Does weirdo need to get home to stare at the movie stars?" Arthur wiggles his fingers, failing to seem menacing.

"How was the audition?" I ask.

"I got it." Arthur gives me a half smile that tells me he doesn't want me to make a scene on the playground.

I pick up his backpack. "Let's get out of here before I do something embarrassing."

BERNADETTE IS OUT of her mind as we round the last curve of our driveway. Arthur is committed to trying to seem like he's too cool for the biggest stars in Hollywood. They'd be lucky to meet him, he seems to want us to think. He's got a major role in *Oliver Twist* after all. "Mom, she's so embarrassing. Everyone at recess and lunch was asking me about this movie. We're like freaks in town."

We pass the Airstream trailer and two eighteen-wheelers before we can even see our garage. A table with pastries and sandwiches blocks my way. I roll down the passenger window and indicate the garage. A young man in a red trucker hat happily agrees to move his operation onto my porch, but not before giving each of my kids a donut.

"This is epic," says Bernadette.

"It's a donut," says Arthur.

I close the garage door before we're even out of the car, happy to be back in my cocoon. Everything outside feels infested with noise and tires and people making decisions who are not me. When I get upstairs, I'll pull all of the curtains. There will be homework, dinner, *Wheel of Fortune*, bed. Their contract says they have to leave by six.

As we climb the stairs into the kitchen, Bernadette goes into overdrive. "Did you meet Naomi? Is she as pretty as she was in *The Mariner's Wife*? Is Leo here yet? Is he tall or not? Frannie says he's short and stands on a box when they . . ." She stops when we get to the top of the stairs and see Leo sitting at our kitchen counter. She's probably out of breath anyway.

Leo stands slowly, rolling up to his full height of about six feet two inches. He gives Bernadette a stern look. "I am not short, young lady." Bernadette smiles and blushes and covers her face all in a single instant.

"Ha! There it is!" Leo motions to her with his beer. Which is my in-case-Kate-and-Mickey-stop-by beer, I notice.

"What?" Arthur asks, a little alarmed.

"The missing dimple. I've been looking all over the house for it. Your mom's missing dimple is right there on your sister's cheek." Bernadette can't stop smiling, and Arthur rolls his eyes.

I realize that I haven't moved since we came up from the garage. I'm frozen with a half a donut in my hand. "Yes, well done. That's where I keep it."

Leo goes back to his beer, and after a silence that seems

to only be uncomfortable for me, I say, "So, I'm Nora. I'm the writer, and this is my house."

"Leo."

"I'm Bernadette, and this is Arthur."

"Cheers."

"Are you supposed to be in here?" asks Arthur.

"I filmed my bit for today, now they're doing a few scenes with Naomi alone. Dark stuff, this film."

"Well, yes. I was in a mood."

"She's in a better mood now," offers Bernadette.

"Yes. And we need to get started with homework," I say.

"I'll just be a little longer. My trailer is hot and I was working on this crossword." He indicates the crossword that I'd been saving for tonight. It's Wednesday, and that's my favorite crossword day, not too easy and not too hard. My kids know this and look at me in tandem, neither seeming like they could predict what comes next.

"Well, okay," I say. Lawn, beer, crossword. I'm keeping score.

I stand by the sink, donut in hand, watching the three of them. Leo working my puzzle. My kids pulling folders out of their backpacks, trying to act normal. Bernadette needs markers; Leo hands her some. She watches him as she colors. Arthur has a sheet of fractions he needs to do within a minute, so he pulls up the stopwatch on his phone. I watch this incongruous threesome, a scene out of I don't know what.

"So, what do you usually do now?" Leo breaks the silence.

"Oh, I start dinner." Grateful for the reminder, I begin to move around the kitchen. I ditch the donut, wipe the counter, open the fridge. The ground turkey has defrosted on the counter so I just need an egg. I place the turkey in a bowl and crack the egg into it.

"Dear God, what are you doing?" asks Leo. Where other people get his famous smolder, I get the scrunched-up look of disgust.

"It's meatloaf Wednesday," Bernadette tells him.

"That can't be right," he says, mesmerized.

I chop an onion and add it. I throw in some bread crumbs. Leo cannot take his eyes off my bowl. "That is truly the most disgusting thing I've ever seen." And then as I begin to mix it with my hands, "I stand corrected." My kids laugh.

Weezie comes looking for him at about five o'clock and doesn't seem too surprised to find him tipsy. "Come on, let's get you back into makeup. We need to reshoot a few things before dark."

Leo makes what I can only call the agony face, the face my kids make when I tell them we're having fish for dinner. "No. Please. Don't tell me there's more."

"Of course there's more. We have one, maybe two days left here before we wrap."

Leo clutches his beer. "But it's so depressing. You guys, your mom is so depressing. I just can't take it."

"She's actually fun," Arthur says. "And the rest of her movies are kinda dumb but with super-happy endings."

"He's right," I admit. "Dumb and happy. This was kind of a one-off, sorry."

He studies his empty beer bottle. "Can't he just come back? Like have an epiphany or something and come back?"

Arthur hides his face by pretending to review his fractions. Ben having an epiphany would be a salve to Arthur's open wound. "He's not coming back," I say.

ABOUT THE AUTHOR

Photo © Jo Bryan Photography 2021

Annabel Monaghan is the author of LibraryReads pick and national bestseller *Same Time Next Summer* and Indie Next and LibraryReads pick *Nora Goes Off Script*, as well as two young adult novels and *Does This Volvo Make My Butt Look Big?*, a selection of laugh-out-loud columns that appeared in *The Huffington Post, The Week,* and *The Rye Record*. She lives in Rye, New York, with her family.

VISIT ANNABEL MONAGHAN ONLINE

annabelmonaghan.com
AnnabelMonaghan
AnnabelMonaghan
AnnabelMonaghan